tHRe3

T.J. Connor

iUniverse, Inc.
Bloomington

tHRe3

*This is a work of fiction. All of the characters, names, incidents,
organizations, and dialogue in this novel are either the products
of the author's imagination or are used fictitiously.*

iUniverse books may be ordered through booksellers or by contacting:

iUniverse
1663 Liberty Drive
Bloomington, IN 47403
www.iuniverse.com
1-800-Authors (1-800-288-4677)

ISBN: 978-1-4759-3159-4 (sc)
ISBN: 978-1-4759-3161-7 (e)
ISBN: 978-1-4759-3160-0 (dj)

Library of Congress Control Number: 2012910101

Printed in the United States of America

iUniverse rev. date: 9/13/2012

1

Janice purchased a roast and some potatoes from the small country store on Main Street. She drove the beat-up red pickup truck a half mile up a bumpy dirt road before taking a right into a massive field in the mountains. The field was surrounded by dense woods. As she drove through the field, a feeling of uneasiness overcame her.

Janice and her husband, Denny, had moved to this location in the early 1930s to get away from the big-city life in New York that had been so unkind to them. In New York, Denny had a good job working in marketing at a large corporation in the city, but like many people in the roaring twenties, he thought he could strike it rich in the stock market, and he lost nearly everything in the infamous market crash in 1929.

They took what they had left and headed south, ending up in the small town of Burnsville, nestled in the mountains of North Carolina. Initially, they stayed in a hotel, and they fell in love with the quaint little town. One summer day, by happenstance they stumbled across the field while looking for a site to picnic.

The field was beautiful, surrounded by massive oak trees, and it was a good five acres. Denny, with the assistance of some locals, built a modest, two-story house on the far side of the field. They didn't have much, but they were happy.

Janice drove through the field and stopped the truck in front of the house. She grabbed the bag of food off the passenger seat before opening the door and stepping outside. As the rickety door to the truck shut, she paused for a moment and stared at the front door with a profound look of concern on her face. She opened the front door and walked into the house. The uneasiness and consternation she felt abated as Denny walked toward her with a welcoming smile.

"Hey, baby, what did you get for dinner?" asked Denny.

"Just a roast and some potatoes," responded Janice.

Denny's prize possession was an antique pistol used by the Confederate army in the Civil War. It had always hung above the fireplace in the living room.

Janice put the roast in the oven and then walked into the kitchen and sat at a small, round table. Her face was at once consumed with terror and confusion. The gun was on the table.

Denny walked toward the table and, looking deep into Janice's eyes as he approached her, quipped, "It is a beautiful gun, isn't it?"

"Why is it on the kitchen table?" responded Janice with a distinct tremor in her voice.

Following the murder-suicide, the only activities at the site over the next thirty years were Klan gatherings. On a couple of occasions, people of color were hung in the oak trees surrounding the field, and there were remnants of burned crosses at various locations. This seemingly was a place where the devil reigned supreme and that God had abandoned long ago. The eerie feel in the air was palpable.

In the spring of 1960, God met Satan in front of the house in the field. God stood five feet in front of Satan with a stoical look on his face and stared deeply into Satan's eyes as if he knew what was coming.

"It's time," said Satan with a large smile on his face. "The Antichrist has been born."

"Why now?"

"That's easy. Mankind's morals and values have deteriorated significantly over the last generation. Man is selfish; he cares only about himself. Countries have attempted to destroy countries. Ethnic groups have attempted to destroy ethnic groups. Does the Holocaust ring a bell to you? Look around you at this incredible field and these beautiful woods that you created. Man has slaughtered man here merely because of the color of his skin."

"That was your doing."

"Oh no, my old friend. You know very well that I just plant the thoughts in their minds. They make the conscious decisions to carry them out."

"First, don't ever refer to me as your friend. You are dark and evil. Second, why must you take such joy out of human suffering and corrupting the world?"

"Hey, that's why I'm the devil," laughed Satan. "Also, let's not forget that you plant good thoughts in their minds and they choose to act on mine. Man does not deserve to exist. I will over the years fill this field with the most wicked of men. You must choose a man to defeat them on three separate occasions and walk out of this field alive. If he can do that, he then will be free to go after the Antichrist. If he doesn't walk out of the field three times, or he does but doesn't get to the Antichrist by the summer of 2037, the Antichrist will launch the weapons of mass destruction that will precipitate the end of the world. Also, when your chosen one fails and the process of world destruction is complete, we in hell take over heaven, and I will sit on your throne."

"I will choose my man to engage in these battles, but if he wins, you will leave man alone and cease corrupting him."

"Well, those are very high stakes indeed. Consequences befitting the ultimate battle between good and evil. If you win, I go away and man flourishes. If I win, man and the world perish and I take over heaven."

"My only other condition is that if my chosen one miraculously finds a way to walk through your valley of evil, not once or twice, but three times, his son, if I elect, takes on your Antichrist."

"That's it," laughed Satan robustly. "I will agree to those terms. Is the world really that important to you?"

God grimaced and looked down before looking back at Satan and saying sternly, "Agreed. Game on. But you know I will never let you prevail."

"There's nothing you can do about it, my old friend," laughed Satan with an impious look on his face. "The odds are too stacked against you. Your man will be lucky to make it through the valley once, much less three times." He then disappeared in an explosion of smoke and fire.

"What a jackass. Did he really expect that to impress me?" God stared at the farmhouse as he contemplated that heaven and earth were very much at risk.

2

It was a frosty day in early 1994 in the small town of Burnsville, North Carolina. The main topic of discussion for the last three decades had been the motorcycle gang, the Dreadnaughts, whose members regularly rode by town. The group had been established in 1960 in Asheville and five years later moved its headquarters to the location in Burnsville, forty-five minutes up the mountain. Jimmy, the leader, reasoned that the group was safer there, as it would be much harder for their rivals to attack. Additionally, it would be almost impossible for any government agencies to put surveillance on the gang in the mountains.

The three leaders of this group were called disciples. The disciples were like the CEOs of corporations, except no one ever questioned their authority or decisions. They laid down the law, and that was it. They managed the Dreadnaughts' burgeoning marijuana business and had begun the process of expanding into the cocaine trade. Those Dreadnaughts who showed great courage and loyalty over a prolonged period of time were designated cowboys. There were only seven of them. They were inaugurated at a ceremony in which a circle symbolizing a wagon wheel was tattooed onto their right shoulders. Thereafter, whenever a cowboy performed a function of great importance to the gang, he received a spoke in the wheel. When the wheel had six spokes, he was elevated to a disciple.

The drug ventures of the gang pulled in as much money as a midsized corporation, and the members lived well. The group's business plan was simple. They eliminated all the major middlemen and dealers; then the disciples or cowboys would meet with the big suppliers and take over the supply lines.

Jimmy was the head disciple. He was six foot three with straight salt-and-pepper hair that flowed just over his shoulders. With the exception

4

of his jeans and cowboy boots, he was a bit of an anomaly. He was clean shaven. He wore a neat, long-sleeved, white button-down shirt, which was his trademark, and there were no discernable tattoos on him. He had hazel eyes that penetrated whomever he was speaking to as if he were staring into the individual's very soul.

Jimmy was fifty-five years old and smart as a whip. He had grown up in a well-to-do family up north. He was the youngest of five children, and he was always thought of as the black sheep of the family. His older brothers excelled in sports, whereas he was content to hang out with his friends, frequently finding his way into minor trouble with the law as a juvenile. His brothers made good grades in high school, and they all attended the state university. Jimmy, although the smartest of the brothers, never applied himself academically, and as a result, his grades were less than stellar. He was fortunate to get accepted into the state university merely because his older siblings had gone to school there and were well respected.

Jimmy managed to do well enough to stay in college and get his degree. Although he really wanted nothing to do with the corporate world, he was provided a job working for a trading firm on Wall Street by two of his older brothers. Although he was making good money, he was not happy. He was ultimately caught handing out insider information and charged with securities fraud, and he spent two years in jail for the offense. He left the firm in disgrace, lost his trader's license, and was disowned by his family.

After his release from jail, Jimmy purchased a Harley and headed south. A few months later, in 1964, he met up with the Dreadnaughts. They were a fledgling organization committing small-time crimes for small-time money. Although not the academic or corporate suit-and-tie type, Jimmy always had big dreams. He began to help increase the gang's membership and steer it toward more lucrative endeavors.

One night in 1965, when Jimmy was twenty-six, the Dreadnaughts drank at a little bikers' bar on the outskirts of Asheville called Bikers and Babes. The Warlords, a rival gang who had controlled the marijuana business in the northwestern area of North Carolina for years, walked into the bar and confronted the Dreadnaughts for attempting to move in on their business. Jimmy, without hesitation, walked up to the leader of the Warlords and shot him in the forehead. The remainder of the Warlords dropped their weapons and summarily joined the Dreadnaughts, and from that moment on, he was the unquestioned leader of the gang.

Jimmy was a brilliant businessman, and the group thrived under his leadership. He was ruthless toward the group's adversaries, and anyone who tried to cut into the gang's market share was eliminated promptly. The Dreadnaughts had become the largest and most feared motorcycle gang in the southeastern United States. Nobody, not even the renowned Hells Angels, messed with them within their territory.

The disciples had recently determined that the group was going to expand into the cocaine business. Jimmy knew that this endeavor would prove far more challenging than their taking over the marijuana business. The main dealers in the marijuana business were small-time players, whereas the cocaine trade was ruled by much bigger fish from a notorious crime family based in New York.

The Dreadnaughts rode their Harleys from Asheville toward Burnsville up the road that wrapped around the mountain. As they reached the small city, rather than take a right onto Main Street and ride their choppers into town, they took a left and proceeded a half mile up a dirt road before taking a right into the five-acre field. They drove their motorcycles through the field to a farmhouse. This was the Dreadnaughts' headquarters.

The front of the farmhouse faced the bikers as they rode through the field toward it. A plain, nondescript white van was nearly always parked at the back of the farmhouse. There was a narrow clearing in the woods leading from the back of the farmhouse that was about a hundred yards long and emptied into an opening in the woods the size of a basketball court. Leading from the opening was an even narrower pathway that was wide enough for a Harley to negotiate, but not a larger motor vehicle, and ran back down the hill to the road just outside the small mountain town below. This route leading from the back of the farmhouse was to be used as an emergency escape in the event it was ever needed. Also, the opening in the woods that connected the narrow clearing leading from the back of the farmhouse and the narrower pathway going down the hill was used to bring those whom the leaders of the Dreadnaughts determined needed to be addressed to a location outside of the presence of the other members of the gang.

The city of Burnsville was a tranquil, peaceful place seemingly far removed from the world stage and its problems. It was an unlikely setting for epic battles between good and evil. These battles would never be referenced in mankind's history books, but they would be major events in celestial history.

Burnsville had a population of 1,644, largely consisting of people over fifty. Each year, about thirty kids graduated from the town's high school. Upon graduating from high school, most left the town, going down the mountain and settling in bigger cities with more opportunities. Main Street ran through the middle of town. On each side of Main Street there were several one- to four-story buildings, many of which were built between the late 1800s and early 1900s. There was one bar with a pool table where many of the younger members of the population congregated each night to drink, play pool, and tell stories.

The only real drama in the sleepy little town of Burnsville occurred in 1989 when a sixteen-year-old high school girl went missing. There had been much speculation that the motorcycle gang had something to do with her disappearance, although others believed she merely ran away. At the time of her disappearance, the town mayor, Bill, convened a town hall meeting to declare that the Dreadnaughts had nothing to do with her disappearance and in fact were helping with the search for her, although there were no visible signs of this. Bill had agreed to allow the Dreadnaughts to purchase the old farmhouse, and it was rumored that he was receiving cash payments from them. The story that was often told in the bar was that the Dreadnaughts took the girl to the farmhouse, where they held her against her will, and Bill was receiving money to conceal this and deflect criticism of the gang.

Bill was in fact as crooked as they came. He was in his sixties, and he had run the town for nearly twenty-five years. Nobody really seemed to ever question his authority. He was the mayor, sheriff, and judge, and he resolved disputes according to who could put a few dollars in his pockets. Nobody seemed to care; this was the way it had always worked in Burnsville. Before Bill, his father ran the town in much the same manner. The only real criticism Bill had faced was when the girl went missing, and for a brief period of time he was accused of helping the Dreadnaughts cover up the crime. He, however, without too much effort was able to largely dispel the criticism and convince the townspeople that the Dreadnaughts did not take the girl and that she merely ran away. Several months passed, the rumors subsided, and life returned to normal. The girl, however, was not found. The bar was the only place where the theory of the Dreadnaughts kidnapping and holding the girl survived.

A year after the girl disappeared, several of the town's young males were drinking late one night at the bar and, emboldened by alcohol, decided to get in a couple of pickup trucks and drive up to the farmhouse to look around. As they approached the farmhouse on foot, they were surrounded by bikers who beat the hell out of them. The following day, bruised and battered, they went to Bill's office to complain. Much to their dismay, he sternly lectured them about trespassing on the Dreadnaughts' property and reiterated his position that the girl simply ran away and the Dreadnaughts were good people who should not be disturbed.

The year 1993 was dismal by any account. In February, a terrorist attack was launched on the World Trade Center when a van exploded beneath it, killing six and injuring a thousand. Two months later, a joke of a man pretending to be God torched the Branch Davidian compound in Waco, Texas, resulting in the deaths of seventy-six people, including twenty-seven children. As 1994 rolled in, it was hoped that better things lay ahead.

The gang typically met the first week of every month for a party that lasted a few days. A day or two before the parties, Jimmy would call the two other disciples and two or three of the top cowboys to the farmhouse for a meeting to discuss important matters regarding the gang's affairs. These discussions were confidential, and their contents were not shared with any members of the gang not in attendance. A couple of days before the party the first week of March of 1994, Jimmy had called a meeting with the two other disciples and the three top cowboys.

One matter on the disciples' agenda at the March meeting was Skinny. He was the bookkeeper and treasurer for the gang. He was also Jimmy's cousin. Jimmy had heard that he had been skimming some of the profits from the gang's marijuana business. Jimmy had assigned one of the cowboys to investigate the matter and report back to him. The rumors proved to be true. Skinny had been using the money on parties where drugs and strippers were plentiful. Although he had been spending the skimmed money on parties that benefited the gang, he had done so without the disciples' authorization, and his indiscretion would have to be addressed in a meaningful way that sent a message to all gang members.

It was briefly discussed whether Skinny should be executed in front of the gang members at the upcoming get-together, but this was not a real option, because he was a very likeable and popular member of the gang. Jimmy, being the shrewd leader that he was, knew that it was important that he show some degree of compassion toward him. Jimmy ruled the gang with undisputed authority, the gang prospered under his leadership, and he was a feared and respected leader; however, he knew this could change rapidly.

After much debate, it was ultimately concluded that Skinny's hand would be severed and placed in a jug of formaldehyde on the mantle over the fireplace of the farmhouse for all to see. He was called and advised to come to the headquarters the following day, a day before the gathering of the entire gang.

Second, the gang was in the process of moving into the cocaine trade, and Jimmy knew that a crime family from New York monopolized this trade in the Southeast. The man who had run the business for the mob was Don Gambotti, who had his headquarters in Atlanta. He had recently been eliminated by the gang, and the disciples were discussing what further

8

objectives they needed to accomplish to take over the cocaine trade in the Southeast.

The third and last issue to be discussed regarded the gang's need to have an attorney exclusively represent it in a wide array of matters. The disciples knew that it would not be easy to persuade a top-flight attorney to agree to exclusively work as the gang's legal counsel. The disciples had a plan to accomplish this that had been in operation for ten months, since May of 1993, and they would meet with the attorney at the upcoming party involving the whole gang.

The day after the meeting, Skinny came in and was given the bad news. Although he wasn't thrilled about the punishment, he was happy because he knew it could have been a lot worse. At least he talked the disciples into severing his left hand instead of his right, and he was able to keep his position as bookkeeper and treasurer.

The next day, the small town in the Carolina mountains reverberated with the roar of motorcycle engines just outside town. The motorcycles ascended the half-mile dirt road that emptied into the huge field. Sprinkled sporadically around the perimeter of the field were tents of all sizes, and there were Harleys everywhere.

The women at this gathering were scantily clad in leather; some were even attractive. The men were typical bikers. Most of them had spiderwebs in varying stages of completion tattooed on their left shoulders. Each link of the web represented a killing, which was a highly touted accomplishment for the Dreadnaughts. With rare exceptions, the women didn't have much say over with whom they slept. They were the property of the gang, and they were shared liberally. The drink of choice was Jack Daniels or Budweiser, the smoke Marlboro and marijuana.

Inside the house, the atmosphere was surreal, with men and women alike chugging Jack Daniels and smoke wafting through the air. On the mantle over the fireplace sat two large glass jars. One contained Skinny's hand floating in formaldehyde, the other a head. The head belonged to an investigator who had been poking his nose in the wrong place. These decorations were reminders to all not to betray or mess with the brotherhood.

The disciples were upstairs engaged in conversation with a young trial attorney named Trey Jackson Jr. He was the attorney whom Jimmy had selected to be the gang's legal counsel. Jimmy was not happy with Trey's responses to his questions. He ordered the three cowboys in the room to take him to the van behind the farmhouse. Toby, one of the cowboys, lacked only one spoke before becoming the fourth disciple. As Trey, wearing jeans, a sweatshirt, and a Yale baseball hat turned backward, sat in the van across from Toby, his thoughts drifted. He was strangely calm and at peace with the knowledge that he was certainly within minutes of meeting his maker. He thought of the life he once had. He pictured his wife Tara, who was eight months pregnant, and he got a forlorn look on his face as he envisioned the times he would be missing with his son-to-be. He wondered how his life had sunk to such depths in four short months.

3

Four and a half years earlier, in August of 1989, Trey had met Tara at Yale in their first year of law school, when they were twenty-two. When his eyes met hers for the first time, he was nearly knocked off his feet. She had dark brown flowing hair and the greenest eyes he had ever seen. She carried herself in a manner that said she was important, yet she had a humble and modest way about her. Trey marveled at how she looked into the eyes of people with whom she was engaged in conversation in a way that indicated that she respected and cared about them.

Tara was not only from a wealthy family residing in Charleston but was from old money. Her grandfather was a cofounder of the New York Stock Exchange. Her father was the CEO of a major corporation, and her family was widely known for its philanthropic efforts. Trey was amazed to find an article about her father in *Forbes* magazine, and he was awestruck as he read the article about him and his family.

Trey's father had left when Trey was two. He vanished, and Trey had never even received a letter or a birthday card from him. Trey's mother had frequently worked two jobs and done the best she could, but there had barely been enough of the essentials to provide for him. Looking back on his youth, he believed that he had to have set a record for eating bologna sandwiches. In good times, he had milk with which to wash them down.

When Trey was young, he and his mother, Missy, lived in Marion, South Carolina, and his mother would sometimes take him to the beach on the weekend. He would sit on the beach and look out into the surf and try to picture what his father looked like. He would find himself wondering why his father had abruptly disappeared from his life and totally abandoned him. Did his father not love him? Why did his father care so little about him that he had made no effort to contact him or see him over the years?

When Trey was eight, his mother had saved some money to buy him a surfboard for Christmas. Prior to that, she could see the pain in his eyes as he stared out into the ocean, and she thought that this would give him something to do and make him happy when they went to the beach. He became a proficient surfer over the next five years, and he met friends while he surfed. His trips to the beach became much more fulfilling.

Trey entered a surfing contest when he was in the eighth grade, and although he only surfed one or two times a month when his mother took him to the beach, he placed third and was delirious when he beat the many boys who lived on or near the beach and who surfed regularly. When he went to high school he made the basketball team, and his trips to the beach and surfing were much less frequent. He always looked back on those weekend trips to the beach when he was in grade school and middle school with much delight.

When Trey made the high school basketball team as a ninth grader, he was only five feet eight inches tall. He had found a new sport to which to dedicate himself, and he frequently stayed an hour after practice was over to work on his skills. Also, he was a fierce competitor. What he lacked in size, he made up for with hard work and heart.

By his junior year in high school, Trey had grown to six feet three and had chiseled features. From a very early age, Trey knew that he wanted a better life. He was more dedicated to his studies than most kids were. He was also a very attractive kid. He was tan with sandy, wavy blond hair and dark blue eyes. It was easy to picture him walking down the beach with a surfboard under his arm. All of the cheerleaders wanted to date him, and he had become the leading scorer and star of the varsity basketball team. He did not date much, as the majority of his time was spent playing basketball and studying. When he did go out with a girl, he went out with one from his study group or a member of student government, to which he also belonged. He shunned the cheerleaders because he was looking more for a friend with whom to hang out and talk. He would occasionally go with a girl or his friends on the team to the beach, where he had such fond memories of his earlier years.

In Trey's senior year of high school, his team made it to the state tournament, and the school was abuzz with excitement. The team won its first seven playoff games and made it to the state final, where it played a team that was ranked number one in the state all year and was undefeated. It had five players who had received Division I scholarships, which was unheard of. Suffice it to say, Trey's team was a huge underdog, and nobody really expected them to win the championship. It was a great accomplishment for them just to make it to the championship game.

As the clock wound down, everyone was surprised that Trey's team trailed by only two points with twenty seconds remaining. The other team had the ball, however, and it did not look good. With ten seconds remaining, one of Trey's teammates stole the ball, dribbled down the court, and as he was cut off by two defenders, passed the ball out to Trey, who was standing just beyond the three-point line. He let the ball go with two seconds on the clock. As the ball went in the basket, resulting in his team winning the state championship by one point, the place was bedlam with the stands emptying onto the court to celebrate with the team. Afterward, as the team sang on the bus ride home, he thought that the only thing that could have made it better would have been if his father were there to see it and be proud of him.

Trey went to a small state college on a basketball scholarship. He knew that his chances of playing basketball professionally were not good, so he focused on his grades and graduated number two in his class. Going to a law school like Yale was a pipe dream for him, but one of his professors encouraged him and helped him with his application. He was in shock when he opened the letter and realized that he had been accepted to Yale Law School. With a partial academic scholarship, student loans, and a part-time job, he was able to attend the law school of his dreams.

The first time Trey spoke to Tara, he was mesmerized. Afterward, he could not even remember what they were talking about. *She must have thought I was an idiot*, he said to himself. He frequently dreamed of being with her. One day he learned from a friend that she was interested in him and looked forward to seeing him at a Halloween party later in the week. He had a very difficult time focusing on his studies that week, as all he could think about was Tara. When he saw her in school, she looked at him, smiled, and said, "Hi, Trey," in a way that made him feel fuzzy and tingly inside.

At the party, Trey, his courage inflated by a couple of beers, asked Tara to dance. She was so graceful and elegant, and he was horrified every time he stepped on her toes. However, she just laughed and looked into his eyes in a manner that made him feel like in her arms was where he belonged. Afterward, they went to a hill off campus where they could look up at the stars. It was a beautiful clear night, and they talked for hours.

At one point, as they sat holding hands, Trey looked at Tara and said somberly, "Tara, my father left me when I was two. I was raised by my mother, and we never had much money, and you come from a very wealthy family."

Before he could continue, Tara put her hand over his mouth and said, "Trey, you must find me to be very shallow. It's not what you have or don't have that is important to me. It's what's in your heart, and you have an awesome heart. Besides, I see great things when I look into your eyes. It's not where you're from that is important. It's where you are going that is important, and I think you are going to do great things in life. I believe in you."

With that, Trey was deeply and totally in love with Tara. She made him feel like he was someone special. She had his heart, his mind, and his very soul. At the end of the night, they embraced in a passionate kiss. Trey had never been kissed like that before. They were together from that moment on, almost inseparable, like soul mates.

Trey beamed when he took Tara home over spring break to meet his mother and his friends from high school. Missy and his friends fell in love with her. She was an incredible girl, and most important, it was obvious how happy she made Trey. He had never been this exceedingly happy, and he had a constant smile on his face.

One afternoon Missy sat on the porch with Tara as Trey left to go play basketball with some of his former high school teammates. Missy thanked her for making her son so happy, and she proceeded to tell her about how she took him to the beach when he was young, and that at times he had an emptiness about him. She knew that it was because he anguished over never knowing his father and his father abandoning him. Trey had never spoken to Tara about his feelings regarding his father except for the brief reference to him the first night they spent together. After the discussion Tara had with Missy, she felt as if she knew him even better, and she was even more determined that they would have an incredible life together and a family one day.

Their relationship was not without its bumps in the road. Although Tara was deeply in love with Trey, her parents had a hard time accepting him. They had envisioned her marrying someone who, like Tara, came from old money. Her parents did not fret much, because they never thought the relationship would last, but when Trey and Tara announced their engagement in the fall semester of their third and final year of law school— along with their intention of getting married right after graduation—her parents did everything they could to dissuade her.

Shortly after announcing their engagement, there was terror and high anxiety on campus. Over a two-month period there had been a string of murders on and around the campus. All of the victims were attractive females who had been tortured, raped, and sadistically murdered. They were left posed in demeaning positions that led the police and FBI to speculate that the murderer was someone who had experienced rejection and humiliation by attractive young women in the past. The number of victims had grown to seven, and the serial killer was attacking almost weekly. The entire campus and the town of New Haven were on high alert, and the story was carried on all of the national news networks daily. The killer was labeled the "Polo Killer" because most of the young women were college students clad in preppy clothing.

Trey would not let Tara go anywhere without him. She was very happy to have him around, as she, like all the other women on campus, was on edge. She lived in a small house just off campus with two other girls. Tara's parents, although not very happy with their relationship, instructed Trey to be with her at all times.

Tara's father, Richard, called Trey and said, "Trey, I want you to sleep at her house. Don't you leave her there by herself, not even for a second."

Trey, well aware of Richard's feelings about him, responded sarcastically, "Do you want me to sleep with her? I mean in her bed?"

"Yes, do whatever you have to do to keep my baby safe. Do you understand me, Trey?"

"Yes, sir. Consider it done."

The police and FBI had made no progress with the case. Far away, in a little biker bar, five bikers were sitting around talking, smoking pot, and drinking whiskey. They began talking about the case and how inept the FBI was.

One of the men was extremely intoxicated and said, "I'm going to tell you guys something. I know who the dude is."

"How in the hell would you know that?" laughed one of the men.

The man leaned over the table slightly and said quietly, "I was at a family reunion last weekend, and my nephew and I were out in the barn drinking whiskey and hitting the crack pipe when he starts spilling his guts to me. He says he's the Polo Killer. I laugh and say bullshit. He then breaks open his wallet and starts showing me the pictures of these girls. He was bragging about it." By this point, he had the others full attention.

"Do you have a picture of your nephew?" asked Animal, one of the bikers.

"Whoa, I'm not saying any more."

Animal then grabbed him by the back of his hair and slammed his face into the table. He grabbed his wallet and rifled through it before finding a photo that he believed may be of the nephew. He then looked at the man with blood dripping from his nose and mouth and asked, "Is this him?"

The man babbled, "Screw you."

Animal grabbed the back of his head by the hair and again slammed his face into the table, sending particles of his teeth airborne. He then said, "I'm going to ask you politely one more time; then I'm going to get violent. Is this him?"

The man screamed, "Isn't anybody going to help me here?" The ten other bikers in the bar just stared, not saying a word. As Animal grabbed him a third time by the hair, he blurted out, "Yes, yes, that's him, you bastard."

"I'm only going to ask you once. What's his name?" Animal then drew his gun and put it underneath the man's chin as he pulled his head back by the hair with the other hand.

The man screamed, "Bobby Blanchard."

Animal then motioned to the others to take him away. He instructed them not to off him until they got his call.

Animal wiped the blood spray from the picture before placing it into his vest pocket. He then looked at a third man at the table and said, "Let's go, Reapor. We're going on a ride." Reapor got a wide smile on his face as though he was very excited about this journey.

Thirteen hours later, the men arrived in New Haven, Connecticut, and checked into a hotel. They looked in a phone book and found a Robert Blanchard, a B. Blanchard, and a Bob Blanchard. They went to the address of Bob Blanchard. They knocked on the door, and an elderly man with a walker opened it. They moved on to the address of B. Blanchard. He came to the door, and again no match with the photograph. They arrived at the apartment of Robert Blanchard. No one answered the door, and the men picked the lock and entered the apartment. Reapor opened a drawer and motioned for Animal to come over. Buried beneath several neatly stacked shirts were numerous photographs. They had their man. Animal placed a call and said simply, "Do him."

It was 9:00 p.m., and the two men sat in chairs with guns with silencers attached waiting for Bobby Blanchard to come home. They passed a whiskey bottle back and forth in a nearly pitch-black room as they waited.

A couple of hours later, Bobby unlocked the door and walked in. He turned on a light, and as he looked up, he saw the two black-leather-clad men sitting on the couch of the small apartment, guns in hand. He turned and tried to run out. Reapor grabbed him from behind and sat him down in a third chair directly across from the men.

"What do you want from me?" asked Bobby as he quivered in fear.

"Maybe we just wanted to see up close what a serial rapist and killer looks like," responded Animal.

Reapor, who was a beast of a man but who had the IQ of a twelve-year-old, said, "He don't look like much, do he?"

Bobby, still shaking, said, "What are you talking about? You think I am the Polo Killer?"

Animal showed Reapor the picture and said, "He sure looks like him. What do you think, Reapor?"

"Yep, that's him."

16

Animal then flipped the photograph onto the floor before Bobby, who picked it up, looked at it, and exclaimed, "So it's a photo of me. How does that mean that I am the Polo Killer?" Animal then threw the photographs of the women on the floor. Bobby had a look of terror on his face as he said, "You guys aren't cops or the FBI. What do you want?"

Animal and Reapor looked at each other and laughed. Animal said, "How does it feel to torture, rape, and kill defenseless young women? What kind of sick bastard poses them to be found like that? How does it feel to know that you have less than five minutes to live?"

Bobby, clearly panicking, said, "Who are you guys? We can work something out, can't we? What do you want?"

Animal grinned and responded, "I'll tell you what I'm going to do. I'm a fair man. If you can rape and kill Reapor, I'll walk out of here and never reveal your secret."

Reapor laughed as he said, "Yeah, Bobby, why don't you try to rape and kill me?"

Bobby jumped up off the chair and ran for the door. Animal shot him in both legs as he fell to the floor. He then went to him and stuffed a small towel in his mouth so that his crying could not be heard. He put his gun in his mouth and said, "Beg, Bobby. Beg like your victims did." As Bobby tried to speak, Animal pulled the trigger.

The two men put on their sweatshirts and sunglasses, pulled their hoodies over their heads, and walked out the door. As they exited the apartment, two men from an adjoining apartment stood in the hall looking at them.

"What just happened in there?" asked one of them.

Animal responded simply, "Call the police. The Polo Killer is dead."

Within minutes the place was swarming with police and FBI. The two men who saw them leave could only say that they drove away on Harleys.

The following weekend, Tara's parents, Richard and Edith, came to visit her. Everyone was relieved that the Polo Killer was dead, although the circumstances continued to be a mystery. They arrived at her place at 5:00 p.m. and were greeted at the door by Tara, who gave them a big hug.

Richard and Edith took Trey, Tara, and her two roommates out to dinner. At one point, all the women excused themselves to go to the restroom. Richard asked Trey if he was staying back in his dorm room now that the Polo Killer was dead and the threat was gone.

"Oh, I thought I would stay overnight a while longer just to make sure."

"Trey, I know we don't have the best of relationships, but you need to respect my daughter and my wishes. You shouldn't be staying at her place—actually my place, as I bought it for her to live in while going to school—unless there's a need for it. The need is gone."

Just then the girls returned, and their faces were pale. Richard asked, "What's wrong, girls?"

Tara said, "I just got a call from one of my friends, and she says that there has been another killing, just like the others. Either they got the wrong guy or he has a partner."

Richard immediately turned to Trey and said, "I'm sorry. You're right. Until we're sure that this thing is over, you're with her 24/7, okay?"

"Richard, in all seriousness, you have nothing to worry about. I love her, and I'll protect her at all times. You've got my word."

The paper indicated that the FBI was speculating that the remaining killer or killers may have ties to a local motorcycle gang, as their best information was that two bikers were seen leaving the dead man's apartment. Anybody on a motorcycle was looked at suspiciously.

The most powerful gang that controlled the northeastern United States, Hell's Fury, had been friendly with the gang who controlled the southeastern states, the Dreadnaughts. They had worked together on drug deals and taking each other's enemies out, and it worked so long as they respected each other's territories. However, Jimmy, the leader of the Dreadnaughts, got an angry call from the president of Hell's Fury complaining that the Dreadnaughts had come into their territory and caused this problem. The Dreadnaughts' leadership had proudly shared the information with Hell's Fury that two of its members were responsible for killing the Polo Killer. Initially, everyone was happy about this. However, with another murder and the FBI all over them, Hell's Fury was now extremely upset.

Jimmy called Animal and Reapor to the farmhouse and told Animal that this had become a bad situation and that he needed to make it right.

"We thought we were doing a good deed and having some fun."

"I know, and at first it was all good. We and our friends to the north were all proud that one of our own killed the son of a bitch that the FBI couldn't find for two months. Unfortunately, with the additional murder and the heat they are taking, they are demanding that we fix it. We definitely don't want to be on bad terms with them and have this thing escalate into a war."

"What do you want us to do?"

"You need to go find the second killer."

The following day, Animal and Reapor were shaved clean, had haircuts, and were given new wardrobes so that they could assimilate into the Yale surroundings without looking too out of place. They got into the white van out back and embarked on their mission.

On the drive to New Haven, Animal reflected on how they were going to find the second killer. He looked at Reapor and said, "Did we miss anything, Reap? If this dude is a copycat killer, he is going to be almost impossible to find. If he was Bobby's partner, did you see anything in the apartment that may tell us who he is or give us a clue?"

"Well, I did keep one of the pictures, but I don't think it helps us. It's just the picture of one of the girls before anything was done to her. She's smiling and happy. She's in her underwear. I didn't think it would hurt if I took that one."

Animal hit the brakes hard and pulled off the road. "Give me the photo, Reap." He inspected the photo carefully before saying, "Damn, Reap, look at the bottom left-hand corner of the picture."

"Yeah, I see him, and that ain't Bobby."

"Exactly. We may have just got a lucky break. I bet Bobby took the photo, and this picture shows the second killer's face in the background." He slapped Reapor in the head and said, "Reap, good thing you are a perverted son of a bitch. You may have just saved our hides."

Upon arriving in New Haven, Animal and Reapor went directly to Hell's Fury's headquarters. They were immediately surrounded. Animal took off his shirt and showed them the wagon wheel on his shoulder and the Dreadnaught insignia on his chest.

They were taken to the group's president, who said, "So you are the Carolina Animal. I've heard all the stories. Although I admire your courage and work, you've caused big problems for us up here. How are you going to fix it?"

"Do you have an in with anyone in the local police force who has access to databases of criminals?"

"Yes, but how is that going to help you? The police and FBI have been searching databases for over two months trying to find these assholes."

"Don't worry about it; it's just a hunch I have."

"I'll set it up."

Animal cut out the portion of the photograph with the man's face. He left Reapor in the hotel room and went to meet the police connection. He walked into the station and asked for her. She met him and took him into her office.

"What's this about?" she asked.

"I have a picture, a piece of a photograph, and I need to know if there is any way you can run it through something and get me an ID."

"I can try, but it may take a few minutes."

The fragment of the photo was placed into a processor, and pixels began to slowly form on the computer screen. Several minutes later, the man's entire face was formed and his name and address popped up on the screen.

Animal excitedly asked, "Can you print that out for me?"

"Sure, but can you tell me what this is about?"

"I wish I could. I'm sure you'll figure it out in the next couple of hours. Thank you so much for your help." He took the printout and left.

It was early evening, and Animal awakened Reapor and they set off for the man's house. After some searching, they found the address on a mailbox located at the top of a dirt road in a remote area on the outskirts of town. They parked the car at the top of the road and made their way on foot down the dirt road. After several minutes, they spotted a small house with the lights on. As they approached the front door, they heard loud screams coming from within. They kicked in the door and went in with guns drawn. As they entered a hallway, they encountered a man standing naked ten feet in front of them with a large knife in his hand. Animal immediately recognized the man as the one in the printout.

Animal smiled widely at the shocked man and said, "Didn't anybody ever tell you not to bring a knife to a gun fight?" He then shot the man between the eyes.

Reapor said, "Damn, why did you do that? I thought we were going to torture him a little bit."

"I'm too tired for fun."

They walked toward the room from where the screams emanated, expecting to find the worst. When they rounded the corner, they saw a beautiful young girl wearing only panties with her hands tied to a bar above her head. They had arrived just in time, before he had cut or physically harmed her. Animal explained that she could relax because her assailant was dead and they were there to free her. They untied her and found her clothes.

As they drove away from the house, the hysterical young girl thanked them repeatedly. "He was getting ready to rape and cut me," she said as she continued crying. Animal explained that they were going to drop her in front of the local police station and that she needed to give the officers the location of the man's house.

She said, still in shock and crying, "I don't know the address or remember how to get there."

Animal said, "Here, take this," and handed her the printout with the man's name and address on it.

As they approached the station, the girl said, "Thank you for saving my life. Who are you guys, FBI?"

"Something like that," responded Animal.

When Animal and Reapor returned home, they were greeted with a huge party at the group's headquarters in the mountains. Jimmy took them inside and said, "I have no idea how you two pulled this off. You have now killed both Polo Killers, and most importantly, our friends from the north are extremely pleased."

"Yeah," said Reapor, "and we saved the lives of many young girls."

"Yeah, that too," said Jimmy as he slapped Animal and Reapor on their backs and instructed them to join the party in their honor.

A few months after the Polo Killers were taken out, Tara and Trey were visiting her parents in Charleston over spring break, a couple of months before graduation. Her high school friends persuaded her to come to a party with Trey. The party was thrown at an expansive mansion on the battery. This was one of the houses that had been passed down for generations. Trey could not believe that this house was even much bigger and more opulent than Tara's.

After doing his best to mingle with the crowd, Trey was made aware by one of Tara's girlfriends that the boy who grew up in the house was an old boyfriend of Tara's. They had started dating when in high school, and they continued throughout much of college, although going to different universities. Trey was curious as to why she had never mentioned this to him, but he didn't give it much thought.

As the night progressed, many of the kids grew boisterous as the effects of the alcohol started to get the better of them. At one point, as Trey was speaking to two of Tara's girlfriends, he noticed that a crowd of several of the more intoxicated guys were looking and pointing at him. He knew that this was not a good sign, although he wasn't too worried about it, as he was a tough kid who had never backed down from anyone.

Eventually the pack approached him, making references to his being Tara's boyfriend. As their comments went in a demeaning direction, Trey just looked at them and smiled. The biggest of the bunch, Charles, was Tara's ex-boyfriend. He was about six feet six inches tall, three inches taller than Trey, and slightly bigger.

Charles, with five of his friends behind him egging him on, chirped, "I hear you were raised in a shack. Is that true?"

As Charles's friends cackled, Trey responded, "That may be true, but who is Tara leaving with tonight?"

Tara came rushing over and grabbed Trey. As Trey stared down Charles with a smile on his face, Charles challenged him to step out back so that they could settle the matter like men. Although Tara implored Trey to leave with her, he would not back down.

The crowd moved out back in anticipation of the impending brawl, and Trey and Charles stepped onto the concrete drive. There was a basketball lying on the drive, and Charles, having been a very good high school basketball player himself and unaware of the quality of player Trey was, declared, "This is your lucky night. I'll give you a choice. Either I can kick your ass, literally, or I can kick your ass in basketball. What will it be?" Trey laughed, took off his shirt, picked up the ball, and threw it to Charles. He then proceeded to make Charles look like a laughingstock on the court. Charles, slumped over and being ridiculed by his friends, stuck up his hand as if to say enough. Trey grabbed Tara's hand, and they left.

The following morning at breakfast, Tara recounted how Trey had handled the situation with Charles. Richard looked dismayed as he listened to the story, slightly embellished by Tara, as he had always hoped that Tara would end up with Charles one day.

Richard, upon realizing that there was nothing he could do to derail the marriage, sat down and had a long talk with Trey. He thought it best that upon graduating, Trey take a respectable job with a Fortune 500 company, which of course he could arrange. When Trey responded that he was going to pursue his dream of being a personal injury trial attorney, Richard was aghast. He considered personal injury attorneys to be the scum of the earth. They robbed corporate America and gave the money to the common man. He could not fathom how he would explain this to those at the club. When Tara's parents realized that she was going to marry Trey despite their best efforts to prevent it, they were determined to have a lavish wedding with all the bells and whistles.

Although virtually resigned to the realization that Tara would wed Trey, Richard, being the cold-blooded snake that he was, had a trick up his sleeve—one last-ditch effort to prevent the wedding.

After graduating in the middle of May in 1992, Tara and Trey returned to Charleston for the wedding in late May. Trey was staying at a small hotel with his two best friends from high school, who had made it down for the wedding. Two days prior to the wedding, Tara's friends picked her up in a limo for her bachelorette patty. Trey and his buddies were merely planning on going to a sports bar. A knock on the door came, and Trey stood flabbergasted as Charles and the five who had taunted him a couple of months ago stood outside the door with a limo behind them.

Charles said, "Hey, man, let's be buds. She loves you, and there is nothing I can do about it. Besides, where in the hell did you learn to play basketball? Anyone who can play like that is a friend of mine. Let's go party." Trey, although not totally enthralled with the idea, figured that he couldn't say no, and anyway, he thought, it didn't hurt to become friendly with friends of Tara's family.

As the night at the strip bar progressed and Charles ordered seemingly nonstop rounds of drinks and shots, Trey and his two buddies were getting rather intoxicated, which was a rarity for Trey. He generally refrained from drinking, and when he did, he drank moderately. Unknown to Trey and his two buddies, Charles and his friends were feigning intoxication and pouring out their drinks and shots.

After Trey had reached a level of intoxication where he could barely talk or walk, Charles and two of his cohorts slipped him into a back room at the club while Charles's other friends occupied his old high school buddies. Trey, lacking any sense of lucidity, was placed on a couch while two dancers were summoned to enter into provocative poses with him. Charles snapped the pictures, which were extremely graphic.

The following morning, Trey and his friends awakened around noon with pounding headaches. As they pieced together the night before, the memories slowly surfaced for Trey. He didn't remember with total clarity the details of what happened, but he remembered enough. At worst, he had a sexual encounter. At best, he acted highly inappropriately with the dancers in the back room.

Charles went to Tara's house to proudly hand over the photographs to Richard. Tara greeted him at the door. She took him out back by the pool and had a conversation with him, at the end of which he clearly and the first time understood the depth of her love for Trey, and he suddenly grew a conscience. He showed up at Trey's hotel room and explained everything. He handed the photographs to Trey and indicated that all the sexual positions were staged. Trey hadn't done anything. He also explained that this was Richard's plan.

"Why are you helping me?" asked Trey.

"It's real simple; I just had a conversation with Tara. She loves you."

As Charles walked away, Trey said, "Charles," and as he turned, Trey said only, "Thank you."

"You're welcome." He then smiled at Trey and said, "Screw Richard."

Charles went to Richard's house later that day, and as he stood outside the front door, he told Richard that despite his best efforts, he couldn't get Trey to drink or do anything inappropriate. "The guy's a stand-up guy," he told him. Richard shut the door in his face, whereupon Charles, staring at the door, mumbled, "The hell with you, old man."

The wedding took place at a church built in 1868. It was attended by over two hundred people. Trey had only his mother and a handful of friends in attendance. Tara's parents invited everyone from the club, many of whom had on jewelry that cost more than Trey's car. He didn't mind that the wedding was essentially for her parents; he was getting his dream girl, and Tara knew that she was home after walking down the aisle and looking into his eyes. They were twenty-four and ready to begin their lives together.

4

Trey was hired in June of 1992 by a medium-sized, prestigious personal injury law firm in Asheville, North Carolina. He had received offers for much more money from bigger firms up north, but Tara loved Asheville, and they would be only four hours from her family in Charleston and three and a half hours from his mother in Marion. This made her parents somewhat happy, as he had also interviewed with firms in New York and California. Although they wanted her in Charleston with them, at least she was only a few hours away.

Although Trey worked long hours and spent a large part of the weekends studying for the state bar exam, Tara was happy. When he had free time, he spent it all with her. Unlike the other young attorneys in the firm, he did not spend any of his time going to bars after work or going to social gatherings without her. She found a job working for a local charity, which made her parents happy. The newlyweds were very content and deeply in love. He still felt tingly all over when she looked at him, and she could not wait to see him after work. When they kissed, she felt the same electricity coursing through her body that she felt that first time after the Halloween party. Life was good.

They lived in a modest house in a middle-class neighborhood, not what Tara was accustomed to, but a step up for Trey. She did not really mind; she would have lived in a tent with him. He knew that she was raised in much more affluent surroundings with all of the amenities, and he badly wanted to provide her with a life more consistent with that to which she was accustomed. He also had a burning desire to prove to her parents that she had made the right decision in choosing him.

In August, a couple of months after moving into their home and settling into their new jobs, Trey passed the bar exam and began to get some of his own cases. The firm held a meeting every Monday at 7:30 a.m., at which time they discussed current cases and assigned the new cases. A new case involving a Coke bottle was on the table. An eighteen-year-old girl with a promising modeling career had a Coke bottle inexplicably explode in her face, causing serious facial scarring and effectively ending her modeling career. The partners explained that this was a very difficult case. They were aware of this happening a few times before, and Coca-Cola had always vehemently denied any responsibility. Every case that had been tried before a jury resulted in a verdict of no liability for Coca-Cola. For a successful result, it would have to be taken to trial; it would not be settled, and the chances of obtaining a favorable jury verdict were slim. However, the partners stated, this was a nice girl for whom they felt bad, and if the jury found Coca-Cola liable, the damages would be in the millions, as it was projected that the girl would have easily made six figures for many years.

Something about the case grabbed Trey, and he eagerly volunteered to take it. The partners, knowing that Coca-Cola would bring experienced trial attorneys to the table who would not play fairly, questioned the wisdom of giving him the case a few months out of law school. After much discussion, they determined to give him his shot. The case was set for trial the first week of December.

In preparing for the trial, Trey took the deposition of the leading chemist for Coca-Cola. During the deposition, he learned that an associate chemist had been recently terminated. The reason for the termination seemed suspect to him, and he knew that if he found this person, he may find the smoking gun that would allow him to take Coca-Cola down. The company apparently did not know where the chemist was, and Trey knew from reviewing transcripts of previous legal proceedings involving Coca-Cola that they would not voluntarily provide him with useful information. They had a reputation for being uncooperative in the discovery process. As the trial neared, the investigator Trey had hired to find the fired chemist had not been able to locate him. Without him, Trey knew he had no chance.

Trey had been obsessed with this case, working day and night for a couple of months. He and Tara felt as though it would be a good idea to get away for a weekend to relax. In early November, they drove to the Grove Park Inn, her favorite hotel. They spent two entire days together, and he was able to put things into perspective.

"Tara, even if I lose this case, I have you, and that's all that matters."

Tara, having had a couple of glasses of wine, quipped, "Yeah, and you can always go work for my dad."

"Now that's funny. You should drink more often."

The following morning, as they were packing their bags, Trey's cell phone rang. "Trey," he heard, "you need to get here right away. I'm in

Atlanta with your guy, the chemist, and you're not going to believe what he's telling me. I think you've got your smoking gun."

Upon arriving in Atlanta, Trey met with the investigator in his hotel room. They drove to the chemist's house in the suburbs, and he welcomed them into his home. The chemist's wife was in the kitchen, and his children were running through the house playing. Trey and the investigator followed the chemist to the back-porch patio, where his wife brought them all a glass of tea. Trey began to inform the chemist about the details of the case. Most importantly, he described his client in detail. He knew that to get the chemist to completely open up to him, he needed to invoke the chemist's empathy for his client.

Initially, the chemist seemed hesitant to provide detailed information. He spoke to Trey in generalities as to Coca-Cola's knowing that the bottles could explode, without providing any details regarding how they might explode or how the corporation knew this. Trey feared that the chemist was not going to give him the type of specific information he required.

Trey calmly opened his briefcase and took out two pictures. He stoically handed them to the chemist without uttering a word. One picture was a close up of the model's face prior to the incident; the other was a close up of her badly scarred face following the incident. After viewing the photographs, the chemist looked up at him with a sullen look on his face. Trey leaned forward in his chair, looked the chemist square in the eye, and said, "Sir, this beautiful young girl needs your help. Prior to this incident, she had a modeling career that was getting ready to take off. The doctors anticipate that even with extensive surgical scar revision procedures, her face will still be marred for life, and her career is over. Also, she was engaged to be married, but because of her depression and perhaps her altered appearance, her fiancé called off the engagement last week. What you need to decide is if you are going to do what is right here. If you want to help this girl, I need details. I need to know everything."

The chemist spent the next hour explaining the secret meetings Coca-Cola had, which included a few of the chemists and high-ranking executives. He indicated that the CEO and president were present at a couple of the meetings. He went into detail as to the chemists' testing of bottles and what was discussed at the meetings. He also revealed what the executives decided at the conclusions of the meetings.

After the chemist was done spilling his guts, Trey passionately said to him, "I very much appreciate your honesty. I know it takes a lot of courage to reveal all of that information. Most important, my client appreciates your courage. What I need to know from you is whether are you willing to take the stand and testify to all of this, to testify fully to the matters you revealed to me today. Are you willing to help this girl? Are you on board?"

The chemist looked down at the ground for a moment before looking up and staring at Trey and stating, "Yes, I am on board."

The trial was still four weeks off, and Trey excitedly flew back to Asheville. Although he was ecstatic at the prospect of being the first attorney to defeat Coca-Cola at trial, he also knew that four weeks was a long time, and he had concerns that the chemist may change his mind. Upon arriving home, he recounted to Tara everything related to his meeting with the chemist. At Tara's suggestion, when he sent the subpoena to the chemist requiring him to be at the trial to testify, he enclosed the photographs of the girl that the chemist viewed at their meeting.

Tara's family had a long tradition of going snow skiing in Colorado the first week of every December, but much to Richard's dissatisfaction, Tara elected to stay behind and support Trey, as this was his first big trial.

At trial, Coca-Cola tried to block its former chemist from testifying. It argued that the chemicals and ingredients in Coke were a trade secret that could not be revealed pursuant to its contract with its ex-employee. Trey, knowing that this ruling would make or break his case, stood and argued, "Your honor, what is more important to this court? The right of Coca-Cola to protect the secret ingredients comprising its product, or the right of this beautiful young girl who has had her face marred and a promising modeling career ruined to seek justice in this court?" The court ruled in his favor and allowed the chemist to testify.

The chemist testified that Coca-Cola knew that two of the chemicals used in its Coke drink, at a certain temperature, in rare instances, had the possibility of causing an explosion that would shatter the bottle. Further, because it would cost tens of millions of dollars to change the chemicals and it would alter the taste slightly, the executives decided it would make more sense and be cheaper to defend the cases in court in the rare instances when a bottle exploded and injured someone. There was a collective gasp in the courtroom as the chemist testified. Trey knew he had them.

The jury awarded the girl 4.8 million dollars for her injuries and 10 million dollars in punitive damages. This was by far the largest jury award the firm had ever obtained, and Trey was treated like a rock star as he returned to the office.

Unbeknownst to Trey, Jimmy, the leader of the feared motorcycle gang, the Dreadnaughts, had attended the entire trial. He was extremely impressed with Trey's performance. Unfortunately, as Trey would find out in a future meeting with Jimmy the following December, this was not a good thing.

The week after the trial, Tom, the founding partner of the law firm, had Tara and Trey over for dinner. His house was incredible. It was designed after an old southern mansion. A porch wrapped around the entire first and second floors, and the front was graced by eight large pillars. The house was white with charcoal accents. Tara gushed with excitement as Tom's wife, Dotty, gave them a tour of the house.

Afterward, Tara and Dotty went into the kitchen to finish preparing the dinner. Tara explained that her parents named her after the southern mansion depicted in the movie *Gone with the Wind* because it was her mother's favorite movie. She told Dotty that her house reminded her of the mansion in the movie and that her mother would be in her glory at the house.

Dotty explained to Tara that shortly before Trey was hired, Tom had a massive heart attack and was in a coma for a few weeks. He was on life support, and the doctors had encouraged her to have the plug pulled because he had no chance of surviving off of the life support apparatus. She had gone home to pray about it, and the next morning she showed up and he was sitting up in bed looking great and off of life support. He made a full recovery, and the doctors indicated that it was a miracle.

As the women spoke, Trey and Tom were in the billiards room, where they shot pool and had a couple of cocktails. Tom was savvy, and he knew that hot young associates like Trey were apt to leave the firm after they figured out that they could handle cases successfully on their own and pocket the proceeds themselves. He explained that Trey's future with the firm was very promising and that the benefits were great once he became a partner in the firm. The reason Tom had Trey over was so that he could see the benefits for himself. After speaking with Trey, Tom knew that he was extremely ambitious and that he would need to be elevated to partner soon or the firm would risk losing him.

The men then joined the women in the dining room for a wonderful dinner. The dinner table was an antique twenty-foot-long wooden table with fourteen antique chairs surrounding it. It was graced overhead by the most gorgeous and elegant crystal chandelier Tara had ever seen. Tom explained that the table had been taken from an old southern mansion and refurbished. After eating, Tara and Trey thanked the couple for having them over and left.

On the drive home, Trey was weary from the long day and had to listen to Tara rave about the house the whole way home. Although he was happy that she was so thrilled from seeing the house, he also knew that they were returning to one that was not much bigger than the mansion's garage.

As Christmas neared, Tara went shopping with some of the wives of attorneys in Trey's firm. She had a limited budget, and finding gifts for her father, mother, and sisters would be difficult, as they seemed to have everything. She ultimately decided on ornate picture frames in which she would insert a photograph of her and Trey. Although she knew that her parents were not enamored with him, she held on to the belief that one day their perception of him would change.

After a couple of hours of shopping, the wives told Tara about a beautiful house for sale on their side of town. They insisted that they take her to look at it. Tara rebuffed them, indicating that she and Trey could not afford such a house until he, like their husbands, made partner in the firm. The wives insisted, and she reluctantly agreed to go with them. The house was incredible. It was a beautiful brick colonial house with white pillars and redwood floors. It was three times the size of her current house and was surely too expensive for Trey and Tara.

As Trey and Tara dressed for the firm's Christmas party, she described to him the house her friends had shown her after lunch that day. "Trey, it's my dream house," exclaimed Tara. Trey replied that one day, when he made partner in the firm, such a house would be within their reach. She had a secret. She had heard from the other attorneys' wives that there would be a surprise announcement at the party. She could barely contain her excitement.

The Christmas party was exquisite. There were ice sculptures, an extravagant buffet, and a band playing the classics. Although Tara was accustomed to such things, Trey was not. As the clock neared midnight, Tom, seventy-two years old, took the stage. He quieted the crowd of nearly one hundred and declared that he had a few announcements to make. He thanked the attorneys and staff for their dedication and hard work. As Trey was drifting off thinking of how fortunate he was to have a wife like Tara, he heard his name. Tara whispered in his ear, "Congratulations; you just made partner. I love you."

That night, Trey and Tara lay in bed holding each other for hours and talking. He could not believe that such good things were happening to him. It seemed that he was truly the luckiest man alive.

Trey and Tara went to Charleston over the holidays to visit with her family. He obstinately refused to stay at her parents' house, and this made her very upset. Although she understood that he and her father did not get along well, it was unlike him to be unwilling to make the best of a situation. After much discussion, she angrily agreed to check into a hotel a few miles away.

Later that afternoon, they drove the short distance to the house. Tara's face clearly indicated that she was still very upset, and she didn't speak a word to Trey during the drive. He had never seen her get this angry with him, or anyone else for that matter. He despised seeing her that way, and he wanted to tell her about what Richard had attempted to orchestrate at his so-called bachelor's party to prevent their wedding, but he thought better of it.

Later that evening, Tara suggested that she and Trey go to a local hangout where several of her friends were going. He knew that he had to go, as he was in no position to further agitate her, and besides he was very happy to oblige just to get out of the house. During their two hours at the house, he had done his best to avoid Richard. The couple of times he briefly encountered him, he just stared at him without saying a word.

While at the bar, Charles showed up, and Trey was happy to see him. He, after all, could very easily have shown Tara the pictures from the bachelor's party and not only derail the marriage but their relationship altogether. In the end, he explained everything to Trey and did the right thing. He had chosen Tara's happiness over kissing Richard's ass, and Trey respected that. Charles, in spite of his shortcomings, seemed to be a pretty good guy.

Tara was pleased to see Trey and Charles get along so well. As the night wore on, she was in a much better mood, and she went to Trey and Charles and asked Trey to dance. He was not much of a dancer, but the mood was light, she had that loving look on her face, and Charles egged him on. After the pair danced for several minutes and shared a few intimate kisses, Charles tapped Trey on the shoulder and asked if he could cut in. Trey obliged, as he was totally comfortable with him at that point.

As they danced, a few of Tara's girlfriends gathered around Trey. One asked him to dance, and Trey, slightly intoxicated and feeling great about the night, danced with her. It was 11:00 p.m., and he was having a great time dancing when Tara forcefully grabbed him from behind by the shoulder. As he turned, she grabbed him by the arm and stormed outside. She screamed at him, "Why didn't you tell me what my dad had done? Now I know why you don't want to be around him." Before he could utter a word, she shoved him into the car and sped off. Trey's thoughts had quickly gone from fantasizing about his night with Tara upon returning to the hotel room to wondering what was about to happen. As they approached her parents' house, he knew this wasn't going to be a pretty scene.

Upon pulling into the driveway, she said fervently, "Get out."

"What did I do?"

"You didn't tell me." As Trey began to try to explain, Tara stated, "Trey, shut up. We're going inside to talk to my father."

Once inside, Tara stormed up the spiral staircase and began yelling at Richard, waking him from his sleep. As Trey stood downstairs, he muttered, "I'm definitely not getting any tonight."

Tara, Richard, and Edith came walking downstairs. As Richard passed him, Trey winked at him and said, "Man, I wouldn't want to be in your slippers tonight."

"Trey, shut up," yelled Tara. "You're not out of the woods yet either."

As Tara grilled Richard about what he did, he would periodically begin to protest and deny the accusations being made about him, but she would cut him off and talk right over him. Richard, realizing he had been caught, eventually sat and took her tongue lashing.

When Tara was done laying out the entire story, Edith looked at Richard in disgust and said, "How could you, Richard? I didn't think even you could stoop so low."

"Yeah, how could you be such a snake in the grass?" quipped Trey.

Tara, for the third time in the last twenty minutes, sternly admonished Trey to keep his mouth shut. She demanded that Richard apologize to Trey. She made him say it three times until it sounded as if he actually meant it. Trey got up, gave Richard a hug, and said in the most sarcastic way he could, "Dad, it's okay." Tara then yelled at him to go get into the car and wait for her. Trey, for the five minutes he was in the car before she came out, laughed as he imagined the verbal assault Richard was receiving from Tara.

When Tara entered the car, Trey said, "I thought that went rather well." She glared at him, and he considered it to be in his best interest to not say another word.

Much to Trey's astonishment, as he walked into the hotel room, Tara jumped on him, saying only, "Don't say a word." It was the best, most animated sex that he had ever imagined possible.

The following morning, as Tara opened her eyes, Trey was staring at her. "I was hoping you were the same girl from last night. That was incredible. By the way, I love you more with every passing day."

"I love you too, but that girl from last night, she only comes out about once a year."

Tara told Trey to pack his bags, and she instructed him that they would be spending the remainder of the week at her parents' house. He didn't mind, because there was no doubting that he had the upper hand on Richard. Richard was on his best behavior for the remainder of the visit, and he went out of his way to be kind to Trey. *What did Tara tell him after I left?* thought Trey.

5

One Friday evening in late January of 1993, shortly after Trey and Tara moved into their dream house, Tara's parents came to visit at the new house. Tara was so proud of the home, and she had gone shopping and purchased the finest steaks she could find. This was the first instance in her life when she had something of which she was really proud to which her parents had not made any financial contribution. The home was not yet fully furnished—that would come with time—but nonetheless she beamed with excitement as her parents' car pulled into the circular drive.

As Tara proudly showed her mother the house, Richard approached Trey as he was grilling the steaks. It was obvious from the beginning of Trey's relationship with Tara that Richard was not thrilled with the prospect of his daughter being with him. Trey's occupation as a plaintiff's personal injury trial attorney was the antithesis of everything Richard held dear. As he engaged Trey in conversation, the tenor of his words was unexpectedly upbeat. Much to Trey's surprise, Richard began to tell him that although he was disappointed at his choice of career, he did respect what he had accomplished, and most of all, he made his daughter exceedingly happy, and he was very appreciative of that. Respect, after all, is what Trey lived his life for, and to hear this from Richard felt like a huge victory to him.

Trey had no intention of alluding to the events of his bachelor's party, as they resulted in no harm to him; however, it did make him suspicious of Richard, and he was very aware of the chicanery of which he was capable.

Richard grimaced and then said, "Trey, about the bachelor's party. I don't know quite what to say. What I did was despicable. I can only hope that you understand that what I did was out of a misguided love for my daughter. I thought I knew what was best for her, and I did not. I now know, without question, that she loves you, and you are what is best for her. Perhaps one day you will be able to trust and respect me and we can be friends."

"I'll work on that, sir," said Trey as he shook his hand. "I have just one favor to ask you. It would mean a lot to me if you would make things right with Charles. He is a great guy, and he deserves your and my respect. He did do the right thing, you know."

"Yes, yes, you've got my word. Consider it done."

After dinner, Trey and Richard played a few games of pool while having a couple of beers. Trey had talked Tara into allowing him to purchase a pool table and create a playroom for himself. Richard and Trey were both very competitive and more alike than Richard would care to acknowledge. As the games became more competitive and they started to talk trash, Tara and her mother looked at each other and smiled. It was a clear sign to Tara that Trey was gaining the acceptance of her father.

Later that evening, after Tara's parents had left, Trey informed her of his conversation with her father. Things had been working out so well for them, and now, her father had accepted her husband, which she had doubted would ever happen. They were both so overwhelmed with joy at their overall good fortune that they first held and then began caressing each other. They had both been so busy at work and with the new house that intimacy had been put on the backburner recently, but on this night, they made love passionately. Prior to dozing off, Trey thought to himself that life doesn't get much better than this. He seemed to have it all.

The following day, Saturday, Tara talked Trey into going furniture shopping with her. They proceeded to a street on the outskirts of town known as Antique Row. Antique Row was lined with shops and a few restaurants. Although Tara was excited to get shopping, Trey was famished, so he persuaded her to eat at one of the restaurants before shopping, declaring that he would be much more pleasant and agreeable about spending money if he had a full stomach.

As they ate, a biker-looking woman came through the small restaurant passing out coupons. She stopped at their table, smiled, and handed Tara a coupon for 30 percent off at a store called Apache.

"Where is the store located?" she asked the woman.

"It's on the second row about in the middle."

Tara slipped the coupon in her purse, and she and Trey finished their brunch. She had little intention of going to the second row of shops, as that row had a flea-market-like atmosphere and she was looking for a couple of substantial pieces of furniture for the new home. Trey thought it would be a good idea to go to the Apache store first since it was offering a 30 percent discount, but Tara declined, telling him that the first row of shops was more suitable for what she was looking for. Trey sarcastically accused her of being a snob, and they engaged in some playful teasing before paying their bill and embarking on their shopping journey.

Trey hated to shop, and Tara knew that his attention span and patience were of short duration. After they exited the third shop, Trey, already looking weary from the ordeal, declared that he was going to go to the Apache store, and he advised Tara to call him on his cell phone if she found something of interest to her. By this time, he was impeding her shopping, so she was happy to send him on his way to the second row.

As Trey neared Apache, his phone rang and Tara summoned him back to look at some furniture she had found. He made it back to the store, and she showed him two pieces of furniture she wanted to buy for the house. Before looking at the items closely, he checked out the price tags. He then walked to Tara and reminded her that there was a 30 percent off deal at Apache. She admonished him to be serious.

As Tara stared intensely at the pieces of furniture, studying them from every angle as only a woman could, Trey began to negotiate with the well-attired saleswoman.

"Are you offering 30 percent off?"

"No, sir. The stores on Antique Row do not offer discounts."

"That's not true; Apache is offering 30 percent off."

The saleswoman, with a glum look on her face, said, "Sir, this is the finest of furniture. Apache and the other stores back there sell lower-end items."

As Trey turned to look at Tara, she had her arms crossed and a look on her face that he understood clearly to mean that he was embarrassing her and needed to be quiet. He meandered over to her and whispered, "She's a snob too. Maybe we should go to Apache."

Tara looked at him with a menacing look on her face and whispered softly, "If you say one more word, you will be on the couch for a week."

On the way home, Tara was so excited with her purchases that she told Trey that she would forgive him for his boorish behavior. She then said, almost in a manner that seemed as if she was trying to convince herself more than Trey, "By the way, I am not a snob." His countenance feigned disagreement, and they began laughing.

Upon arriving home, Tara reminded Trey that they were having some people over. He grimaced, as he was not particularly fond of entertaining. He would rather relax and drink a bottle of wine with her by the pool than make aimless conversation with people.

As their guests arrived, Tara showed the women the house and described the furniture that she had purchased earlier. Trey and the men retreated into his playroom, watching a Super Bowl show and shooting pool. After some time passed, the men could hear the women laughing uncontrollably in the family room. As the men went to see what was happening, Tara was telling the story of her and Trey's earlier shopping adventure, taking the liberty of exaggerating slightly when describing his conduct. Trey and Tara bantered back and forth as he playfully portrayed her and the saleswoman as stuck up. Everyone laughed heartily as he mimicked the saleswoman and Tara and even harder as she mimicked him and his request for a discount. After their guests left, they lay in bed holding each other and laughing.

On Sunday, Tara awakened Trey to get ready for church. He was not very religious, but she reminded him that he had much to be thankful for, and Trey, knowing that she was right, got ready for church without further complaint.

The pastor's theme that day centered on how materialistic people had become. As he preached that people had to have bigger houses, better cars, and expensive jewelry and furniture, Trey turned his head to stare at Tara. She had a smirk on her face, and she grabbed his hand and squeezed it as hard as she could. She then turned and whispered playfully in his ear, "That's it; you're on the couch for a week—make it two."

Later that afternoon, Trey got a call from one of the members of the law firm. He and his wife were Buffalo Bills fans, and the Bills were playing the Dallas Cowboys in the Super Bowl. They were on their way to meet up with a couple of the other younger associates of the firm at a local sports bar to watch the game. Trey, a Cowboys fan from an early age, had planned on lying low with Tara and watching the game at home. As the attorney on the other end of the line antagonized him about not being man enough to come watch the Cowboys get whipped, he couldn't resist.

As he and Tara donned their Cowboy attire, he could only stare at her as she dressed. She put on a dark blue Cowboys jersey with "Aikman" on the back and a skimpy pair of white shorts. After she put on her pumps and stood up, he was overwhelmed with her sexiness. She was one of those rare women who could dress a little on the trashy side and yet still look so elegant. She exuded sexiness, class, and grace all at the same time.

Upon arriving at the crowded bar, Trey was relieved to see that his friends had gotten there early enough to get a table. As they walked through the crowd, Trey, walking behind Tara, couldn't help but notice all the heads turn and the male eyes affix themselves on her as she walked by. Tara, although twenty-six and several years older than some of the college girls at the bar, was clearly the hottest.

As they sat down, it was thirty minutes before kickoff, and already the trash talking started. The other four at the table were either hard-core Bills fans or they were rooting for the Bills.

Trey had become obsessed with the Cowboys when he was seven and turned on the television one day. When the Cowboys came running onto the field wearing their blue-and-silver uniforms with the blue star on the helmet, they became his team. He was thrilled when the announcer made reference to Bullet Bob Hayes, once the fastest man in the world, who had retired a few years ago and was being honored at half time with a star on the interior of the stadium. Ever since, it had been all about the Cowboys for him. Tara, not being much of a sports fan, adopted the Cowboys as her team.

As the game progressed and the beer flowed, the Cowboys began to blow out the Bills in a decisive fashion. Tara cheered loudly throughout the first half, much to the chagrin of the others at the table. By half time, the game was essentially over. Tara and the other woman went to the restroom while Trey went to the bar to order one last pitcher of beer. He didn't really want to order more beer, as he had to get up early the following morning, but it was his turn, and the disgruntled Bills fans at the table were not about to let him slide. As he stood at the bar, two very attractive girls from the college nearby came up on each side of him and began to flirt with him. Tara was gorgeous, but Trey was no slouch himself. He was almost always the best-looking guy in any crowd.

Tara and her friend came back from the restroom and sat at the table. Tara immediately looked up at the bar and saw Trey standing there speaking with the young girls standing on each side of him. The pitcher was on the bar in front of him, but he hadn't left the bar, and he looked as if he was having far too much fun. The other woman whispered in Tara's ear that she better get up there and pull him away from the bar. Tara, not at all the jealous type, indicated that she would leave him up there for a while. A couple of minutes had passed when she whispered in her friend's ear, "Watch this," as she got up from her chair and walked toward him and the two youngsters.

When she reached them, she stood to the side of one of the girls and ordered a beer. She then thrust herself into their conversation, initially asking the girls what school they attended. As the girls introduced her to Trey, he wondered what she was up to. After the four continued to talk for a couple of minutes, she looked past the girl at Trey and said, "You know something, what's your name again? Oh, that's right, Trey. You are so damn hot." She then pushed her way around the girl, and as the two college girls stood there with their mouths wide open, she grabbed him and began to make out with him as though they were still in high school. A minute later, with the girls still standing there in disbelief, she grabbed his hand, and as they began to walk away, she looked at both girls and said, "See, girls; that's how you do it."

As they returned to the table, the others were laughing and amazed at what Tara had done. Before they could even sit down, Trey threw a one-hundred-dollar bill on the table and exclaimed, "Ladies and gentlemen, the tab's on me. We're out of here." Trey was all over Tara before they even reached the car in the parking lot. She was everything that he could ever dream of, and more.

6

February through June passed by uneventfully. Trey and Tara were immersed in their jobs and in each other. Outside of work, they would run, work out, and just hang out at the new house watching movies and enjoying each other's company. They didn't need much else.

They were invited to go to Tom's house for a Fourth of July party. He lived on five acres, and his Fourth of July parties were legendary. Tara and Trey had gone the year before, but at the time Trey was a new associate, having only been with the firm for a few weeks, and he was in training with no cases of his own. He was the proverbial low man on the totem pole.

This Fourth of July was different. Trey had won the multimillion-dollar Coca-Cola case, and he had been elevated to partner status in December. He was much more excited about this party.

The guests arrived around two in the afternoon for an elaborate barbeque, and the fireworks started at nine. The fireworks were always magnificent, as Tom had them professionally done. They lasted half an hour.

At 8:30 p.m., as people were making their way farther out back with their chairs and blankets in anticipation of the display, Tom approached Trey and told him to go upstairs with Tara and watch the fireworks from the upstairs terrace. "It's the best view," he said, "and you can watch them in private. It's very romantic. You and Tara need to start working on a family."

Trey was not sure what Tom was suggesting, but he took Tara's hand and led her upstairs to the terrace. They indeed had the best location from which to watch the display as they stood at the railing looking at the crowd in the distance.

As the fireworks got underway, Trey moved around behind Tara and put his arms around her. After a few minutes, he began to slowly unbutton the top three buttons of her white shirt. He gently grabbed the back of her hair and turned her face toward his. They kissed while he caressed her bra. He then began inching up her red knee-length dress and softly rubbing her inner thighs. They continued kissing passionately as they made love while the fireworks exploded in the distance. At one point, Tom turned around and looked back toward the terrace and smiled.

On the drive home, Tara said, "Trey, that was incredible. The fireworks and sex at the same time. I am not so sure Tom would have approved, though."

"It was his idea."

"What?"

"He thinks we need to start working on a family. He instructed me to take you up there so we could have some privacy and romance."

"That's crazy. I'm on birth control anyway."

"Yeah, but the sex sure was good."

"No disagreements here."

Later in July Trey sat at the kitchen table finishing his coffee. Tara came down the stairs dressed casually and advised him that she was taking the day off to go shopping and spend some time with Debbie, a friend whom she had met through her charitable work. As was his custom, he hugged her and told her how much he loved her before departing for the office.

Tara went to Antique Row looking for a few pieces of furniture to fill spots in the family room. She was thirty minutes early to meet Debbie, so she went into a restaurant for a glass of tea. As she fumbled through her purse looking for her money, she pulled out the coupon for the Apache store.

She stepped out of the restaurant and phoned Debbie, who informed her that she was running late and was at least twenty minutes away. As Tara put her phone back into her purse, she pulled out the Apache coupon and stared at it momentarily before instinctively setting off for the store.

The store was filled with rows of wood carvings of Indians, ships, animals, and fictitious creatures. There was a strange aura about the place, and Tara was uncomfortable while at the same time amused. As she neared the end of an aisle, she was startled by a soft raspy voice: "May I help you find something?" As she turned, she saw an old Indian lady with long, unkempt gray hair. She was about five feet tall and was dressed in old jeans and a black sweatshirt. The old lady, who appeared to be in her midsixties, stared at Tara with a strange smile on her face.

She beckoned Tara to follow her as she began ambling toward the back of the store. Tara, although apprehensive, followed the woman, as she seemed harmless. The woman led her to a small back office and motioned for her to sit down. As Tara sat in an old musty chair covered with what looked like a black cowhide, the woman knelt on both knees in front of her. She then grabbed Tara's right hand and began to study it intensely. The expression on the woman's face was at times happy and at times concerned as she studied Tara's hand. She then repeated the process with the other hand.

When the old Indian woman was done, she stared into Tara's eyes for what seemed like minutes before Tara exclaimed, "What is it? What do you see?"

"You have a kind heart, you like adventure, you are from a wealthy family, and you are with the one who is your soul mate. You will be with him forever. There is also a surprise coming right around the corner."

"What surprise?"

"You will find out soon enough." She then began to reach for Tara as she uttered softly, "You are full of life." This startled Tara, and she hurriedly got up and scurried toward the door.

As she neared the door, Tara looked back at the office as she ran into someone who had just entered the store. He was a scruffy biker-looking man who looked to be in his midforties. He was wearing jeans and a black leather jacket and had a bandana on his head.

"Whoa, what's the hurry, young lady?"

"Nothing. I'm okay," responded Tara with a hint of anxiety in her voice.

"Oh, you must have met the old Indian woman. Did she read your palms and tell your fortune? Don't be scared. She does that to anybody who will follow her into the office. She's pretty good at it. She was diagnosed with a cancerous tumor in her head over a year ago and given only two months to live. Since then, not only has she gotten better, but she can see the future too." This unsettled Tara further, and she hastily made her way out the door and went on her way to meet Debbie.

As Debbie and Tara were laughing and carrying on over lunch, Tara related her experience with the old Indian woman.

Debbie laughed and told her, "You shouldn't go to that back row. There are freaks back there. I hear some of the store owners are members of cults and think they are psychic. What does that mean, 'You are full of life'?"

"Well, I am a week late. Maybe she meant I am pregnant." They looked at each other with wide eyes and then laughed at the notion that the old woman could know that. "Besides," said Tara, "I've been taking birth control pills for three years. That's not even possible."

On her drive home, Tara kept thinking of the old lady and picturing her in her mind. She recalled that the old lady was reaching for her stomach when she got up and ran out of the store. She pulled into a supermarket a couple of miles from her house and purchased a home pregnancy kit; although she felt like an immature kid at the checkout line, she just had to know.

Tara sat at the kitchen table anxiously waiting to see the results of the test. Her heart sank as the positive indicator appeared on the box. She was at once jubilant and terrified. She stared at the box for a couple of minutes to see if the positive sign would disappear. When it did not, she got up and walked around the house as if she was in a daze.

Knowing that it would be another hour or two before Trey got home, Tara ran to her car, backed out of the driveway, and began driving the two miles back to the supermarket. Once there, she studied the row of home pregnancy kits before grabbing three of them.

Upon returning home, Tara stared at the row of tests as they all turned positive. She heard Trey's car pull into the garage, and she nervously gathered all the tests and placed them on a table in the bedroom.

As Trey walked into the living room, he looked at Tara sitting on the sofa. Her face was radiant, almost glowing.

"What's going on?" asked Trey.

Tara ran to him and jumped into his arms before whispering in his ear, "I'm pregnant."

"How do you know? Did you go to your gynecologist today?"

Tara took Trey's hand and led him into the bedroom. He looked with bemusement at the four positive tests scattered on the table. She looked at him, anxiously awaiting his response. He grabbed her hands and stared into her eyes before saying, "I love you so much. You're going to be the best mother."

That weekend, Trey and Tara drove to Charleston. She wanted to announce her pregnancy to her parents and sisters in person. She felt comfortable doing this, as the relationship between Trey and her parents had improved so much since the wedding.

As they sat around the table drinking coffee after dinner, Tara stood, took her fork, and struck her water glass three times, declaring that she had an announcement to make. As she proclaimed that she was pregnant, the room was silent. After a few seconds passed, both of her sisters and their husbands offered subdued congratulations. It was clear that everyone was waiting to get Richard's reaction to the news.

Richard stood, looking first at Tara with an expressionless look on his face and then at Trey. He said to Trey, "I have just one question. Are you going to send him or her to business school or law school?"

Trey looked down, pausing for a second, and as he looked up at Richard responded, "Yale School of Management of course; no question about it."

Richard chortled and declared, "Let's celebrate."

Later, as the four men sat in Richard's study smoking cigars and sipping brandy, Richard said, "Trey, you know that I am not fond of personal injury attorneys, and I continue to hope that one day you will see the light and join your brothers-in-law in the corporate world, but I must say, at least you have proven yourself to be a great injury attorney, and I respect you for that." The brothers-in-law had looks of consternation on their faces as the thought that Trey was becoming Richard's favorite crept into their minds.

Trey and Tara returned home, and she began to prepare a room for the baby. Trey didn't really understand why she was obsessed with preparing for a baby eight months away, but it made her happy, so he went along with it.

It was a beautiful Saturday morning in late August, and Tara was out back on the pool deck reading a romance novel. Trey was at work preparing for a trial the following week. She imagined that she and Trey were the main characters in the book, which made it all the more interesting. She was so engrossed in the book that she almost did not hear the phone ringing. It was one of her friends, Linda, whose husband was also a young attorney at Trey's law firm. She invited Tara to come to the park where some of the wives of the attorneys in the firm were taking their children.

Tara met them at the park. The women sat at a picnic bench and watched their young children playing. Tara glowingly watched the children as she envisioned her own child playing on the playground in a couple of years. She wondered what he or she would look like. She smiled as she tried to imagine a one-year-old Trey hanging from the monkey bars as he admonished her that he did not need any help.

The women munched on food they had brought, and they teased Tara as she pulled out her mainstay during her pregnancy, peanut butter and carrots. As they watched her dip her carrot into the jar of peanut butter and laughed at her, one of the women looked up and could not find her six-year-old daughter. As the women ran around in a panicked state, a policeman pulled up to the curb, and Tara ran to him, frantically explaining that a six-year-old girl was missing. The officer ran to the playground and began questioning the mother as to what color hair the child had and what she was wearing. By now, the entire playground was in chaos as everyone was feverishly looking for the child.

Suddenly, Tara looked up and saw a scrappy-looking man with tattered jeans wearing a bandana walking toward them holding the missing child's hand. As she and Linda ran toward the child, the officer grabbed the man and threw him to the ground, cuffing his wrists behind his back. As another police cruiser with additional officers arrived, the man calmly announced, "It wasn't me. I was going into the men's room over there to relieve myself when I saw the pervert walk in with the crying girl. I beat the hell out of him and walked the girl back. I swear. Go in the restroom, and you will find him there. I beat him pretty bad."

Two officers ran to the restroom. A couple of minutes later, they came out with the man handcuffed, his nose and mouth bloodied. The little girl identified him as the man who brought her to the restroom and confirmed that the man with the bandana on his head had helped her.

As the officer uncuffed the man who had saved the girl, Tara and Linda thanked him repeatedly for his good deed. The man said simply, "Nothing to it. I was just doing my civic duty." The man looked at the officer who had thrown him to the ground and said derisively, "By the way, where were you guys when you were needed?" He then walked away.

As the man got on his Harley, Tara stared intensely at him; he looked eerily familiar to her. As she tried to imagine where she had seen the man before, it suddenly came to her that he was the one she had run into as she exited the Apache store on the second row of Antique Row four weeks ago. This perplexed her, as her encounters with the man in such a short period were either a major coincidence or he was following her. After further thought, she concluded that it must be a coincidence; there was no reason for the man to be following her.

As she drove home, Tara could not get the man off of her mind. She remembered that he spoke to her about the old Indian woman at Apache as though he knew her well. Tara, thinking that the woman knew the man, drove to the store determined to speak with the woman in hopes that she could learn the man's identity. The old woman had made her uncomfortable before, but she seemed harmless, and Tara had been intrigued as to how the woman had apparently known that she was pregnant.

As Tara stepped into the store, the old lady stood smiling a few feet before her. She slowly came to Tara, held her hand, and walked with her back to the office, the site of their prior meeting.

As she sat down, Tara looked at the woman and said, "You knew I was pregnant, didn't you? How did you know that?"

"That is not important," responded the woman as her face took on a somber expression. "There are some troubled waters around the bend, and you will be tested. You must remain strong. Remember what I told you before. You are with your soul mate. Do not give up on him, no matter what happens."

Tara, with an uneasy look on her face, coaxed the woman to give her details as to what she meant, but the woman would say no more other than to repeat that she would need to be strong.

Tara, realizing that she was going to get no further explanation from the woman regarding the troubled waters that lay ahead, asked her about the biker-looking man she had run into the last time she was at Apache. "He is a friend; do not fear him," stated the woman. Again, with no success, Tara questioned the woman further about the biker but could get no additional information. As she left the store, she convinced herself that the woman was not playing with a full deck and that her two brief encounters with the biker were purely coincidence. She resolved to put it all out of her mind and to never go back to the Apache store.

It was 9:00 p.m. on Tuesday of the following week, and Trey was still at work working on some cases. Tara called, and he promised her that he would be home in an hour. They had not been intimate in a couple of weeks, and she told him that he may want to hurry home, as she had gone shopping earlier and she had a surprise for him.

"You got something for the baby's room?"

"No, I went clothes shopping," responded Tara in a soft but sexy voice.

Trey needed to hear no more. He hurried out of the building and into the garage parking lot.

The lot was almost empty this time of night. As Trey approached his Porsche and began to open the door, he felt something stick into his back, and a deep gruff voice said, "If you value your life, you'll do exactly what I tell you to do. Slowly turn around." Trey had never before avoided a confrontation, but the man either had or pretended to have a gun sticking in his back, and he was not about to find out whether the man really had one. As he complied, slowly turning around, the man struck him in the left eye with the handle of the pistol, knocking him to the ground. As the man began to rifle through his pockets, he heard several footsteps approaching. When he looked up, three bikers were standing a few feet away, glaring at him.

The assailant said, "Hey, what's going on? I've got cash, a Rolex watch, and some credit cards. We can split them up. I'm not greedy." The three bikers jerked him up, threw him against the concrete garage wall, and mercilessly pummeled him until he slid down the wall unconscious onto the ground. As Trey looked up, holding his left eye, the men walked to him and handed him his belongings before walking away.

Trey called the police on his cell phone as he exited the garage to report the incident and tell them where they could find the battered man. He looked into his mirror and saw that his eye was swelling badly. When he arrived home, Tara was frantic as he lay on the couch trying to explain what had transpired. She prepared a bag of ice and applied it to his eye. He looked at her running around the house in the new black negligee she had purchased earlier, and he was not sure if he was more upset with the man for giving him a badly swollen and rapidly blackening eye or for ruining his night with Tara.

At 10:30 p.m., two police officers arrived at the house and took a statement from Trey. After he gave the details of what had occurred and the officers left, he was discouraged as he looked at Tara, who had changed into an old pair of sweat pants and baggy shirt.

By 11:00 p.m., the ice had reduced the swelling significantly and the eye was turning shades of purple and black. The Advil Tara had given Trey an hour before had reduced his headache and pain, and he talked her into putting on her black negligee. He played the part of a policeman who had just pulled her over, and he mock cuffed her. He took some degree of satisfaction in knowing that at least his assailant had not ruined his night with Tara and her new negligee.

The following morning, Tara took Trey for an x-ray to make sure nothing was broken around the eye socket. The x-ray was negative, but he was left with a badly bruised eye.

Trey didn't know why the three bikers had rescued him, and he really didn't care. He wished he could thank them, but they disappeared into the night, and he didn't even get a good look at them.

When Trey awoke on Monday morning of the following week, he found that his eye had almost completely healed, with some minor discoloration remaining. As he and Tara were leaving for work at 7:30 a.m., she reminded him that her mother was coming to stay for a few days and that she would be arriving in the midafternoon, while they were gone. She also stated that she was going directly from work at the Coalition for the Homeless to the first of the four classes on childbirth for which she had enrolled them without consulting him. She reminded him to meet her there at 5:45 p.m. and not to be late. They would meet her mother afterward at the house.

Later that day, Trey, intensively reviewing a deposition, looked up and realized that he had lost track of time. It was 5:30 p.m., and he knew he could not make it on time for the class. In addition, he had no desire to go. Suddenly, he had what he thought was a good idea. Since the location of the class was only ten minutes from his house, he called Tara's mother and explained that he was in a jam and asked her if she could fill in for him. He told her to inform Tara that he promised he would make the other three classes. Edith agreed and left to meet Tara at the class. When he hung up the phone, he leaned back in his chair, admiring his craftiness. *Three out of four classes isn't bad anyway,* he thought. Boy, was he wrong.

At 8:15 p.m., as Trey was relaxing in his recliner watching a college football game with a glass of lemonade, Tara walked through the front door. Judging from the rapidity of the clanking of her shoes on the floor, he for the first time appreciated that she may not be very happy with him. She stormed into his playroom and stood directly to the left front side of his chair. He didn't have to look to feel her staring a hole right through him.

As he slowly and apprehensively looked up and to his left, he said, "Oh, hey babe, how was the class? I'm sorry I had to miss it, but at least I did the next best thing and called your mom, right?"

"Trey, how could you? You called my mother to fill in for you?"

"Yeah, and she is going to fill me in on everything I missed, so I won't be behind when I go next week."

"Trey, you know how important this class is to me. I don't ask that you do much for me, but you couldn't find the time to do this one thing. If you didn't want to go through this with me, if it wasn't important to you, then why didn't you just tell me that?"

"Oh, but it is. I promise, baby," said Trey as he scrambled to save himself as Tara turned and walked away. "I'm going to go to three out of four, honey. That's pretty good, isn't it?"

"No, Trey. That's pathetic."

Trey, now fully realizing the severity of his miscalculation regarding the importance of the class to Tara, gave her a few minutes to cool off. He brought her, sitting on their bed with tears in her eyes, a plate full of carrots with a jar of peanut butter and a single flower he had picked out of a vase in the family room. She looked at him and couldn't help but smile.

"I just want this to be as important to you as it is to me," wept Tara.

"I'm sorry. I screwed up, but I promise you, Tara, that this baby is as important to me as he or she is to you. You gotta know that."

"I do."

They then hugged and all was forgiven. As for Trey, he was there at 5:45 sharp for the last three classes.

7

Four weeks later, in late September, Trey sat in his office at 5:00 p.m. catching up on some paperwork. As he reclined in his chair, a call from the receptionist came through: "Mr. Jackson, there is someone here to see you. His name is Toby. He has no appointment." Trey replied that this gentleman should call him tomorrow as he was getting ready to leave the office. "He insists on seeing you now," responded the receptionist. "He says it will only take fifteen minutes."

"Send him back." Those would be fateful words.

As Toby, who appeared to be between forty-five and fifty, walked through the door, there was no mistaking who he was. He wore a navy bandana on his head so that you could not see his hair. On the bandana were small white skull and cross-bone emblems. Red sideburns protruded from the bandana and extended down the sides of his face until they merged with a scraggly red beard. His face was rough, reflecting a hard life. He had the bluest eyes Trey had ever seen. He wore an old tattered black T-shirt with the words "Harley-Davidson" adorning the front. Over the T-shirt was a rather worn, sleeveless, black leather jacket. He had on a weathered pair of jeans, ripped in places, and a brown leather belt with a large belt buckle in the shape of a skull. He wore black leather boots, and the pungent smell of stale cigarette smoke enveloped him.

He shook Trey's hand, introduced himself, and took a seat. He apologized for coming by without an appointment and indicated that he needed his help. He explained that he had been drinking in a bar on the outskirts of town the night before and that he met up with a former client of Trey's who had been rear-ended in an automobile accident a year ago. The fellow raved about him, and Toby figured he could help him too.

47

As Toby began to explain that he had been charged with assault and battery stemming from a barroom brawl a few months ago, Trey stopped him and explained that he was not a criminal attorney and that he would be happy to refer him to an attorney who may be willing to help him. Toby convinced Trey to listen to the rest of his story.

At the conclusion, Toby indicated that he merely needed Trey to file a motion to dismiss the charges against him, as the prosecutor had no evidence. Trey responded, "I'm sure they took the statements of witnesses and charged you based upon those statements." Toby insisted that it was self-defense and again asked Trey if he would file the motion to dismiss the charges against him. Trey reluctantly agreed to file the motion and show up at court to see what evidence the prosecution had, but again he explained to Toby that it wasn't going to be that easy, as the prosecutor had to have witness statements and wasn't going to drop the charges simply because he filed a motion. Toby handed him a sliver of paper with his cell phone number and said, "Call me when you know the date and time of the motion hearing."

Later that night, as Trey and Tara sat down in the living room to relax after dinner, he related his encounter with Toby to her. As he referred to Toby as a biker and recounted the entire story, she couldn't help but think of the biker-looking fellow who she had run into at the Apache store two months earlier and saved her friend's child a month ago. She interrupted his story and asked him to describe the man.

"He is a biker. What difference does it make what he looks like?"

"Just describe his face. What did it look like?" As Trey described Toby's face, Tara just stared at him with a blank look on her face.

"What is it? Don't tell me you know this guy."

Tara then described to Trey the events at the Apache store and the park over the last two months, and she indicated that the person he was describing seemed uncannily similar in appearance to the man involved in those episodes. He looked at her with a perplexed look on his face before declaring that the two could not possibly be the same biker.

"Tara, do you know how many biker-looking guys with red hair there are in this city? What are the chances that we are talking about the same guy?"

"Yes, I guess you are right. What are the chances?" The subject was dropped, and Tara put it out of her mind.

Trey met Toby at the courthouse in mid-October thirty minutes before the hearing on Trey's motion to dismiss. Trey emphatically told Toby that this would be his last involvement in the case and that he would have to find another attorney when their motion was denied. Toby responded that the case would be dismissed after the hearing and that he was not worried.

48

At the hearing, Trey argued that Toby was merely acting in self-defense, as he was reacting to an imminent threat of harm from his assailant. The prosecutor scoffed at this statement and indicated that he had eight witnesses whom he had subpoenaed to the motion hearing who had all given written statements immediately after the incident indicating that Toby's assault was totally unprovoked.

The first witness called by the prosecution testified that he didn't see anything. "Then why did you give a statement to the investigating officer at the scene describing the attack in detail?" angrily demanded the prosecutor.

"I don't know. I guess I was drunk."

When the second witness took the stand, the prosecutor initially asked if he saw what happened, and the witness said that he did. Looking relieved, he then asked, "What did you see?" He then had a shocked look on his face as the witness indicated that the other gentleman was drunk and provoked the fight and Toby was merely defending himself. The judge looked down from the bench at the prosecutor and tersely asked if there were any witnesses who would actually testify against Toby. The lawyer requested a fifteen-minute recess.

The prosecutor returned after the recess, stood, put his hands in the air, and stated that the state was dropping all charges against Toby. As he walked past Trey, he merely shook his head and exited the courtroom.

Once they got outside, Trey looked at Toby with a befuddled look on his face and asked, "What just happened in there?"

"It doesn't matter. Congratulations; you won your first criminal case."

"My last criminal case."

"Oh, come on. It wasn't that bad. How much do I owe you?"

"Nothing. Just don't call me again unless you've been hit by a truck and seriously injured."

Toby laughed, patted Trey on the back, and walked away.

As Trey watched Toby walk away, he yelled, "Hey, Toby!"

Toby turned and looked at Trey for a second before saying, "Counselor," with a quizzical look on his face.

"What are the chances that you were in the park about two months ago saving little kids? Do you hang out in parks and save kids?"

Toby paused for a moment before laughing robustly and responding, "Counselor, I don't know where you got that idea. I don't do parks, and I don't save kids." He then turned and disappeared around the corner.

A few days later, Trey bumped into the prosecutor while out at lunch. He, like Trey, was in his midtwenties. When Trey saw him standing on the other side of the small restaurant, the prosecutor just smirked and shook his head. Trey smiled and held his hands out as if to say he didn't understand what happened. The prosecutor laughed before sitting down to eat.

After eating, as Trey was exiting the restaurant, he found himself behind the prosecutor. They stood outside for several minutes talking about what had taken place in court. The prosecutor stated that he had never seen anything like it in his career. Although he had only been practicing, like Trey, for a little over a year, nobody in the prosecutor's office, not even veterans of twenty to thirty years, had ever seen anything like it.

The prosecutor revealed to Trey what had happened during the fifteen-minute recess at the motion hearing. "Of the six left who hadn't yet testified," he said, "I asked who had seen what had happened. Two of them said they didn't really get a good look at what happened. I then asked the remaining four what they saw. They all responded one by one that after leaving the bar and reflecting on the events of the attack, they felt that Toby was defending himself after all. I instructed all eight that there could be consequences for giving false statements to the police after the event, and they all looked down and shrugged. It was obvious that someone got to them. They all were very scared."

"That may have been the case. It was certainly bizarre. As for me, that was my only and last criminal case. I didn't even want to help the guy, but he insisted, and I told him I would file the motion and appear at the motion hearing; then I was out. Believe me, had I even thought that witnesses were being tampered with, I would have had nothing to do with the case. I feel really bad. I apologize." The prosecutor stated not to worry and that he understood that Trey had no part in getting the witnesses to change their stories. He laughed as he departed.

As he walked back to his office, Trey was grateful that the prosecutor harbored no ill feelings toward him due to the events at the motion hearing and was confused as to how this scraggly, biker-looking dude could have exerted so much influence over not one or two but eight people. He played over in his mind the prosecutor's words: "They all were very scared. It was obvious that someone got to them." Although he marveled at Toby being able to pull this off, he was also at the same time repulsed by it and a little dismayed that he allowed himself to be used that way. After he reached the office, he convinced himself to put the events of that day behind him and not think about it.

A couple of days later, Trey got home from work at 6:00 p.m. and began putting on his basketball shorts and T-shirt. As he was lacing his high tops, Tara walked in and said, "Oh, this is your basketball league night. I'm sorry; I forgot and made plans to go to dinner with a couple of the girls. Do you mind?"

"No problem. We're playing the police team. They are not very good, just throw a lot of elbows and play a little dirty. I'll be okay. Go ahead and have fun with your friends, and I'll see you back at the house later."

Trey was a much better player than anyone in the league, but a couple of the teams had gone out and found some former college players to try to stop him. The police team was no different. Their team, although not very good, had some large players with larger egos, and they were tired of losing to his law firm team. They had recruited three new players, including a fast point guard who had played college ball and was given the assignment of shutting down Trey.

As the game began, Trey started out taking it easy, as was his custom. In past games, he didn't want to go out and score thirty or forty points and take most of the shots. He passed the ball around and played at about half speed. He would pick up the pace and do his thing only when, and if, the team needed it.

After three quarters, the new guy on the police team who was covering Trey, Demps, had about fifteen points, and the police team was up by five points. As they walked off the court, Demps and the two other new players on the team began to taunt Trey, telling him they had heard he had game but they didn't see it. He just smiled and walked back to his team's bench. As they gathered to start the fourth quarter, all the attorneys looked at Trey and indicated simply, "It's time; do your thing."

Trey began the quarter by easily maneuvering around a trash-talking Demps and then going up and over another defender for a thunderous dunk. Demps had challenged him, and he loved it. He did not let up for the entire quarter. They couldn't stop him even when they double and triple teamed him. By the end of the fourth quarter, he had put twenty points on Demps in that quarter alone, and he stole the ball from him a few times. The steals were punctuated by dunks of all varieties. Trey's team won the game by twelve points, and they remained undefeated in the league, a streak extending into its second season.

After the game, a few of the officers invited Trey's team to go down the road for a couple of beers. Trey and most of his team accepted and joined them at the bar. Upon arriving, Demps walked up to Trey, handed him a beer, and said, "Man, you played me for three quarters. I didn't think an attorney could have that kind of game. Sorry about all the trash talking. I was wondering why a few of my teammates were telling me not to do that to you. Now I know."

"Not a problem. You made it fun. That was the first time I've been challenged out there."

"Well, it wasn't much of a challenge."

51

Trey sat at a table with a couple of the officers, including Demps. He asked them to tell him about their jobs. Demps indicated that he was an undercover officer assigned to investigate gang activities and gather the evidence needed to file charges against them. This intrigued Trey, especially since he and Tara had been running into bikers with uncommon frequency.

Trey described to Demps his and Tara's encounters with bikers and asked him if there was an influential motorcycle gang prevalent in the city. "The Dreadnaughts," responded Demps. He explained to Trey that the Dreadnaughts had increasingly become a problem over the last several years and that they were very violent and dangerous people. "We've been trying to gather the evidence to put most of them away for distribution of marijuana and cripple them," said Demps. "Also, they are getting more violent and are expanding into the cocaine trade. We also believe they have been involved in many murders, and it's getting worse. What I find troubling about your stories, Trey, is that one saved a little girl at the park where your wife was, three saved you, one bumped into your wife while she was leaving a store, and one of them just out the blue showed up at your office one day asking for help. That doesn't make any sense, unless these were merely chance encounters involving bikers who are not Dreadnaughts. If they were Dreadnaughts, my fear is they chose you for some reason. You need to be very careful. This gang is not only violent; they are also very well organized, almost like a well-run business, and their leadership is very smart."

As Trey drove home, he played over in his mind his experience with Toby and the situation with the three bikers who saved him from certain grave harm or even death. He thought about Tara's experiences with them at Apache and the park. He wondered if Toby's explanation for obtaining his name at a chance encounter with one of his former clients at a bar was a fabrication. He mulled over what possible reason the Dreadnaughts could have any interest in him. What possible purpose could he serve for them?

As Trey pulled into the driveway, he thought better of relating his conversation with Demps to Tara. He concluded that the Dreadnaughts could not possibly want him for any reason, and these episodes likely had nothing to do with the Dreadnaughts, or if they did, they were pure coincidence.

Trey came into the house and found Tara watching the news. He gave her a kiss and sat down beside her. She asked how his game went. He indicated that it went well and that the cops had asked them out for a couple beers after the game.

Tara said she figured as much and then stated, "You won't believe what happened tonight. When we were ready to leave we asked the waiter for the bill. He advised us that the gentleman at the bar had already picked it up. We asked him to point him out so we could thank him. He looked around before pointing to a man walking out the door. He had a helmet on, and all we could see was his back."

"What was he wearing?"

"He had a black leather jacket on. That's all I could see."

"Did it have any lettering on it?"

"Yes, but I couldn't really make it out. It was something silly like Dreadful or Dreadhead."

As Trey, who had just a few minutes earlier convinced himself that these Dreadnaughts had no connection to him or Tara, stared straight ahead, she looked at him and asked, "What's wrong?"

"Nothing. Let's go to bed."

8

It was now the first week of November, and Tara was packing a suitcase. She had not seen her best friend and college roommate, Kim, since the wedding, and she was preparing to fly to San Diego to spend a few days with her.

Trey drove Tara to the airport. Prior to boarding the plane, they embraced and said how much they would miss each other. They had not spent a night apart in a very long time. Trey knew he would have difficulty sleeping without her by his side.

Late that night, Trey and Tara spoke on the phone. Predictably, he tossed and turned, having a rough night with little sleep. He kept thinking of his encounter with Toby and what Demps had told him that night at the bar. He had tried to block Toby and the Dreadnaughts out of his mind for the last week, but his mind raced this night with thoughts of what happened in court and how several people had apparently changed their stories. Although it seemed that Toby was a member of the Dreadnaughts motorcycle gang, how could they influence a bar full of people to completely change their stories in a town this big?

The following morning, while Trey was doing some research in the firm library, a call came through from the receptionist, "Trey, Toby is on the line." How ironic, he thought, that Toby would call the day after he had been thinking of him. Trey, who was tired from his sleepless night, instructed the receptionist to take a message. He had not planned on calling Toby back. He hoped that if he didn't return his call, he would not hear from him again. It wasn't as though he disliked him; he actually found him to be a rather amusing and likable fellow. But he also knew that it was not a good idea for him to have any further communications with him.

It was 4:00 p.m., and although not accustomed to leaving this early, Trey, weary from his lack of sleep, was preparing to leave for the day. Just as he was about to walk out the door from his office, the receptionist rang him. It was Toby again. He knew that Toby would just continue to call, and he also wanted to know if any of his suspicions were correct.

He answered the phone in an almost sarcastic manner, "What can I do for you today, Toby?"

"Counselor, I just wanted to repay you for the favor you did for me. Meet me out at Bikers and Babes, a little bar on Edge Street on the south side of town. Just make sure you find me right away. You'll be safe if you're with me."

"I'll see what I can do."

Trey had no intention of meeting Toby for beers anywhere, much less at biker bar. He laughed heartily when he hung up the phone.

As Trey got into his Porsche 911 and began to drive home, he inexplicably punched in Bikers and Babes on the navigation system. He had never heard of the place, and he had rarely been to the south side of town. Reflexively, he began to proceed toward the bar. As he drove down the remote road on which the bar was located and neared the bar, he mumbled to himself, "What in the hell am I doing? This is crazy."

There it was, in the middle of nowhere, a big lighted sign with a white background and "Bikers and Babes" in red. As Trey pulled in, he observed an expansive area with a partially paved parking lot, bikes spread around the exterior, and at least a hundred black-leather-clad bikers partying at various locations in the parking lot. The bar itself was a small wooden ramshackle structure that didn't look as if it would hold more than fifteen to twenty people.

As Trey pulled farther into the lot, it seemed as if the entire party stopped and stared at him. It occurred to him that his was the only car, and to make matters worse, it was the only imported item on the property. Realizing that he had made a big mistake, he threw the car into reverse and was on the fast track out of there. Before he could shift the Porsche into first gear, two burly bikers stepped in front of his car as the crowd began to shout from various parts of the parking lot, "What are you doing here? Your old lady ain't comin' home tonight."

Just as Trey realized he was in serious trouble, the bikers blocking his car walked off to the side, and there he was, square in his headlights—Toby. "Good evening, counselor," he said. "I'm glad you could make it. Park your car right there in front. I promise no one will touch it."

Trey followed Toby into the small building. Eight wooden barstools lined the bar. Across from it stood a round wooden table with six more chairs surrounding it. It was chilly in the bar, as there was no heat. The bartender, Jack, asked Trey what he was having, "Jack Daniels or Bud?" Trey ordered a Budweiser, and before he could pay, Toby slapped two dollars on the bar and pronounced, "Tonight's on me, counselor."

As time passed, Trey became more comfortable with the surroundings. He was surprised that the bikers were such fun-loving people who treated him so well. One lady, Lois, revealed that she had been a legal secretary in a law firm downtown with which he was familiar.

As 10:00 p.m. approached, the table across from the bar began to fill as a poker game was forming. Jack made all of the players put their guns and knives on the bar prior to taking a seat. Toby smiled and said, "The games get pretty lively at times. Best they limit it to fist fights." Also, two beautiful young women in their early twenties entered in trench coats. Trey stared at them for several seconds before looking back at Toby.

Toby said, "The entertainment has arrived. It's okay to check out the merchandise, but let's not forget that you are happily married."

"Very happily."

By this time, Trey had consumed a few beers and done a couple of shots of Jack Daniels. He was readying himself to thank Toby for the night out and make his way out the door as Toby became engaged in a heated argument with three very drunk and rather big bikers. Trey, although fortified by the alcohol and acting cool, was petrified inside. As best he could tell, Toby had apparently been messing with the wrong girl.

When Toby uttered, "She said I was the first real man she had been with in years," Trey knew he was in deep trouble.

One of the men broke a bottle and pointed it at Toby, yelling, "That was the last time you'll mess with one of our girls."

"Whoa, just a minute. Before you boys see fit to gut me like a fish and hurt my friend here, step into the bathroom, I have something I need to show you."

Trey turned to Jack and said, "Shot, please."

Jack looked at the three so eager to do serious bodily harm to Toby and said, "Gentlemen, you have a choice to make. You can either kill him now or go into the bathroom and see what he has to show you. I strongly recommend you go to the john with him before you decide to kill him, but it's your choice."

The three men grabbed Toby, picked him up off the bar stool, and threw him several feet into the bathroom door. Trey downed his shot and nervously looked at Jack. "It'll be fine. He gets out of worse than this all the time," said Jack. "Here, have another shot on the house."

As Trey sat on the bar stool contemplating how much he was going to miss his wife and never see his child be born, much to his astonishment and delight Toby and the three men walked out of the john laughing loudly and slapping each other on the back.

Shortly thereafter, Toby walked Trey outside to his car. "What the hell happened back there?" asked Trey. "I thought you were going to die in that restroom and that I was next just for knowing you. And did you really have to tell them I was your friend? I was trying to act as if I didn't know you." Toby laughed before getting into the passenger seat of the car and pulling up his right shirt sleeve. There was inked on his right shoulder what appeared to be a wagon wheel with five spokes.

"Anyone kills someone with this on his shoulder, he is tracked down nonstop until he is killed himself."

"How do I get one?"

"You don't want one."

As Trey, tired and clearly having had too much to drink, traveled down the poorly lit isolated road several miles from the highway, his cell phone rang. It was Tara. She was upset with him, as she had been calling him for hours. As Trey, accustomed to thinking fast on his feet in the courtroom, fabricated a story about having to go out for dinner and drinks with a client, a Harley flew up behind him. After a couple of minutes the chopper passed him, accelerating rapidly down the road. One of the women in trench coats was on the back.

A couple of minutes later, as Trey was getting off the phone with Tara, he saw the chopper pulled off the road. As he slowed further, he saw the man strike the woman, knocking her to the ground.

Trey immediately pulled over, jumped out of his car, and yelled, "Leave her alone. If you want to hit someone, hit a man, you coward."

As Trey walked closer, the biker responded, "When I'm done with her, I'll be happy to tend to you."

The biker picked the woman up by the coat and was rearing his right arm back to strike her again when Trey took two steps, coiled, and struck the biker with his best left-handed hook, dropping him to his knees. As Trey reached back to hit the man again, the man fell over onto his face.

Trey consoled the woman, who indicated that they had better leave before the biker's friends showed up. They jumped in his Porsche and within a couple of minutes were on the highway.

The woman was not only young but was one of the most beautiful women Trey had ever seen. As she gave him directions to her apartment, she explained that she was a student in college who danced two or three times a week to pay her way through school. One of her fellow dancers persuaded her to go to the Bikers and Babes bar, as she could make an easy thousand dollars in cash. After the near altercation involving Toby, some of the bikers got aggressive with her, and she asked one to please take her home, as the other dancer did not want to leave.

Upon arriving at her apartment just off campus, she asked Trey if he would come in for a few minutes. Although knowing he shouldn't accept her invitation, he felt that he would make sure she was okay and then leave. The woman poured each of them a drink, and they sat on the couch talking for several minutes. The more he looked at her, the more beautiful she looked. One of the shoulders of her trench coat gradually fell down her arm, revealing the large part of an incredible breast.

Trey became so enthralled with her sexuality that he couldn't hear what she was actually saying. The woman suddenly straddled him and began French kissing him passionately. Before he knew it, he was having hard and lustful sex with her on the couch and then the floor.

Trey awakened on the couch at seven the next morning with a splitting headache. He found some water and Tylenol. The girl was gone. He began to realize the full events of the night before, and he hurried out of the apartment.

Two days after Trey's experience at the Bikers and Babes bar and his encounter with the young woman, he sat at his desk reflecting on the events of that night and lamenting his conduct. Tara was the one true love of his life and his best friend. He sat pensively at his desk hoping that his unfaithfulness was a bad dream from which he would awake shortly.

Trey's mind was filled with so many unanswered questions. He thought of Toby's involvement in his life and questioned if it was just coincidence or if something more was going on. He couldn't help wondering whether Toby was the biker Tara had run into at Apache and who had saved Tara's friend's child at the park. He thought of the young woman with whom he had sex, and he wondered if she was okay.

Trey left work early and set out for the woman's apartment. Perhaps, he thought, she might be able to provide him with some answers. Upon arriving at the apartment, he knocked on the door, and a young woman answered. As he began to talk, she smiled and said, to his surprise, "Yeah, I know who you are. You're Trey. Come on in. My name is Becka. I assume you are here to see Stacey. She's in class. She should be back in about fifteen minutes. You can wait if you want." He went into the apartment and sat on the couch. Becka came out from the kitchen and handed him a bottle of water. They sat on the couch and began talking. Becka, like Stacey, was very beautiful and extremely personable. She put him at ease as she talked about her studies and what she wanted to do upon graduation.

As Stacey came through the door, she heard talking. She had a puzzled look on her face as she looked across the room and saw Trey and Becka staring at her with smiles on their faces. Becka got up from the couch and went into a back bedroom, and Stacey, books in hand, sat down next to Trey.

Stacey looked into Trey's eyes briefly before saying, "Why are you here, Trey? I am assuming that you are not leaving your wife for me. What do you want?"

"I want to apologize for the other night. That was not me. You are gorgeous, and any guy would be very lucky to have you, but I am not the kind of guy who gets drunk and cheats on his wife."

"Trey, that was not your fault. First of all, I owe you a big favor. You saved me from that fat, disgusting, pig of a biker. I made a mistake that night. I had rent to pay, and I figured I would make some easy money dancing at the bar. You've got my word—no more dancing for me. That guy was beating me because I refused to have sex with him. No telling what would have happened had you not shown up. Besides, once we got back here, I came on to you. I can tell that you're a good guy, and that night was an aberration for you. Look, everyone makes a mistake from time to time. Don't be so hard on yourself. It was a one-time deal, and I am fine with it. One day, I'll find a great guy like you, get married, and have a family."

"I appreciate your comments. You're a beautiful girl. If I were not married, I would love to spend some time with you to see where it would go. What do you know about the bikers at the bar that night?"

Stacey looked Trey squarely in the eyes and said emphatically, "Trey, they are bad characters. You saw what the one did to me that night. I don't know much about them, but I know that you should stay as far away from them as possible. Let's promise each other that neither of us will ever again have anything to do with them."

"Agreed."

Trey stood, hugged Stacey, and left. He was satisfied with the conversation he had with her, and he felt much better about what had happened. He convinced himself that he had made a one-time mistake and that he would never go around Toby or the bikers again. He told himself to put it in the past and forget about it.

After Trey left, Becka came out, stared at Stacey, and said, "You didn't tell him, did you?"

"I couldn't."

Over the course of the next three days, Trey could not stop thinking about Stacey. For the first time since meeting Tara, he considered whether another woman was as beautiful as she. He was agitated and disappointed with himself that he would even think of another woman as being Tara's equal. He contemplated what this meant. Did his obsession with Stacey mean that he did not love Tara? If he loved her, why did he have sex with another woman, and even more troubling, why could he not get her off of his mind?

Trey fidgeted as he waited for Tara to come through the door. He was not the nervous type. He was a model of composure as he stood before a jury arguing that his client should receive large amounts of money, but as he sat waiting for her, he was an emotional wreck.

Tara came through the door, put her bag down, and ran to Trey, screaming as if they had been away from each other for weeks. As he held her, he at once became calm and comforted. He then held her hands and looked into her eyes, and any doubts he had about her and their relationship raced from his mind. He realized with total and complete clarity how much he loved her and how she made him feel. Without saying a word, he led her to the couch by the hand, and despite her being over four months pregnant, they made soft and delicate love. All he needed was to see her again. Nobody would ever compare to Tara.

A few days later, Trey was at the office when he got a call from Demps. He insisted that Trey come down to the station to speak with him.

"What's this about, Demps? Unless it's important, I really don't have the time right now. Is my wife okay?"

"Yes, she's fine, but I am not at all sure that I can say the same for you. You need to get down here immediately. I can't tell you more over the phone."

Upon Trey's arrival, he was led into an office and seated across from a desk. There were pictures on the desk of Demps and his wife, and on the walls hung pictures of him playing college basketball.

Demps walked in, sat in his chair, and stared at Trey for a few seconds before asking, "What in the hell is going on, Trey? What have you got yourself into? Are you the legal counsel for the Dreadnaughts?"

"That is preposterous. Why would you even think such an insane thing?"

"Don't bullshit me, Trey. This is serious business. You have no idea what you're dealing with here. You were seen at Bikers and Babes, the Dreadnaughts' hangout. What would you have been doing there?"

Trey explained to Demps that the same night they had gone out for beers after the basketball game, he thought that Tara had seen Toby, who he assumed was a Dreadnaught, at a restaurant where she was eating with some friends. "He even picked up their bill," said Trey. He went on to explain the phone call from Toby as he was leaving the office. "I don't know what I was thinking. I guess I figured if I went there, I would get some answers. Were they following me? Were they following Tara? What, if anything, did they want from me? Then I had too much to drink, but Toby asked nothing of me. He just wanted to thank me for the case I handled for him. I swear, he didn't ask me for anything. I honestly don't think I'll hear from him again, but if I do, I will not meet him anywhere. I'll call you immediately."

"That would be very wise."

Demps lectured Trey sternly, "I'm only going to say this one time Trey. You're a smart guy; I don't need to repeat myself. These are extremely dangerous people, and you and Tara need to stay as far away from them as possible. We believe that they kidnapped a sixteen-year-old girl from the town below their headquarters five years ago, although we haven't been able to prove it. She has never been found. Am I making myself clear, Trey?"

"Crystal clear. You've got my word."

Demps gave Trey his cell phone number and instructed him that if anything suspicious happened or he was contacted by Toby or the Dreadnaughts again, to call him immediately. "Don't think about it, Trey. Don't wait; call me," he said firmly. Trey stood, shook his hand, thanked him, and walked out of the office. As the door shut, Demps mumbled to himself, "Christ, I hope he's right."

The following morning, Trey got to work and opened the paper. He nearly fell out of his chair. On the front page was a picture of Demps with the headline, "Veteran officer gunned down." He trembled as he read the article. The article didn't give much information other than relating that a passing motorist called 911 at about 1:30 a.m. when he passed Demps's unmarked police car pulled off the side of the road. When fellow officers arrived, he was found off to the side of the car, face down, with a single bullet shot to the back of the head. It resembled an execution, the paper reported.

Trey closed the paper and leaned back in his chair in shock. He was extremely distraught at the death of someone he considered to be a friend, and he was concerned as to what was coming next, knowing that the one person who he could trust to protect him and Tara was now dead.

Trey and Tara went to Demps's funeral. Trey couldn't help but continue to look across at Demps's grieving widow. He knew that the Dreadnaughts were responsible for Demps's killing. He wondered if Demps was killed because he was caught by the Dreadnaughts investigating them, or was it directly related to the Dreadnaughts somehow having knowledge of the conversation he had with him earlier that day? Either way, it was a bad situation.

After Demps's burial, Trey encouraged Tara to go visit her family in Charleston for a couple of days. He needed some time alone to think and figure it all out.

Immediately after Tara left the following morning, Trey went to work and called an investigator who did work for him on cases. He got the number of a former CIA employee who was an expert on detecting phone-tapping devices and bugs.

Trey met the expert after work at 6:00 p.m. at his house. The expert pulled out a device that looked as though it was a wand and began walking through the house. When he walked into the kitchen the wand lit up. He uncovered two bugs in the kitchen before looking at the phone. He pulled apart the phone and pulled out a tiny chip, which he held up and showed to Trey. He then wrote on a piece of paper for Trey not to say a word because any conversation was likely being monitored. The same routine was repeated throughout the entire house, and several more bugs were found. All of the phones were tapped. Trey shook his head with disgust as a bug was even found in the bedroom. The expert combed the house thoroughly a second time to make sure that he got everything. As he was doing this, Trey went outside and called a locksmith to come to the house to change all the locks.

An hour had passed before the expert finally spoke a word. "Who are you? I've never seen anything like this in a private residence. Whoever did this could hear any conversation in any part of your house and listen to every phone conversation. This was a professional job."

If there had been any question at all in Trey's mind as to whether the Dreadnaughts and Toby were behind the happenings of the last few months, there was no longer. The only question at this point was why.

9

Tara returned from her parent's home in Charleston, and things were quiet for a couple of weeks. There were no signs of Toby or the Dreadnaughts, and Trey hoped for the best.

One Friday evening in the first week of December, Tara was preparing to go to Hawaii with her family. They usually went snow skiing in Colorado this time of year, but she was five months pregnant, so the plans changed.

Trey wanted to go, but he was on the trial docket for Monday. He was representing the family of a juvenile who had died while in a state-owned detention facility. The youth had been restrained by four detention officers and beaten badly. He died of his injuries, and Trey had filed a wrongful death suit on behalf of the family. The state was tough when it came to settlement negotiations, and he had little hope that the case would settle in the upcoming week.

Trey awoke early on Saturday to make Tara breakfast and help her finish packing for the trip. He carried her luggage to her parents' car when they arrived and hugged her and promised to catch the first plane out if his case settled at some point during the upcoming week. He spent the remainder of the weekend preparing for the trial on Monday.

Trey met with his expert witnesses early Monday morning to go over their testimony one more time. At the courthouse, he began his opening statement. He knew that this phase of the trial was extremely important, as it was the first opportunity to introduce his case to the jury. It also allowed him to explain that although the juvenile was a troubled young man, surely he did not deserve to die as a result of the excessive and unnecessary force used by the brutish juvenile detention officers. As Trey concluded his opening statement, he heard a faint slow clap. As he looked in the direction of the clap, much to his consternation, he saw Toby nodding his approval with a wide smile on his face.

As Trey listened to the state's opening statement, he glanced back, but Toby was gone. He carefully observed the jurors during his and the state's openings, and he felt very good that they were leaning his way. After the state concluded its opening, it was nearing noon, and the judge instructed everyone to break for lunch. As Trey was leaving the courtroom, the state's attorneys motioned him over. They wanted to talk.

They moved to a small conference room where they asked Trey what it would take to settle the case. He replied that they had his final figure two weeks ago and that he believed that his case was looking very good. The state, knowing that it was in a bad position, begrudgingly agreed to meet his figure, and the case was settled.

As Trey returned to the office, he was congratulated by everyone—the attorneys, secretaries, and paralegals. He was in a celebratory mood. He had obtained a big-dollar settlement from the state, which was not easy to do, and he could catch an evening flight out to Hawaii to be with Tara. Just as he was about to make his airline reservations, the receptionist buzzed his phone. Toby was there to see him. He knew he could not avoid Toby. He needed to know what Toby wanted from him, and he needed answers.

Toby walked through the door applauding. "Well done, counselor. You were incredible. Not just anyone can bring the state to its knees the way you did."

"Look, Toby, I appreciate the kind words, but you obviously want something from me, so let's quit dancing around it and you tell me what it is."

"Fair enough."

Toby proceeded for the next fifteen minutes to explain that his initial meeting with Trey was no accident. Sure enough, he had been involved in an altercation, but any attorney could have handled the matter, as his superiors, the disciples, had seen to it that all the eyewitnesses had changed their stories. No, it was no coincidence. Trey had been selected by the disciples for a purpose.

"For what purpose?" asked Trey as his cell phone rang. It was Tara.

"Better tell her that your trial's still going on and you can't leave yet."

Trey complied, lying to Tara. Toby then explained that the disciples needed to speak with Trey, and then everything would become clear. Before Trey could protest, Toby indicated that if he wanted this thing over with and Toby and his people out of his life, he needed to come with him. "Besides," said Toby, "I'd hate to see anything happen to that pretty girl of yours, Tara." Although Trey knew that the Dreadnaughts had bugged his house in the past, he sat dumbfounded as Toby raved about the house and described certain aspects of the interior that one could only know from having been in the house. Trey understood that he was in deep, for reasons still a mystery to him, and that he had no choice but to go with Toby to meet the disciples.

As they drove in Toby's pickup truck through town and onto a road leading up into the mountains, Trey's mind was occupied with thoughts of what this could possibly be about, or whom he may have wronged in the past who may have some connection to these outlaws. After traveling up the mountain road for forty-five minutes, the truck came upon a small town and turned left up a long dirt road before turning into a large open field. The truck jostled across the field before stopping in front of a dilapidated two-story wooden farmhouse at the far edge of the field.

Trey entered the house and followed Toby up the stairs, down a narrow hall, and through a door. As he entered the room, his eyes locked on three individuals who looked as if they could be Toby's brothers. "The disciples," said Toby. The three were seated at a table. The big one, who looked to be in his midfifties, sat in the middle. Trey surmised that he was the leader. He said, "Welcome, Trey. Have a seat." As Trey sat down across the table from him, he said, "Relax. We have no problem with you. To the contrary, we picked you out because we were impressed with your abilities as an attorney, and you have done us a favor by helping Animal in his battery case."

"Animal? I thought his name was Toby."

"Animal is his biker name."

"In any event, it wasn't much of a favor. You got all the witnesses to recant their stories."

The large man laughed and said, "Nevertheless, you're a good man and in good graces with us." He identified himself as Jimmy and instructed Animal to roll up his shirt sleeve. "What do you see?"

"Yes, I've seen it," responded Trey with an irritated look on his face. "It looks like a wagon wheel. It supposedly has some sort of protection powers."

"Very good, but what do you see?"

"It has five spokes with what looks like a space for a sixth."

"Good again."

Jimmy then explained to Trey that Animal had the honor of being a cowboy. Cowboys were chosen based upon ability and loyalty to the group. There were only seven of them in the Southeast, which is where the Dreadnoughts operated. Once they received six spokes, they were elevated to the status of disciple. The disciples performed the leadership function of the group. If anyone ever messed with a cowboy or a disciple, the entire group hunted him down. Consequently, nobody in the biker or criminal world ever knowingly harmed a disciple or cowboy, as it would result in a death sentence.

"Yes," said Trey as he grew more agitated, "I've seen it in action."

"So you have," laughed Jimmy.

"What do you have to do for a spoke?"

"Well, you have to perform a function of great importance, usually killing one of our enemies."

"So cowboy is a nice word for hit man."

Jimmy laughed again, folded his hands, leaned over, stared Trey in the eyes, and stated simply, "Yes."

Jimmy then proudly explained to Trey that the Dreadnaughts had been formed thirty-three years before. Under his leadership over the last twenty-eight years, they had developed a successful marijuana distribution business and slowly eradicated most of their main rivals in the Southeast. They had recently expanded their illicit dealings to include cocaine distribution. The competition was more fierce, ruthless, and violent. He felt that the Dreadnaughts needed to make this leap, as this was where the big money was. They needed to follow the same business model that had proved so successful in their marijuana business. Basically, this called for a structured and systematic elimination of their rivals. The first large rival to be whacked was in Atlanta.

The mark in Atlanta was the biggest and most difficult hit the gang had ever undertaken. While growing the dope business, the marks involved small organizations that wielded minimal power. They were not very organized or difficult to get to. This, however, was different. The mark in Atlanta, Don Gambotti, was a big-time cocaine distributor. He ran the cocaine trade in the Southeast for a major crime family headquartered in New York City. This family distributed cocaine nationally. The organization was a well-oiled machine, and Don Gambotti was highly guarded at all times. This was no ordinary hit, and Jimmy knew he had to be creative.

Jimmy indicated that Trey must accompany Animal and help him create a strategy to successfully hit Gambotti. As Trey began to protest that he could not even contemplate participating in murder, Jimmy raised his hand and stopped him.

"Perhaps you should look at these," said Jimmy as he slid a big envelope across the table to Trey. He looked inside and was shocked to see numerous photographs of himself and Stacey engaged in sex acts.

"If you think you can use these to get me to commit murder, you're crazy. I'll tell my wife, and we'll work it out."

66

"Now, Trey, I don't have to make threats and make this any uglier than it has to be, do I? By the way, how's that pretty little wife of yours and her family doing in Hawaii?"

"If I do this, then what?"

"Then you're out. You'll never hear from us again."

"How do I know you'll keep your word?"

"I'm a man of honor. My word is my bond. I didn't get where I am by not honoring my word. You'll have to trust me." After pausing, Jimmy said, "If you and Animal work efficiently together, you'll be back home in time for Tara's return from her trip." Trey and Toby, or Animal, immediately set out in a van for Atlanta.

As they drove, Trey felt as if he were in the middle of a bad dream. How insane was this, he thought, that he was headed toward Atlanta to assist Toby in carrying out a hit on a rival drug lord.

Upon arriving in Atlanta, they went to a seedy motel just outside the city. Immediately after checking in, the two went to the lounge downstairs and ordered drinks. As Trey drank heavily, he and Toby did not utter a word to each other. Trey had a glazed-over look in his eyes, as though he was in shock. "Hey, it's not that bad, counselor," remarked Toby. "You help me with this one job, and you'll never hear from us again. You'll resume your fairytale life with Tara, and everything will be grand." Trey, staring straight ahead, said nothing. As he ordered his fifth drink, Toby reminded him that they had a very important task to perform tomorrow and he should not drink anymore. "There will be plenty of time to celebrate at the conclusion of our mission," said Toby.

The following morning, the wake-up call came at 8:00 a.m. Trey, having a touch of a hangover, popped a few Tylenol. "Let's rock," said Toby. "Today's the day."

That day, the two seemed to aimlessly wander the streets of downtown Atlanta. Toby was on his cell phone much of the time. At 6:00 p.m., they stopped at an Irish pub to eat. As they ordered their meals and beers, Toby's phone rang. After listening for a few seconds, his eyes lit up. "Very good," he said. "We're on." He looked at Trey with a smile on his face and declared, "Have a couple of beers, relax, and get focused. It's nearly show time."

A couple of hours later, they approached a group of nightclubs with brightly lit signs and long lines waiting to get in. Eventually, they reached a club with a sign in bright blue letters and stood at the back of a long line. As they stood in line, Trey's stomach began to turn. He had stood in front of a packed courthouse, at the center of the stage, but he had never been this nervous. After almost an hour, which seemed like an eternity to him, they entered the club.

The club was like nothing Trey had ever seen before. Young girls were in skimpy bathing suits on swings overhead, beautiful women in negligees walked around and served shots of alcohol, and more women danced in cages suspended above the dance floor. The music was pulsating in an almost trance-inducing beat. Couples were grinding on the dance floor and groping each other.

Trey and Toby eventually found a small table to one side of dance floor, close to the men's restroom, which was a good thing, because Trey felt sick to his stomach. He consumed several beers and had a few shots. He was beginning to relax and enjoy the scenery when he remembered why they were there.

Trey turned to Toby and remarked, "Surely we are not going to do anything here. This place is packed."

"You see the fellow seated at the table on the other side of the dance floor? The one in the red shirt with all the girls around him? He's our man."

"What are you, nuts? How in the hell are we going to get to him in a crowded club with all those people around him? You've seen *Scarface* a few too many times."

Toby laughed and responded, "He's got to go to the restroom sometime."

Upon hearing that, Trey angrily got up from his seat and said, "I'm out of here. This is ridiculous."

"Before you go, take a seat; there's someone you may want to talk to."

Toby calmly hit several numbers on his phone, waited a few seconds, and handed it to Trey. On the other end was a voice unpleasantly familiar to him.

"How are you doing Trey?" asked Jimmy. "My, Hawaii certainly is beautiful this time of year. The beach is fabulous. By the way, a picture doesn't do Tara justice. I walked right by her on the beach an hour ago. She has an incredible smile. I would hate to see anything happen to her. You will complete your mission, Trey. Don't do anything stupid."

Trey handed the phone back to Toby. He knew he was boxed in, resigned to his murderous fate. There was no way out. He would die before he would let anything happen to Tara. He loved her more than the air he breathed.

"Are we good, counselor?" asked Toby.

Trey stared straight ahead and responded tersely, "Kiss my ass, jerkoff."

Within a couple of minutes, Trey began to mumble, his eyes rolled up into his head, and he slumped over onto the table. Toby carried him outside, hailed a cab, handed the cabbie a hundred-dollar bill, and instructed him to see that Trey made it back to the hotel room.

Toby returned to the table, and as he downed a shot, he saw Gambotti begin to move. Toby's steely-blue eyes followed the man as he made his way around the dance floor. As he walked past him, Toby took one last shot of Jack Daniels, turned, and headed toward the restroom.

Upon entering the restroom, Toby went to the urinal as if he were relieving himself. The men to each side of him flushed and left. He immediately turned, opened the door to the toilet, and fired two shots from his silencer into the chest of Gambotti. He walked out of the restroom with no one observing what had just taken place.

The following morning, Trey awoke to a pounding headache. Toby handed him a glass of water and threw a newspaper down on the bed. The headline of the paper read: "Mob boss gunned down in stall of nightclub." Trey stared into the paper for a few seconds before looking up at Toby. "You did it," Toby declared. "Congratulations, you've earned your freedom. Let's go home."

On the van ride home, Trey went over and over in his mind the prior evening. The problem was that he didn't remember a thing after his phone conversation with Jimmy. He did not know that Toby had drugged him and sent him back in a cab. He had no reason to doubt that he had assassinated the man the paper referred to as Don Gambotti, a reputed mobster who was a main player in a prominent crime family from New York.

Trey asked Toby, "How do you know that we will not get implicated in this? You know we will both get fried if we're caught."

"Relax. I'm a professional. There is no way we'll get caught. They will suspect a rival mob family in New York or Chicago, and they'll go to war, which is what we want."

"I need to know what happened. I was too drunk. I don't remember."

"You were great. All you need to know is that I handed you the gun with the silencer in the restroom and you shot him. What more do you need to know? When we get home, relax, pretend this never happened, and go on with the awesome life that you have. You and Tara have kids and live happily ever after."

Trey then inquired of Toby as to why the disciples needed someone to accompany him to carry out the hit and why he was chosen to be his partner. Toby responded that the disciples don't share all the reasons and information with the cowboys but that he assumed that he was chosen because he was smart and because if they needed to get creative to pull off the hit, he could help. Also, if the hit went bad, he would be set up as the fall guy.

Upon returning to the gang's headquarters in the mountains, they parked the van just outside the old house. As they entered the house, several bikers were sitting on the couches and chairs drinking and smoking. Jimmy's voice echoed from the far corner of the room. "Well done, Trey," he said as he and the others began to clap. As Trey turned to face him, he was startled by what he saw.

He stared for several seconds with a glum look on his face before subtly shaking his head and saying, "Stacey, what a surprise. This just keeps getting better and better."

Stacey, sitting on Jimmy's lap, smiled at Trey and said, "Trey, you don't look so good. You need to get some sleep."

"Oh yeah, you volunteering to help me out with that again?"

Jimmy laughed and invited Trey to stay for a while and have some drinks with them. He declined and asked Jimmy if Toby could take him home. Jimmy indicated that Animal was going to stay and celebrate the Gambotti hit with the disciples and said, "I'm sure Stacey would be happy to take you home, Trey. No photographs this time, I promise." Trey rolled his eyes and walked out the door. Stacey stood, Jimmy slapped her on the butt, and she ran out the door.

The first thirty minutes of the almost hour-long drive home, there was dead silence in the car. Eventually, Stacey broke the silence by apologizing to Trey for setting him up in their previous encounter. As they continued to talk and the conversation got easier, Stacey began to speak freely. She was, after all, a young girl, and Trey decided that he would use this opportunity to utilize his trial skills to ply her for as much information as possible. As they neared his office where his car was parked, he had put her at such ease that he was able to get her to reveal that Stacey was not her real name.

Trey got in his car and drove home. He spent the next several hours sipping Jack Daniels as he watched television and attempted to fully absorb the events of the last three days. At 10:00 p.m., he collapsed in his bed and entered a deep sleep.

At 8:00 a.m. on Thursday, his eyes suddenly opened wide as he thought that he had come to a major revelation. He jumped into the shower, hurriedly dressed, and headed toward the library. Once there, he got the microfiche containing copies of newspapers from the surrounding areas. He went back about five years and rapidly scrolled through the articles. After about thirty minutes, he got to a headline and just stared intensely, reading the article for a few minutes. Stacey, whose real name was Erin, was the girl who went missing from the mountain town five years earlier. The story was true. The bikers had taken her and made her one of them.

Trey left the library and drove to Stacey's apartment off campus. He figured that he would not find her there and that he would probably never see her again. He was torn up over his feelings. He wanted to go to the police or her family, but he knew that he could not. He wanted to speak with Stacey, as he felt an obligation to at least make sure she was okay and not being coerced by the Dreadnaughts into continuing her participation with them.

Much to Trey's surprise, Stacey answered the door and welcomed him in. She explained to him that she was doing fine and that he need not worry about her. The Dreadnaughts had not forcefully taken her or kidnapped her when she was sixteen. She was being sexually abused by her stepfather, and the gang had taken her in and treated her well. They were paying for her apartment, living expenses, and tuition. The downside was that she had to do jobs periodically for the gang, like the one she had done with Trey. But the life the Dreadnaughts had given her was much better than the one she had before. They had rescued her from dire circumstances and a bleak future.

Trey, feeling much better about the situation, hugged Stacey and wished her the best. He encouraged her to get her degree and make something of herself. He told her that she would make an excellent wife and mother someday. She grabbed his hand and said emphatically, "Trey, stay away from Jimmy and Toby. Apparently they have given you your out. Whatever it takes, take your out, run away as fast as you can, and never look back. They are ruthless people. They will stop at nothing. Go back to your wife and forget the Dreadnaughts. Erase your experience with them from your mind for good. You're a great guy. Never go around them again." He left with the firm conviction in his mind that he would do just that.

On Friday, Trey found his old full-body wet suit packed in a box in the garage, and he loaded up his old surfboard and headed to the beach. He ran on the beach in his sweat suit and then changed into his wet suit and surfed until dusk. He cleared his mind of the week's events, and upon returning home, he ordered a pizza and watched some television. He fell asleep at 11:00 p.m. on the couch.

It was 6:00 a.m. on Saturday. Trey had only one day prior to Tara returning from Hawaii, and he tried to regroup. He could only hope that Jimmy would be true to his word and the Dreadnaughts would stay out of his life so that he and Tara could resume the lives they led before. The baby was due in less than four months, and he knew that he needed to get it together.

Trey was curious as to how far the Dreadnaughts had gone. He met with the expert who had cleaned the bugs and phone taps from his home at the office at 7:00 a.m., when nobody would be around. The expert began walking around Trey's office with the wand. He predictably found two bugs, and the phone was tapped. As a precautionary measure, Trey had him go through the remainder of the five-thousand-square-foot office, and nothing else was found. The house and the office were now clean, and Trey thought that he could have a fresh start and forget about his encounters with the Dreadnaughts. He told himself it was over.

Prior to Tara's leaving for Hawaii, she had stood with Trey in the baby's room and expressed her interest in changing the color of the room, for the third time. He didn't really understand her obsession with the room, as the baby's due date was still almost four months off and they didn't even know what sex it was. Nevertheless, he wanted to surprise her when she got home on Sunday, so he went to pick up some paint.

Trey spent his Saturday afternoon painting the room a dark shade of blue. It occurred to him as he painted that if the baby was a girl, Tara would want the room repainted once again, but if it made her happy and it kicked off his post-Dreadnaught life on a positive note, it was well worth the effort, he reasoned.

Trey finished painting about 6:00 p.m., and he was exhausted. He ordered takeout from the Italian restaurant down the road. He left early to pick up his order so that he could stop by the Piggly Wiggly and get some flowers for Tara. After arriving back at home, he carefully placed the flowers on the kitchen table with a note attached telling her that he missed her and to go look at the baby's room.

After eating, Trey grabbed a beer from the fridge and reclined in his chair to watch a college football game. As he was about to doze off, Tara called him. She said that she was getting ready to head for the airport and she would see him tomorrow at noon at the airport in Asheville.

Trey awoke at 7:00 a.m. on Sunday. He went for a five-mile run. He then shaved and took a long shower. Things were going to be different now, he thought. He wanted everything to be perfect when Tara got home. He cleaned the house thoroughly and even made the bed for the first time in a week. He struggled with the bed, and it didn't look the way it did when she made it, but she would appreciate the effort, he thought.

It was 10:00 a.m., two hours before Tara was due to arrive, and Trey had one more thing to do to make her homecoming perfect. He went to the mall and visited three different jewelry stores before finding the perfect gift. He found a gleaming gold bracelet on which he could add attachments. He bought three tiny attachments: a man, a woman, and a baby. He knew she would love it.

Trey got home at 11:20 a.m. He placed the gift box next to the flowers on the kitchen table and stood back for a moment and smiled, reveling in his work over the past day and a half making everything perfect for Tara's return. He grabbed his keys and made his way hastily for the door. He wanted to be there when she got off the plane. He then abruptly turned around, running back to the kitchen table to get the jewelry box. He would give it to her in the car; that would be even better.

As Tara came through the tunnel, her eyes shifted around trying to locate Trey. When she saw him, they ran to each other and hugged. They kissed and told each other how much they each missed the other. Much to Trey's dismay, Tara's smile quickly turned on him, and she began to chew him out for not calling her every night as they had agreed. She continued to give him a hard time all the way to the baggage pickup.

Trey waited anxiously for the bags to come down on the conveyor belt, thinking that once he got her in the car and gave her the gift, everything would be okay. Once in the car, he looked at Tara and said as sincerely as he could, "Tara, I'm sorry. You know how obsessed I am when I have a trial going on. I was working nearly nonstop at the office through Friday. I know that's no excuse. I'm so sorry." He then gave her the box. She was expressionless as she opened the box, as she understood that this was merely his obligatory "I'm sorry I messed up" gift. She looked unimpressed as she held the bracelet. She had many bracelets, and this seemed like a gift he ran out and picked up quickly without putting any thought into it. "Look in the box," said Trey. "There's more." Tara's countenance went from glum to one resembling a young child opening a Christmas gift as she picked up the small figurines. "See—there's you, me, and, yes, there's the baby," said Trey excitedly.

Tara stared at the bracelet and the figures for a moment before turning and hugging Trey as she wept. She knew that he had put some thought into the gift, and she was over her anger with him.

Upon arriving home, Tara went to the kitchen and saw the flowers. She opened the card instructing her to go to the baby's room, and she looked up at Trey, saying, "What did you do?" As she walked into the room, she surveyed the walls briefly before putting her arms around him and crying. "I love you so much," she sobbed. *I am the king of comebacks,* thought Trey.

10

The following few weeks were difficult for Tara. Trey seemed aloof, showing little interest in her. On the occasions when she tried to speak with him, he would dismiss her concerns as foolish. He was distracted. He couldn't enjoy his time with her or focus on anything, including work. The holiday season was even an uneventful, dreary time with him. He relived the trip to Atlanta in his mind almost nonstop. He had taken a human life, and he did not know how he would live with it. Nor was there anyone he could talk to about it.

It was the middle of January of 1994, and Tara was having lunch with the wife of an attorney in Trey's firm. She began to discuss her problems with Trey. The woman indicated that her husband and the others at the firm were also very concerned about him.

"It all began in early December when he disappeared for a week. Some thought he had gone to meet you in Hawaii without telling anyone, but we found out that he didn't go. Nobody knows where he was."

"He had a trial that week," responded Tara with a confounded look on her face.

The woman stated that she was sorry and perhaps she shouldn't have said anything because she didn't want to cause more problems. As Tara pressed her for answers, however, it became apparent that Trey was not in trial while she was in Hawaii. She did not understand why he had lied to her. She was confused, and she began to think what seemed obvious to her. He was having an affair. That's the only explanation that would make sense of the last four weeks.

That evening, Tara sat in the living room waiting for Trey to come through the door. As he came in and looked at her, he could tell that something was amiss. "We need to talk," she said. She told him that

74

nothing had been the same since she had returned from Hawaii. They no longer laughed together, did things together, or talked. They had not been intimate. "Furthermore," said Tara firmly, "how was your trial when I was in Hawaii?" Trey stared at her as tears began to roll down his cheeks. He apologized, saying he could not lie to her anymore. He was not in trial that week. Tara then begged him to talk to her and tell her the truth, to tell her everything. She then asked the obvious questions: "Are you having an affair, Trey? Is there someone else?" He indicated that he was not having an affair and that there was no one else. "Then talk to me, Trey," said Tara. "What is it? Do you not love me anymore?"

"Tara, my love for you is so complete and profound that I have always felt as if I was in love with you before I even saw you for the first time. I could never love another woman, but there are things I cannot tell you now. I have to figure them out on my own."

"Trey, you can tell me anything. We'll work it out together. I love you so much. Whatever it is, we will deal with it together."

"I wish it were that simple, but I have to deal with this one on my own."

Tara then instructed Trey to go and come back when he was prepared to talk openly with her, had no more secrets, and was ready to share his life with her again. As he walked out the door with his poorly packed suitcase, she sobbed uncontrollably. She felt as if she was losing him, and she did not know if she would ever get him back. It killed her that he was in serious trouble of some nature, and she had no idea how to help him.

Over the course of the next couple of days, Tara phoned numerous people, including all of the wives she knew of the other attorneys in Trey's firm, searching for answers, but no one seemed to know anything. She remembered the old Indian woman who had known that she was pregnant and who had told her about troubled waters ahead. She was desperate, and maybe, she thought, the old woman indeed had some physic powers and could provide her with the answers she so badly needed.

Tara went to the Apache store. She entered and was almost immediately greeted by the old woman. The two sat on chairs in the back office of the store, and Tara began crying. Upon regaining her composure, she briefly explained the problems that had developed recently with Trey and that she had suspected that he had someone else but she could get no answers.

The old woman held Tara's hand and looked into her eyes for a moment before saying, "You are the love of Trey's life. You are his soul mate, and you will always be his soul mate. There is no other woman."

"Then why, why has he left me?" questioned Tara with tears still running down her face. "Why won't he talk to me?"

"Something has happened in his life that he needs to work through on his own, and he cannot be together with you again until he has figured it all out."

"How long will that take? Will he be back before the baby is born?"

The old Indian woman told Tara that, unfortunately, when a man has a problem like Trey's, there is no way of knowing how long it will take. As Tara got into her car she felt equally relieved knowing that he still loved her and wanted to be with her and horrified knowing that he was living a nightmare of some sort; she did not know how long it would take him to resolve it and be with her again.

One late Friday afternoon, as Trey was in the firm's library researching a legal issue, Stu, one of the firm's middle-aged attorneys, approached him and asked him if he would like to go to the Charlotte Hornets basketball game with him that evening. The firm had season tickets to the games. Although Trey did not have much of an interest in socializing or going out because he preferred to go back to his apartment and dwell in his misery by himself, Stu did not take no for answer, and Trey eventually agreed.

Stu had never been married, and he envisioned himself as a ladies' man, although his belly and balding head belied this image. In any event, he knew how to have fun, and he was frequently in the company of young women who were much more pleasing to look at than he was.

During the first half of the game, Stu and Trey each had a couple of beers. The seats were located near midcourt three rows up. Trey, having been a very good basketball player, was enjoying himself, and he was able to take his mind off his problems as he focused on the game.

The firm's membership allowed them to go to a club within the stadium and have drinks and socialize with the cheerleaders and team executives after the game.

Trey and Stu were standing at the bar in the club having a drink when one of the cheerleaders approached Stu and began conversing with him. Trey had never been impressed with Stu's popularity—it seemed obvious that the women were attracted to his status and money. Trey had always looked at him in a sympathetic way, as he deemed his life to be superficial, but Stu was happy. This lifestyle worked for him.

As Stu engaged in conversation with the woman, Trey was staring blankly across the room, lamenting his problems and his separation from Tara, when he heard a soft and very feminine voice utter, "Hi, Trey, how are you?" As he glanced to his left and focused in on the person addressing him, he stared for a few seconds before remembering who she was. She was Stacey's roommate, but he could not remember her name. "I'm Becka, Stacey's roommate," said the woman after tiring of his struggle to remember her. He was amazed that she was a Hornets cheerleader, and he was at a loss for words, which didn't happen often. Stu was impressed that Trey knew one of the cheerleaders, and the four talked for the next hour over drinks.

As the club closed, Stu, always thinking of prolonging the night and ultimately scoring, suggested that they continue the party back in Asheville at his condo overlooking the city. It was late, Trey was tired, and he knew that continuing the evening at Stu's could only lead to trouble. As he declined and indicated that he needed to get home because he had an early morning, he asked Becka if she would mind letting him ride with her on the two-and-a-half-hour drive home to Asheville. He realized that this wasn't a good idea, but he enjoyed Becka's company, very much the way he did Stacey's, and it beat the alternative of riding back with Stu and his date for the evening.

As they made the long drive back to Trey's office, he revealed that he and Tara had separated, and Becka proved to be a good listener, apparently sympathetic to his problems and even suggesting ways that he and Tara could get back together. She told him that it was obvious that he still loved Tara and that he should do whatever it took to get back together with her.

As they pulled into the parking garage at Trey's office, Becka asked him if he wanted to follow her to her apartment so that they could talk some more, and once again, although understanding that it was clearly not the right choice, he accepted. Once inside the apartment, the conversation continued, and one drink led to a second. Midway through the second drink, she took his drink from him and set it on the table. She looked at him in a manner that made it clear what she wanted. He instinctively grabbed her, aggressively turned her over, and pulled her teal cheerleader skirt up onto her low back. A moment later, he looked up and saw the two of them in a mirror. He paused, and she looked back and asked him what was wrong. He grabbed his shirt and ran out the door as he pulled up his pants.

On the drive home, Trey had a look in his eyes as if he were possessed. Tears ran down his face as he came to the realization of who he was becoming and his second act of infidelity. He loved Tara, so why was he doing this? It seemed as though he was in an ongoing battle with evil, and evil was winning.

It was a Saturday afternoon, and Trey prepared to go into work for a few hours. On his way to work, he altered the plan and decided to go to a bar, drink some beers, and shoot pool. He went to a small weathered-looking bar about twenty minutes from his house. He didn't want to be seen by anyone he knew, and this joint fit the bill.

Trey guzzled beer, shot pool, and joked with those at the bar. He bought several beers and shots for others at the bar, and he seemed to be enjoying his newfound friends. By 10:00 p.m., he and most of the others at the bar were extremely intoxicated.

Four new guys came into the bar at 10:30 p.m., and one put his quarters on the table to claim the next pool game. Trey, by this point inebriated, lost the game he was playing, and Mitch, the winner and one of several who had been drinking with Trey for several hours, began his game. He was not much of a match for the much more sober opponent who had arrived recently.

Mitch's opponent and his friends began mocking Mitch as he swayed back and forth while striking the cue ball with his stick. He and the others who had been drinking for hours with Trey were regulars at the bar, and they were the harmless type. As long as they were drunk, they were happy, and they certainly were not the type to get confrontational over being mocked and derided.

As Trey watched the pool game, his first instinct was to intervene on behalf of his new buddy, but he thought better of it. As the derision continued and he stared at Mitch's opponent, he drunkenly mumbled to himself, "What an asshole." Mitch's opponent and his friends froze and glared at Trey for a moment before approaching him. As they neared, he figured that he was in for a fight and he wasn't going to get much help from his new friends. He determined that he wouldn't wait to hear what the man with the pool stick in his hand had to say. He threw a straight right that caught the man square in the nose. The man dropped down to the ground, and Trey hoped that perhaps the other three would back off. Unfortunately, he wasn't that lucky, and they jumped him and began hitting him. Trey, with all the anger that had been bottled up inside him, began to fight back furiously. As his new friends saw that he was holding his own against all three of them, they became emboldened and jumped into the fray. After they had all beat on each other for a few minutes, the cops stormed through the entrance. Once they were separated, they were all cuffed and hauled off to the county jail.

Trey sat there in the lockup with a bloodied nose and bruised cheek. He looked around and surveyed those around him. One of his newfound friends wearing a tattered T-shirt smiled at him with a couple of missing teeth and said, "Good brawl, man; you did good." Trey closed his eyes, rolled his head to the side, and thought, *What the hell am I doing here?* As Trey remembered times gone by in his house with a smiling Tara, an officer unlocked the cage, pointed at him, and said, "You, come with me."

He escorted Trey down a hall and into a side room. As he entered, he saw three men sitting around a table staring at him.

As he sat down across the table from them, one said, "Trey, you look like shit. You need to listen to me very carefully. We know you are in a very bad situation, and you need our help. We are your only chance of pulling through this with any semblance of a life left."

"What the hell are you talking about? It was a bar fight. Bad judgment, I'll give you that, but let's not overstate the situation."

"Do you have any idea who I am?"

"No, should I?"

"I am Demps's partner. He was investigating the Dreadnaughts when he was assassinated. I spoke to him earlier that day before they took him out. He was very concerned about you. He said you were involved with them in some way and that they wanted something from you."

"And just how do you propose to help me? Besides, they assured me that they would leave me alone. I haven't heard from them or seen them since."

The man laughed, shook his head, and said, "Man, you don't get it. Once they get their hooks into you, they will never leave you alone, Trey. We are your only way out. If you don't help us dismantle them, you will end up dead or, even worse, one of them."

"I'll take my chances. Now take me out of here. I'm not speaking with you gentlemen any further."

Trey was escorted back to the holding cell. An hour later, Stu from the firm showed up to bail him out and take him home. He was the only one Trey knew he could call who would come help him this time of night and, more importantly, not tell anyone about it.

As Stu pulled into the parking lot of Trey's apartment, he grabbed Trey's shoulder as he began to open the car door. "Trey," said Stu, "you've got my word that I will not say a word about this to anyone. But, Trey, you've really got to get it together. You're by far the best trial attorney in the firm, in the city, but people are talking about how you're falling apart, going off the deep end. This shit has to stop. I'm here for you if you need anything. You know that, right?"

Trey, staring straight ahead as Stu spoke to him, responded, "I know that, Stu. You're a good friend. Thanks for helping me out tonight."

As Trey walked toward his apartment, Stu shook his head, put down the window, and yelled, "Trey, damn it. Don't you throw it all away. Call Tara."

11

By the second week of February, Trey had been gone nearly a month, and Tara was growing increasingly distressed. She had heard that he had moved into an apartment. She could not comprehend what was happening, and she could not believe that he had not called her since he had left. They had not been apart for more than a week since they began dating. Her earlier concern that he was having an affair was renewed. The alternative was that he was in serious trouble. Although neither prospect was good, it ripped her apart not knowing.

Tara's mother called one morning, and Tara could not contain her pain. Within an hour of their conversation, her mother and sister were in a car and on their way to Asheville. They arrived at 3:00 p.m., and they were greeted at the door by a wailing Tara. They sat down and had a long talk. The typical questions were asked, and a tearful Tara could merely reply to all of them with, "I don't know." Edith suggested that they hire an investigator to try to get some answers. Tara initially opposed the idea but ultimately agreed because this was the only way she was going to find out what was happening with Trey.

One late Friday afternoon as the clock neared 5:00 p.m., Trey sat at his desk in deep reflection. As he contemplated going to speak with Demps's partner, he suddenly stood and, with one forceful, anger-filled motion of his right arm, knocked everything off of his desk. He went to the parking garage, got in his car, and headed toward Bikers and Babes in search of Toby.

The bar was not nearly as crowded as the first time he was there. There were only about ten bikes in the front of the small bar and a handful of bikers outside. Trey pulled up, slammed the door as he exited the car, and hurriedly walked inside. As he entered, the five bikers inside froze, and all eyes were upon him. They began to walk toward him, at which time Jack yelled, "Hey, back off him. He's a friend of mine and is welcome here."

Jack placed a shot of whiskey and a bottle of beer before Trey and said, "You don't look so good, stranger."

"Yeah, well I don't feel so good. Do you know where I can find Toby?"

"I haven't seen him in a few weeks."

The investigator Tara hired, Harry, had followed Trey to the bar. He had pulled his car off the side of the road about fifty yards before the bar. This was a remote area, and the bar was surrounded by woods. Harry stealthily made his way through the woods and was behind a few small bushes abutting the parking lot of the bar. As he began to take pictures, he stepped onto a branch lying on the ground and there was a loud snap. Three bikers who were standing outside the front of the bar roughly fifty feet from him all turned at once and stared at the location of the noise. They said a few words and then began to walk toward the thatch of bushes behind which Harry was hiding.

Harry began running furiously through the woods back toward his car. When he reached his car, thinking that he had escaped, much to his dismay he found bikers standing and waiting for him. "Wait a minute," said an overweight Harry as he gasped for air, tired from his run through the woods. "This has nothing to do with you guys. I was hired by a woman to find out if her husband was cheating on her; that's all. Please let me go, and you'll never see me around here again." At that time, the three bikers pursuing him through the woods arrived. One of the bikers placed a call on his cell phone and walked away from the group. He returned a few minutes later and instructed the bikers to take Harry to the mountains. He was dragged screaming back into the woods.

Trey, inside the bar and on his second round, began asking Jack questions about Toby. As Jack answered that he really didn't know him well, Trey became disoriented. His eyes started to flutter, and he began to sway on his barstool.

A few minutes after his head hit the bar, Toby walked in, looked at him, and said to the several bikers in the bar, "Did anyone take anything from him? Did anyone disrespect him?"

"No," said Jack from behind the bar. "Everything was fine. He was treated well."

"We need to get him home."

Toby instructed one of the bikers to take Toby's bike and follow him. He and a third biker picked up Trey and placed him in the passenger seat of his car. Toby belted him in carefully and departed. Upon arriving at Trey's apartment, Toby carried him in and put him on the bed. As he exited the apartment, he hesitated, looking over the sparsely furnished apartment littered with TV dinner containers and empty bottles of Jack Daniels. He mumbled to himself, "Jesus, he has got to get his act together." He then stopped and stared for several seconds at the photograph of Tara, the only photograph in the apartment. He shook his head and walked out.

Toby then embarked on the forty-five-minute drive to the Dreadnaughts' headquarters up in the mountains. Once he arrived, he walked up the stairs and into a small room where he found Harry tied to a chair, wearing only his boxers. "Some investigator you are," said Toby with a wry smile on his face. He was in no mood for games.

Toby removed his handgun, pointed it between Harry's legs, and said, "I am only going to ask you once: who do you work for, and what were you trying to find?"

Harry, sweat dripping from his body, cried out, "I was hired by a woman named Tara to find out if her husband, Trey Jackson, was having an affair. I swear, that's it."

Toby looked at the three bikers in the room and stated simply, "Put his head on the mantle," and walked out of the room. As he walked down the stairs, he could hear Harry screaming, "What does that mean?"

As the light shone through the window on Saturday morning and awoke Trey, he sat up in bed with a purpose. He wondered how he got home from the bar the night before, but he quickly dismissed the thought; he just didn't care. Things were going to be different from that moment on. He got up, looked himself in the mirror, and uttered, "No more." He shaved and then took a long hot shower. When he got out of the shower, he retrieved his black WWJD bracelet from his sock drawer and put it on his left wrist. Tara had given him this bracelet in law school. He then cleaned the apartment, throwing away several empty Jack Daniels bottles. After cleaning the apartment, he put on basketball shorts, a sleeveless T-shirt, and his basketball shoes. He went to the park in the middle of town and played two hours of basketball.

Trey went back to his apartment, showered, and put on a pair of dress pants and a dress shirt. He went to the Catholic Church he had attended with Tara, and he sought out one of the priests to confess his sins. He confessed fully. Once seated in the confessional, he stated, "Father, I have sinned. I have committed murder and adultery on two occasions, I have lied to my wife, and I have been a drunk."

After the confession, the priest took Trey back to his office. "Trey, I have known you and Tara for nearly two years, and I always thought that the two of you would be together forever. You look as if you belong together, and I can see the affection you have for each other in both of your eyes."

"I don't know, Father. I love Tara, that's for sure, but I have done so much to undermine our marriage. I don't know how she could ever forgive me and trust me again. I don't deserve her."

"Shouldn't that be her choice? Perhaps you should sit down with her, tell her everything, and then let her decide."

"Yes, I know you're right, but I don't know how to tell her. It will break her heart."

"Just remember, Trey, that if she truly loves you, she will forgive you, just as God has forgiven you for your sins here today to which you have confessed." The priest's face then took on a contorted look as he said, "Tell me about this murder you committed, Trey. You don't seem like the murdering type to me."

"I don't remember anything. A guy in a motorcycle gang named Toby told me I shot a drug lord."

The priest's face contorted even more as he said incredulously, "A guy in a motorcycle gang told you that you killed a drug lord? Trey, I say this with the strongest conviction. You need to go to Tara and talk to her."

The following Monday, upon arriving at work, Trey was called into Tom's office. Tom was leaning back in his chair with a disconcerted look on his face and his hands folded in front of him. Trey could discern that this was not going to be a good meeting. Tom told him that the firm had signed up a big personal injury claim over the weekend and the damages would be several million dollars. The other partners had met at 7:30 a.m. to discuss the claim and who would be the lead trial attorney on the case. The three other partners did not want Trey to be the trial attorney because of the erratic behavior he had exhibited over the preceding two months. They thought the case was too important to risk having an unstable trial attorney.

"You come into the office at times smelling like an empty whiskey bottle, Trey. You don't work as hard as you used to, you have separated from Tara, you don't look good, and you don't seem to have the passion you once did."

"I know, and I'm sorry, but Tom, I promise you that things are different. I awoke on Saturday morning and committed myself to straightening out my life. I played two hours of basketball, and I've quit drinking. I even went to church and confessed my sins. I'll beg you, Tom, if I have to; please give me the case. This is just what I need to get back on track. I am also hoping that Tara will take me back. Please, Tom; you know I can do this."

"Quit begging. I told the other partners that you are a better trial attorney drunk than anyone else in this firm is sober. You've got the case, Trey, but don't let me down. I went out on a limb for you."

"You've got my word. This will be my best work yet."

Trey's life was starting to come together. He had gotten Toby and the Dreadnaughts out of his life, he had made the commitment to stop drinking, and he was playing basketball again and taking care of himself. To some degree, he had come to terms with the killing of the drug-dealing crime boss by convincing himself that the world was a better place without him, but the truth of the matter is that this continued to gnaw at him. Also, he wanted more than anything to go home to Tara, but he didn't know how after everything that had happened. He was better, and he was making a comeback, but he still had a long way to go, as he would soon find out.

A few days later, Tara's mother and sister encouraged her to call Harry to see if he had discovered anything. His secretary answered the phone and said, "We don't know where he is. He doesn't answer his phone. We are very concerned. He has never just disappeared like this." Tara hung up the phone and stared blankly into space, not hearing the voices of her mother and sister. She knew that Trey was in deep trouble, but she had no idea why or how to help him.

Trey got out of bed one morning and walked into the shower. As the hot water ran over his body, he realized that he needed help. He went to the office and called a psychologist who had worked on a case for him in the past. He explained that it was an emergency, and he made an appointment for 11:30 a.m.

The psychologist was known for his ability to bring one's repressed memory to the surface through hypnotism. Trey was not a huge believer in this discipline, but he figured that he had no alternative to find his answers, so he went.

Trey sat in a reclining chair as the psychologist came through the door. "What is the emergency?" queried the doctor with a concerned look on his face.

"First, I want to tell you that the story that I am about to tell is going to be hard to believe, but I assure you that it is true. Second, I want to make it crystal clear that whatever I tell you is covered by psychotherapist-patient confidentiality and that you will under no circumstances reveal the content of our meeting to anyone at any time."

"Sure, Trey, you know our conversations are confidential."

Trey related the events in the nightclub in Atlanta and that he awoke the next morning not remembering anything shortly after getting off the phone with Jimmy. He needed to know what happened in the gap in his memory. The doctor turned off the light so that it was pitch-black in the room. A red dot the size of a dime appeared on the opposite wall. He instructed Trey to focus on the dot. Speaking in a soothing voice, he went through each of Trey's muscle groups, getting him to relax them. He then took him into a deep trance-like state. He told him his arms were heavy, so heavy he couldn't lift them from the arm rests. He then told Trey to try to lift his arms, and much to his astonishment, he could not. The therapist then told him to recount the events of the night at the nightclub, starting with when he entered the club. Trey never felt so relaxed as he described the events in great detail, step by step. He reached the point in the story where he got off the phone with Jimmy; then nothing. He hit a wall and could remember no more about what happened at the club. The psychologist asked him questions, trying his best to get the memory to surface, but still nothing.

After Trey came to, the doctor revealed the extent of Trey's recall. Trey said, "I don't understand. Why can't I remember the end of the story? I remember everything else in great detail."

"Well, unfortunately, sometimes it simply doesn't work. You could have created such a subconscious barrier that your deepest mind will not allow you to let it surface. Or the other explanation is that there is no memory, even at the deepest levels, to come to the surface."

"How is that possible? Something happened."

"I'm afraid I can't answer that," responded a somber psychologist.

Trey left the office more frustrated than ever, thinking he may never know the details of what transpired that night.

Upon arriving home from work, Trey found an envelope attached by a rubber band to his door. He went inside, sat in his recliner, and opened it. There was a copy of a sonogram with a note attached. The note read: "Trey Jr.—Please come home; *we* need you. Whatever you've done, we'll work it out." The bottom of the note stated, "Love always, no matter what, Tara and Trey III."

Trey, smiling from ear to ear, sat in the recliner as he pictured past experiences with Tara. He ran through his mind their first dance when he clumsily kept stepping on her feet, the magic of their first kiss, and the many great times they had shared. He closed his eyes and imagined teaching his young son how to play basketball.

Trey changed into his basketball attire and traveled to the basketball court. He was as upbeat as he had been since the Dreadnaughts had entered his life. He felt as if he was close to coming full circle. Tara, he thought, was the last piece of the puzzle needed to put his life completely back together. As he drove, however, his thoughts turned less upbeat as he understood that he would also need to come to terms with what he had done in killing Gambotti, and this was the only obstacle to him going back to her. He hadn't resolved how he would deal with this, and he fully understood that he may never be able to resume his life with her and be the husband and father he needed to be.

Later that evening, Trey called Tara and they spoke for an hour, which was highly unusual for him, because he despised talking on the phone. He indicated that he had quit drinking and he had been playing basketball every day. He was taking care of himself, and he was feeling much better. He told her about his new case that Tom had elected to give to him, and how excited he was to be working on it. Tara told him about her mom and sister visiting, and how her obstetrician's appointments had gone. It gave him great comfort to know that she and the baby were doing well. He told her how much the note she had left meant to him, and he cried as he told her for the first time in many weeks that he loved her and how much he cared about her.

Tara glowed as Trey spoke to her. He sounded like the old Trey, the one with whom she had fallen in love and shared her life. There was a lull in the conversation, and she whispered, "Trey, please come home."

"Tara, you can't imagine how badly I want to come home and be with you and my son for the rest of my life. There is just one thing I need to find a way to resolve, and then I will be home. I promise, Tara, I'll be home soon. I love you."

Trey was ecstatic when he got off the phone. He became more sullen, however, when he realized he still had one problem for which he had no answer. He knew it would be excruciatingly difficult and painful to tell Tara about the two acts of infidelity, but he thought that they could work it out. Murder, however, was a different story. He knew that he could not go home to her without telling her everything. He respected her too much for anything less, and he couldn't live with anything but the whole truth and a fresh start. Also, even with full and complete disclosure to her, he knew he had to resolve this issue in his own mind or he couldn't be completely there for her and his son. They deserved all of him, and he couldn't give it until he came to terms with his murder of Gambotti, a scumbag, but a human being who had done nothing to him.

Trey tossed and turned that night, getting little sleep. He replayed over and over the trip to Atlanta with Toby, trying to remember what had taken place at the nightclub. He remembered seeing Gambotti across the dance floor. He remembered being very intoxicated, but he had no recollection of shooting him in the stall, or even going into the restroom. He also tried to determine why the Dreadnoughts wanted him there with Toby. Although Toby had given him an explanation on the van ride back, it just didn't make much sense. He also visualized his meeting with the priest, during which the priest didn't seem to believe that he had murdered anyone.

Although Trey for the first time seriously questioned the events of that night and whether he actually killed Gambotti, he couldn't think of a reason why Toby would have lied to him. He thought maybe he was just that intoxicated, or he had irretrievably repressed his memory of it. He was confused. He wanted to go home, but as hard as he tried, he couldn't figure it out. Little did he know that the answers were about to come to him.

12

It was the first week of March in 1994, and Trey's emotional status continued to improve, although he couldn't bring himself to go home. Tara was due on the fourth of April, and he badly desired to be with her for the last month of her pregnancy. One night at nine o'clock, the phone rang. It was Toby.

"What the hell do you want?" demanded Trey. "You have ruined my marriage. You have ruined my life."

"Yeah, I hear you're not doing too well. We need to talk. There are some things you should know, things I really need to tell you. Believe it or not, I want to help you."

Toby instructed Trey to meet him at the old house forty-five minutes up the mountain. Trey was determined to meet with him to confront him and get some answers. Dressed in jeans, a sweat shirt, and his Yale baseball hat turned backward, he cranked the ignition on his Porsche and headed out.

Trey pulled into the field about 10:00 p.m. It was a circus. There were bikers and their women partying everywhere. He pulled over to one side of the field and began walking toward the house, which was the site of his earlier unforgettable meeting with the disciples. On the way, he ran into Toby. Trey, before Toby could get out a word, hit him with a right cross, knocking him to the ground, at which time several bikers jumped on Trey and began to pummel him. "That's enough," yelled Toby. "Get off of him."

Trey slowly got up from the ground, the corner of his mouth dripping blood. He grabbed Toby by the shirt and exclaimed, "No more games. I'm not leaving until you answer all my questions or you kill me; it's your choice."

"I understand; follow me."

87

They made their way into the house. On the mantle over the fireplace sat two jugs. One contained Skinny's hand, which had been severed the day before, and the other Harry's head, with eyes wide open, which had been on the mantle for over two weeks. They walked up the stairs, down the hall, and into the room that was all too familiar to Trey. Upon entering, he grabbed a chair, turned it backward, and sat down before the three disciples.

"How you doing, Jimmy?"

"I'm doing fine. The question is how are you? I hear you're not doing so well. Is that a Yale baseball hat you have on? Can you get me one? I've always wanted one of those."

"Enough of the bullshit. Why in the hell did you assholes screw with my life? I have lost everything I had before I met you. Why me?"

"Well, it's not that complicated. We want you to quit your law firm, open up your own solo firm, and represent us exclusively in a variety of legal matters. We'll pay you well, plus you'll get all our personal injury business. You'll make more money than you ever dreamed of, and we'll get the best attorney around. It's a win-win situation."

"Hell no; that was not our deal. You gave me your word that I was out after Gambotti in Atlanta. I lived up to my end of the bargain."

After Jimmy continued repeatedly with no success to get Trey to change his mind and become the Dreadnaughts' legal counsel, he instructed the three cowboys present, including Animal, to take him out back to the van.

As they drove in the van from the back of the house through the narrow clearing in the woods, Toby, or Animal, looked up at Trey. Trey stared deeply into his eyes and stated calmly, "You betrayed me. Where's the honor in this?" Toby looked away and began to think back about the meeting that occurred at the farmhouse in the first week of May of the preceding year when Trey's name first came up in a meeting involving the disciples, him, and the other top cowboy.

The three disciples had called the meeting ten months earlier with the cowboys to discuss two areas that needed to be addressed. The first issue was simple, involving someone in the gang's drug business who needed stern warnings to fall in line and run his operations more efficiently. Animal was assigned that task. The second issue needing to be addressed was more complex.

Jimmy handed a picture to the second cowboy and explained the strategy. The cowboy would get involved in a bar altercation resulting in criminal charges. He would then present himself at an attorney's office and request assistance. The attorney would later be set up in a way that he would have no other choice than to assist the cowboy in a hit on Don

Gambotti, who needed to be eliminated so that the gang could expand its fledgling cocaine business throughout the Southeast. Jimmy then explained to the cowboy the additional and perhaps most important goal, of then using the hit on Gambotti as leverage to force the attorney to represent the gang exclusively in all future legal matters.

The gang had various legal needs. Every month, a couple of its members faced criminal charges ranging from failure to pay tickets to murder. Also, its members were frequently injured, sometimes seriously, by careless drivers who struck their motorcycles. Last, the gang was getting into some legal businesses and needed an attorney to draft contracts. The disciples had concluded that they needed one very good young attorney who could handle all of these matters for the next thirty or forty years.

Jimmy said that because this was a matter of major significance to the gang, he had undertaken the search for the right attorney. He narrowed his search to three young attorneys, each of whom had graduated from an Ivy League School. He figured that the best attorneys would come from the best schools. He determined when each would be in trial, and he went and observed him. One attorney stood out. He was bright, good-looking, and in total command of the trial proceedings. He took down Coca-Cola and their battery of attorneys at the trial. He was perfect.

Jimmy then began to give the cowboy responsible for this job the details regarding the attorney. He stated the name of the attorney: Trey Jackson Jr.

After he concluded instructing the cowboy, Animal stood and assertively declared, "I want this job. This job is of the utmost importance. I am perfect for it, and I should have to do a job of great benefit to our cause to receive my last spoke."

"Animal, I agree. You are the best one for the job, but you have done so much for us, and I thought I was doing you a favor by giving you a short and easy job for your last spoke and your becoming a member of the high counsel. This mission has many parts, and it will take several months, maybe close to a year, to complete it and get your last spoke. But if you want it, it's yours."

As Toby reflected upon that day ten months ago, the van came to a sudden stop in an opening in the woods. Trey was brought by the two other cowboys to the middle of the opening. The three disciples and Animal stood before him.

"Trey," said Jimmy, "I really like you. Please reconsider what we are offering. You have the opportunity to make a lot of money, and we will always protect you and your family."

"Go to hell. I will not become an attorney for common criminals who will dictate every aspect of my life and threaten my family if I don't consent to their every wish. What kind of life is that?"

"Trey, you disappoint me. We could be so good together. This is your last chance to accept our offer."

"You are all cowards. Death is better than being one of you bastards the rest of my life."

Jimmy looked at Animal and said, "Hey, it's not your fault. I picked him. You did everything you could. You'll still get your final spoke. Hell, at least we got Gambotti. I like the kid, but he's not willing. I've tried to convince him, but it just isn't going to work. Finish him."

Animal took his gun with the silencer, slowly walked to Trey, and pressed the barrel to his forehead. Their eyes locked, and tears began to run down Trey's face. He closed his eyes. Animal then inexplicably knocked him to the ground and shot the two cowboys behind him. He then wheeled around and shot two of the disciples, leaving only Jimmy.

"What the hell are you doing?" yelled Jimmy. "Why? Why are you protecting him? Your loyalty has always been to us."

"Because he's right; there is no honor in this." Animal then pulled the trigger.

Trey got up onto his knees, not fully comprehending what had just happened. Toby helped him up and cut the rope binding his hands behind him. Toby told him to go about half a mile down a narrow dirt pathway leading from the opening. That would lead to the road running beside the small town below.

"Why did you do that?" asked Trey.

"It doesn't matter why. Get the hell out of here. Go now before others come."

Trey turned and began running down the narrow dirt pathway. Once he made it to the road, he was fortunate and a trucker picked him up and gave him a ride down the mountain into Asheville. After being dropped off in Asheville, he made his way on foot the mile back to his apartment, stopping at a liquor store on the corner to purchase a bottle of Jack Daniels. Although he hadn't had a drink in nearly three weeks, he was an emotional wreck, and upon returning to his apartment, he chugged the whiskey from the bottle until he passed out.

After Trey had departed down the pathway, Toby returned to the farmhouse in the van to make sure that everything was okay and nobody had any idea what had just taken place. All of the Dreadnaughts were very intoxicated, and none was aware of the trip with Trey in the van. Toby clandestinely retrieved a shovel and headed back through the clearing in the woods on his chopper. Once he got to the opening in the woods, he positioned his Harley so that its light shone brightly onto it.

As he made his way into the opening, he stopped suddenly. There were only four bodies. He anxiously checked the bodies and quickly learned that the missing body was Jimmy's. He drew his gun and made his way around the opening. He found a blood trail leading down the pathway that Trey had gone down. He ran down the pathway, concerned that Jimmy had got to Trey before he had made it to the road just outside the town below.

As Toby, out of breath from his half-mile run down the pathway, reached the road, he saw no signs of a body or altercation, and he was relieved that apparently Trey had made it out before Jimmy got to the road. *Besides,* he thought, *there is no way that a badly injured Jimmy could have caught Trey.*

Toby knew that he had to find Jimmy and finish him off. He followed the blood trail across the road, and it became clear that Jimmy had gone into the town. Toby made his way into town. It was 1:00 a.m., and the only sign of life came from the bar. He stuck his gun into the back of his jeans and entered the smoke-filled room. There were a handful of kids playing pool and several others sitting at a couple of tables and at the bar. Everyone froze, and there was dead silence as they all stared at Toby. He declared that he was in pursuit of a badly wounded and bleeding biker and asked if anyone had seen him. The people just continued to stare at him as Jimmy came barreling through the western-style swinging doors and shot him in the back left shoulder, propelling him to the ground. Toby's gun went flying, and as he turned and looked up, Jimmy was standing just in front of him with his gun pointing down at him.

Jimmy, slouched over in pain and bleeding badly from the gunshot wound to his chest, yelled, "Animal, you traitor. Why did you do that?"

Animal, aware that these could be his last words, chose them carefully. "Why? Because you cut off Skinny's hand, because you have no honor, and because you kidnapped and raped the girl from this town five years ago."

Before Jimmy could pull the trigger, a pool stick struck the back of his head with a loud crack. As he lay there unconscious, the kid who struck him looked at Toby and said, "She was my cousin." Toby thanked him and told him that she was alive. He retrieved his gun and said, "Excuse me for a second." He shot Jimmy twice in the head before telling the kid where he could find Erin. The boy pointed to the back door and said, "Take him out that way."

Toby spent the next hour dragging Jimmy over the road and back up the pathway. Once at the opening in the woods, he dug a large trench and buried the five bodies. He went to the farmhouse and got Skinny and drove

Trey's car back to his apartment, with Skinny following on his Harley with his bandaged wrist.

As they returned on Skinny's bike to the farmhouse, the sun was coming up. Toby went into the house, and Skinny fixed the bullet wound to his shoulder. He then fell asleep in a chair. He woke up a couple of hours later as fellow gang members made their way about the house.

Toby got together two cowboys who he knew were loyal to him and four other Dreadnaughts, including Skinny, to explain the situation. He knew that some of the membership was not pleased with the manner in which Jimmy and the two other disciples had been running the gang. Many were upset that Skinny's hand was severed and displayed on the mantle for all to see for skimming a few hundred dollars here and there for strippers and drugs, which he shared with them. Others were dissatisfied in general with the manner in which the Dreadnaughts was being run. It was being run like a large corporation with too much structure and too many rules for their liking.

Toby explained that there were two remaining cowboys who were very loyal to the deceased disciples and that they were not going to readily accept their deaths and a change in leadership. After much discussion, he felt comfortable that he had the loyalty and support of the six he had assembled, and he called the two cowboys who were loyal to the deceased disciples upstairs for a meeting.

As the two cowboys entered the meeting room, they knew something was amiss when only Toby sat before them in the seat customarily occupied by Jimmy. They all stopped on a dime and stared at him. One began to reach for his gun when Toby declared, "Wait a minute; don't do that. Let's sit down and talk before you decide you want to put a bullet in my skull." He explained to the two cowboys that he got into an argument with the disciples over their treatment of Skinny and one thing led to another. The cowboys feigned understanding and support for him, but Toby was too smart to buy it.

As Toby stood and began walking out the door, the two cowboys stood and drew their weapons and raised them toward his back. They were unaware that he had three loyalists hiding in the room, with the other three just outside. After several rounds were fired, the two cowboys were dead.

Toby addressed the two hundred bikers outside the farmhouse. He simply told them that it was time for change, for new leadership. He then introduced the two remaining cowboys, other than himself, as the new disciples.

"Are you the third disciple?" yelled one of the members.

"No, I am retiring. I'm too old for this shit." As the laughter died down, he announced, "Skinny, how would you like to be the third disciple?" The members roared with approval.

Toby had a glass of whiskey with Skinny before saying good-bye to him. Skinny implored him to stay, but he would have none of it. He hugged Skinny and then got on his bike and road into the sunset. He went back down the mountain to Asheville where he had a small dingy apartment. There was one more matter he had to take care of before he left the area.

The following morning, Toby went to the diner at the truck stop where he frequently ate meals. He got a newspaper, sat in a booth, and ordered his breakfast. He read the paper as he waited for his food. As he got to the local section, he saw the headline: "Man found hung in the woods." He began reading the article and his eyes got big as he realized that this happened in Burnsville, the little town down the dirt road from the Dreadnaughts' farmhouse. As he continued to read, he got a big smile on his face when he realized that it was Stacey's stepfather who had been hung.

The morning after Toby had killed the disciples and two cowboys, Trey awoke and walked to the window. Sitting outside was his Porsche, exactly where he had left it upon returning home from work the day before. Just as he was thinking that perhaps the events of last night were a bad dream, he first rubbed and then looked down at his wrists, which had rope burns on them. He then looked to his left and saw the half-empty bottle of whiskey on the counter. "No wonder I don't feel so well," he mumbled.

After the night at the farmhouse, Trey got back on track. He quit drinking again, resumed playing basketball after work, and buried himself in his big case at work. Although there were still questions for which he knew he may never have the answers, he felt confident that he had the Dreadnaughts out of his life forever. The disciples and two of the three head cowboys were dead, and the remaining one, Toby, seemed to support the idea that he should be left alone. He did not know why Toby protected him, and he really didn't care. He thought that perhaps he was a motorcycle-gang murdering lunatic with morals. With that thought, he laughed and determined that he would never think of Toby and the Dreadnaughts again.

It was three weeks before the baby was due to be born, and Trey badly wanted to reconcile with Tara, but he simply couldn't convince himself that it was the right thing to do. He figured that he could explain nearly everything to her, but he didn't know how to tell her that he had murdered another human being, no matter how big of a felonious dirt bag he was. Even if she could find it in her heart to forgive him and accept him back, he had to feel as if this was right for her, and that his mind, heart, and soul were in a place where he could give her 100 percent of him, for she deserved that and more. He did not know when, and if, he would feel comfortable going to her. In many ways, he felt as if she would be better off without him and that she deserved better than a life with a murderer.

One night about 8:00 p.m. the following week, as Trey was leaving the city park where he had played basketball, he began to think of Tara and all of the good times they had shared together. He thought of the life they would have had if he had not been involved with the Dreadnaughts. He thought of his son-to-be and wondered what he would look like.

Trey drove to his old house and parked his car across the street. It was dark, and he didn't think Tara could see him. Within a few minutes, his cell phone rang. "Are you just going to sit there all night staring, or are you going to come in?" asked Tara. He got out of his car and walked toward the front door. As he neared the door, she opened it and stepped into the doorway. He had not seen her for two months. She was even more gorgeous than he had remembered. Her stomach was very big, and he stared at her face and then her stomach like a man who had never seen a pregnant woman before. She told him that it was not polite to stare and instructed him to come inside.

The two talked for over an hour. They laughed like old times, and they both smiled throughout the conversation. About 10:00 p.m. there was a pause in the conversation. Tara stared at Trey, subtly shook her head, and said, "Trey, what are you doing? Come home. Stay here tonight."

There was silence before Trey responded, "Tara, I want to, more than anything, but I can't."

"Why?" asked an exasperated Tara. "Trey, just talk to me. You and I, we're best friends. I don't care what it is. You can tell me."

There was a long pause before Trey looked up at her and said, "I killed someone."

"You what? Trey, who did you kill?"

"It doesn't matter." He then got up and left as she stared at him with a deeply perplexed look on her face.

Over the next couple of days, Tara obsessed over what Trey had told her. She could not imagine that he was capable of killing anyone, unless it was self-defense. If he had, however, and it was unprovoked, she knew that he was not the person she thought she knew and fell in love with, and for the first time since she met him, she questioned their relationship and her love for him. She began to accept the fact that he would not return prior to the birth of the baby in two weeks, nor was she sure anymore that she even wanted him to return, now or ever.

Tara worked the final day of her charity job before going out on maternity leave. The job had been good for her over the last two months, as it took her mind off Trey. On her last day, her fellow employees threw a party for her. They had baked her a cake covered with blue icing. She also got a few baby gifts.

As the party was concluding, someone approached Tara from behind and put his hands over her eyes. "Guess who has come to visit you?"

Tara, instantly recognizing the voice, turned rapidly, threw her arms around the man, and screamed, "Charles."

At this point, Tara would have been ecstatic to see the face of any of her old friends from home. Although Charles had been a real rat in the past, even collaborating with her father to try to prevent her wedding to Trey, he had, after all, redeemed himself in admirable fashion, and she trusted him. She gave Charles the key to her house and advised him that they would have a long talk upon her returning home.

When she got home, Tara and Charles hugged for what seemed like minutes as she sobbed. Charles indicated that he had heard about the difficulties that she and Trey were having and had come to help in any way he could. She offered Charles a beer that had been in the refrigerator since Trey left, but he refused, saying that he was there for her, and if she couldn't drink, he would not either. The two eventually made it out to the pool area, sat down, and began to talk.

"Tara, you've been a very special person to me for a long time. We grew up together. I wanted to be with you. No, I wanted to marry you, but when I saw what a great guy Trey was, how happy he made you, and how happy you made him, I knew you two were destined to be together. What happened?"

"I really don't know the details, but it all started when his mood changed dramatically in the middle of December and he became cold and distant. Then I discovered that when I was in Hawaii and he was supposed to be in trial all that week, he wasn't, and nobody knew where he was. I confronted him, thinking the obvious, that he may be having an affair. He denied it but left anyway, saying he had things he needed to resolve. Then I didn't hear from him for nearly two months. When he finally came over to talk to me, he told me how much he loved me and wanted to come home, but he couldn't because he killed someone." She held out her arms, clearly indicating that she was confused.

Charles, with a confounded look on his face, exclaimed, "Killed someone? That's crazy, Tara, unless he was defending himself or it was justified in some way. Trey is not the kind of person who would take someone's life for no reason. What did he say?"

"Nothing. He didn't tell me anything about it. It has been extremely difficult to get him to even talk to me since he walked out over two months ago. I'm so confused."

"Do you want me to talk to him? Maybe I can get some answers."

"No. I'm not sure I want him back anymore. If he killed someone, he's not the person I thought I married and I'll just have to move on without him. We were supposed to be partners. We could tell each other anything and had a marriage based on trust and honesty, and I don't know that we can ever have that again after his actions lately."

The following day, Charles hugged Tara and told her he loved her before departing. Despite her request that he not talk to Trey, he figured that it was worth a shot. He loved Tara dearly and he liked Trey, and he had to at least try to help. He couldn't just leave and go back to Charleston without making the effort.

Charles showed up at Trey's office, and Trey instructed the receptionist to let him in. He walked through Trey's office door, and Trey got up from his chair and shook his hand for a moment as they looked at each other as if trying to figure the other out.

They hugged, and Trey said, "It's good to see you, Charles. I've missed you. I hope you're here on your own volition as my friend and not at Tara's urging."

"No, no. As a matter of fact, she expressly told me not to talk to you, at least about the problems you two are having."

"Charles, I have come to know you as a good friend, but there is nothing you can do to help me now. I want to go home. Not a day goes by that I don't yearn just to be with her, but it's complicated."

"Trey, you and I both know that you have the most beautiful and amazing girl in the world. I would give my right arm just to have a shot at her, but she doesn't feel that way about me. I've seen the way she looks at you. She would never look at me that way. If you have issues to resolve, do whatever you have to do to resolve them and get back home as soon as you can. She needs you. Trey, I say this as your friend: Tara is a once-in-a-lifetime girl. Don't mess this up."

"I know. I'm going to try; I promise you that."

After Charles left, Tara's mother and sister came back to be with her for the last twelve days of her pregnancy and to make sure that she was okay. The topic of Trey eventually surfaced. Tara solemnly looked at them and said, "For the first time, I am not sure that I want him to come home. So much has happened over the last two months, and I'm not sure anything would be the same even if he did come home. I'm not sure that I know who he is anymore." She began to cry, and her mother and sister embraced her as they all began to weep.

Tara was comforted by the fact that her mother and sister were there. Trey would not be at the hospital with her for the birth of the boy, as she had concluded that she didn't want him there even if he wanted to be, and she took great solace in knowing that her mother and sister would be there for her.

Richard unexpectedly showed up one day about noon as the girls lunched by the pool. Although Tara knew that he could be unscrupulous, she also knew that he always acted out of love for her, no matter how misguided, and she ran to him, yelling, "Daddy." After lunch, Richard called all the women into the family room for a talk. He asked Tara if she believed that there was any chance that she and Trey would get back together. She looked down and, after several seconds of silence, looked up and said, "No. Things have gone too far. I really don't understand him anymore. He's just not the same man I fell in love with."

Richard then asked Tara to try to relax and hear him out. He expressed his opinion that after the baby was born, she should begin divorce proceedings. Further, he felt that she should consult with an attorney now, before the baby, to at least understand her rights and what the process would entail. Richard's wife, not one inclined to confront him, proceeded to scold him, indicating that this was not the appropriate time to discuss these matters and that Tara needed to focus on relaxing and her baby. She could address the issues concerning her marriage to Trey at a later time. "No, Daddy's right," said Tara. "It wouldn't hurt to talk to someone now so I know what I need to do after the baby is born."

The following day, Richard took Tara to speak with an attorney who had been highly recommended by some of his connections. They sat down, and the attorney began to explain to her the basics. He explained custody, visitation, property split, alimony, and spousal support.

"Do you think your husband will be difficult regarding these issues?"

"No, of course not. He's really a great guy, and he will be very fair to me."

"Tara, I don't want to alarm you, but I can't tell you how many women come to my office for the first time and tell me the same thing, but once the proceedings start and money and property are involved, things get real nasty."

Tara began to cry and then said, "I don't care about all those other women's husbands. Trey's different; he's not like that." She ran out of the office.

When they returned home, Tara went directly to her room, sat on her bed, and began thumbing through her old photo albums. She wrapped a blanket around her and flipped through the albums. Periodically she would sniffle and tears would run down her face. Edith came in, bringing her a box of Kleenex.

"I'm so sorry, baby. I know this is not easy for you. You just need to take your mind off of him until the baby is born. You can deal with those other things later."

"I know, Mommy. It's just so hard. I love him so much, but I know what I have to do later, and it kills me. I really thought he was my one and only love. I don't think I can ever love another the way I love Trey."

As Tara's mother walked downstairs and passed Richard sitting in the recliner, she said simply, "Jackass." He then looked at his daughter sitting across from him and raised his arms as if he didn't understand. "Oh, Daddy, I don't even want to hear it," she said. "You can be so insensitive at times." She then stormed out of the room and walked up the stairs to console Tara.

Tara's sister sat on the bed with her, rubbing her shoulders and not saying a word. As Tara continued thumbing through the album, she asked, "Do you believe that there is one guy for every girl? I mean, do you believe that for every girl there is only one guy walking around out there who is her soul mate, whom God has destined her to be with, and that most women go their entire lives without finding him, but a few get lucky and do? Do you believe that?"

"Yes, I guess I do."

"I know I have found mine in Trey. Why can't things work out the way they're supposed to?"

"Tara, I don't know exactly what Trey has done the last couple of months, but maybe you can sit down with him and try to work everything out after the baby is born. I'm sure he'll want to come home after he sees the baby."

"I don't know. He's done some things that I don't know if he or I can ever accept. He's different now." She did not dare tell her family that he had apparently killed someone.

It was late March, with the baby due in just ten days. Tara wrestled with her heartstrings. At times, she thought perhaps she would take Trey back no matter what he had done, and this put her in a better mood. Unfortunately, her gut told her that it was over, and the sooner she accepted it, the better off she would be, and her spirit deflated.

Trey was at work one afternoon, and in through the door, unannounced, strode Toby. As he sat down, Trey just stared at him, not knowing what to say or even think.

As Trey regained his composure, he began to speak, but Toby interrupted him: "Just listen, counselor. I am truly sorry for everything we put you through. You will never see or hear from any of us again, including me. You've got my word, not Jimmy's, and unlike Jimmy, I keep my word. Also, go home to Tara tomorrow after work. She'll be waiting for you, and everything will be fine. You two can resume your happy lives. By the way, you didn't tell her that you killed Gambotti did you?"

"Yes, I did."

Toby grimaced and said, "You dumbass. Oh well, no matter. I am going to fix everything. You're going to have to trust me. When you get home tomorrow after work, you'll understand everything. Also, don't talk to Tara between now and tomorrow evening. Again, you're going to have to trust me to make things right." He then abruptly got up and walked out before Trey could say anything.

Although Trey was not comfortable understanding that Toby was going to contact Tara, he knew that he had saved his life, and maybe, just maybe, he could save his marriage. He wasn't sure how, or what Toby could say to change things, but he knew that this may be his last chance, and he was going to have to trust him. As he reclined back in his chair, he couldn't help but think about how surreal this whole ordeal had been, and to cap it off, he was entrusting his marriage to a vicious motorcycle gang member whose gang name was Animal and who had murdered countless people.

As Trey reclined with his head back, he didn't notice Stu standing in the doorway.

"Trey, who was that guy?"

"That guy is both the cause and cure of all my problems over the last few months."

"What?"

"Don't even try to understand. Maybe one day we'll sit down over a few beers and I'll tell you the whole story."

"As long as you're buying."

"By the way, Stu," said Trey with a large smile on his face, "I'm going home to Tara tomorrow night, I think for good."

"That's great. You are a terrible single guy anyway."

13

It was 3:00 p.m. the following day, and Trey anxiously watched the clock in anticipation of going home to Tara, hopefully to stay. The clock moved so slowly. Every five minutes seemed like an hour. He figured he would just show up at the front door at about 5:30 p.m. and see what happened. He couldn't imagine how Toby was going fix everything between him and Tara, but he hoped for the best. Hope was all he had.

As Trey daydreamed about his meeting with Tara and how it might play out, the receptionist rang. Stacey, or Erin, was there to see him. As she walked through the office door, he greeted her with a warm smile. He knew that she had a painful youth, suffering unimaginable horrors at the hands of her stepfather. He did not blame her for what had happened between them in the past. Her involvement with the Dreadnaughts was understandable. It was actually a move for the better for her. He took full responsibility for their act of indiscretion. She was simply acting on orders from Jimmy and the other disciples.

Stacey sat down and indicated that she wanted to talk to Trey one more time before she left. She explained, "The strangest thing happened to me three weeks ago. My cousin came to see me. Apparently, Toby told him where I lived. I told him what my stepfather had done to me, and that is why I left home and never contacted anyone. He went home and told my mother. She confronted my stepfather, and later that day he was found hung in the woods. She called me a week ago, and I went to see her. She apologized for what had happened and for not protecting me. She asked for my forgiveness, and she told me she loved me. She gave me my real dad's phone number in Los Angeles. He's a general contractor. I don't remember him, but we had a great conversation. He wants to get to know me. He asked me to come live with him. He's going to give me a part-time job, and he's going to pay for me to finish college. I just wanted to let you know that I'm going to be okay."

Trey had a big smile on his face as he stared at her for a few seconds, shook his head, and said, "That's incredible. You deserve a happy ending. If you work hard, you can accomplish great things with your life. Do me a favor and send me a postcard from the beach."

"You aren't back with your wife, are you? Trey, you need to forgive yourself for everything that happened. Jimmy played you and messed with your life. In any event, he's gone now. Toby saw to that. You love your wife, Trey; go to her."

"I'm leaving the office at five to go meet with her, and hopefully she'll take me back."

"That's awesome. I know it will all work out. You deserve to be happy too."

After Stacey left, Trey found the number for the Burnsville Police Department and called. Burnsville only had one deputy. He was put on hold for a few minutes before the deputy picked up. Trey inquired about the death of Stacey's stepfather, and the deputy said, "He was pretty beat up. I suspect he was murdered, but nobody's talking, and I'm closing my investigation." Trey surmised that Stacey's cousin and his friends had beat and hung the man. He called not because he didn't know what happened but for the purpose of defending the cousin and any others involved if they were charged with murder.

Just after Trey got off the phone, Tara called. She was due in eight days, and she insisted that he come to the house to speak with her after work. She said she had some very important information to discuss with him. His excitement at the prospect of going home and seeing her, the only woman whom he could ever love, was now so overwhelming that he could think of nothing else for the next hour.

As Trey pulled into the drive, he trembled as he remembered the life he once had. Although he couldn't wait to see Tara's face, he had no idea what she was about to tell him. He wasn't sure how, but he prayed that on this day everything was going to return to normal for the first time since he had the sexual encounter with Stacey nearly five months before.

Tara opened the door, and as Trey looked into her eyes, he felt as if he was home, that this was where he was meant to be. Tears began to roll down his face, and impulsively the words streamed from his mouth, "I love you more than anything in this world. You are so incredibly beautiful." She hugged him, and they both began to cry. He jerked back and looked at her. She smiled and said, "That was your son who just kicked you. Not that you don't deserve it. Now come in."

As they sat down, Trey began to try to explain to Tara that as much as he loved her, she deserved better than him. "I killed someone, Tara," he sobbed.

"Trey, you are no murderer. You've done nothing wrong. I talked to Toby today."

Earlier that day, Toby had called Tara and said simply, "Do you love Trey?"

"Yes, I do. Who is this?"

"If you want him back, then meet me at Apache on the second row of Antique Row in one hour. You know, the one with the old Indian lady."

Tara, although scared to death, did not hesitate, for she knew that this was her opportunity to get an explanation as to why Trey began acting so irrationally over three months ago, and perhaps to save her marriage. Tara, although a slight woman from a privileged upbringing, was tough as nails when she needed to be. She was fearless when something was important to her, and Trey was her everything. She would gladly put herself in harm's way if it meant that she had even the slightest chance of understanding what had happened recently and helping him.

As Tara entered the store, she came upon the small Indian woman, who took her hand and led her down an aisle and into the back room. Sitting on a chair was Toby with a warm and inviting smile on his face. Tara recognized him as the man who had last summer run into her when she was coming out of Apache and who had saved her friend's child, and she became very nervous. The man stood and introduced himself before saying, "My, I can see what the boy sees in you. You are beautiful, and courageous. How's the baby?" Almost immediately, she was put at ease. She didn't know why, but she could sense that he meant her no harm and that he cared about Trey, her, and her unborn child. They talked for nearly an hour about Trey, how he and Tara met, and some of the things they did in law school. His eyes lit up every time she told a story about Trey or described some of his accomplishments. "He's a good kid, you're a great girl, and you two need to be together forever," said Toby.

Toby explained everything to Tara. He told her about the meeting with the disciples in May of 1993 when he insisted on taking the job related to Trey that included the hit on Gambotti several months later in December. If the other cowboy had taken this job, Trey would have been involved in a murder, or worse yet, been killed himself. Trey only went to Atlanta to protect Tara because the disciples had told him that they would harm her if he did not. Toby had drugged him and had him taken back to the hotel room so he would not be there when the hit took place. "Poor fella," said Toby, "he thought he killed that Gambotti fella. He wasn't even there."

Toby explained that the disciples had promised Trey that he would be left alone after the Gambotti job, but unknown to Trey, they had planned to use his involvement in a murder as leverage to coerce him to be the Dreadnaughts' full-time attorney. When he refused, the disciples ordered him to be taken to a field and killed, as he was no longer of any use to them. As the disciples watched, Toby was instructed to shoot him.

"I just couldn't do it. I shot and killed my fellow Dreadnaughts instead."

"Why? Why did you choose Trey over your brothers?"

"I really don't know. What is important is that you know that everything Trey did he did because he thought he was protecting you, because he loves you, and the only reason he hasn't come home is because he thinks he killed someone. You need to meet with him to set the record straight, get him home, and get him together for the birth of your son."

"How do you know it's a boy?"

"The Indian woman told me, and as you know, she knows what she is talking about."

They laughed and hugged and Tara left the store. She was no sooner back in her car when she was on her cell phone calling Trey and insisting that he come home after work.

After recounting the story to Trey, Tara embraced him, and after assuring him that everything was fine now, she asked him if he wanted to grow old with her. He replied, "More than anything." They held each other, alternately crying, kissing, and staring into each other's eyes. He was home, and he finally had his life back.

Their son was born eight days later, on April 4, 1994, without complication. Trey was in love, and life was great again.

Periodically, Trey would reflect about Toby and wonder why he saved his life and gave him back his life by meeting with Tara. He thought he would never know the answers to those questions. It almost seemed, he thought, in a perverse way that Toby was his guardian angel. "Guardian angel from hell," he mumbled as he shook his head.

Trey cut back on his basketball, although he continued to play two or three times a week. He, Tara, and Trey III attended church every Sunday without fail. He had confessed everything to Tara, and she had forgiven him. When she found out that he had also confessed everything to the priest, she was mortified. "You told Father Charlie that you killed someone?" cried out Tara.

Tara dragged Trey into a meeting with Father Charlie and said, "Father Charlie, I know that Trey came in a few months ago and confessed his sins. He has also told me everything, and I have forgiven him. However, there is one thing that he was confused about. He did not kill anyone. He was tricked into thinking he did, but he didn't."

"Tara, I never thought that he did. I am thrilled that the two of you are back together. Trey had told me in my office after his confession that he didn't remember doing it, but, who was that who told you that you killed someone, Trey? Oh yes, a member of a motorcycle gang." The priest looked at Tara and smiled. "I am happy that Trey has overcome his confusion and that he's back where he belongs, with you and in the church."

Two months after the baby was born, Tom called Trey into his office. Tom sat at his desk, and he had two gentlemen sitting across from him. He told Trey to take a seat before introducing him to Winston, who was Tom's college roommate. Winston was the owner of a major construction company in town, and he had done extremely well. He continued to be one of Tom's closest friends. He then introduced Winston's son, Marshall, who appeared to be in his early thirties.

Tom told Trey, "My dear old friend has a very serious problem. Marshall was out on the town a couple of weeks ago. He and a few of his friends ended up on the college campus partying with several of the college kids. He made the mistake of drinking too much and having consensual sex with one of the female students. The problem started the following morning when the police showed up at his front door to arrest him. The girl was legal. She was eighteen, but she claimed that Marshall raped her. I believe she found out who he was and that he was from money, and she fabricated this story to ultimately get a financial settlement from his family."

"Yes, yes, I remember reading about it in the paper, but why are you telling me this?" asked Trey with a befuddled look on his face. "What does this have to do with me?"

"It's real simple, Trey. You are our best trial attorney. Heck, you're the best trial attorney this side of the Mississippi. I want you to represent Marshall as a personal favor to me."

"Whoa, wait a minute, Tom. I am a personal injury attorney, not a criminal defense attorney. There are several very good criminal law attorneys in town who can help him and who are much more qualified than I am in criminal defense. I know virtually nothing about it. Besides, the last time I got involved in a criminal case, a very minor one at that, it almost ruined my life. You can't seriously want me to do this."

"Trey," scoffed Tom, "criminal or civil, it doesn't matter. There is not a trial attorney around who can hold your jockstrap. This is very important to me, and I am asking you to do this."

Trey stared at Tom for a few seconds with the full understanding that there was no way that he could refuse his request. He looked at the two men and said, "Be back at the office at eight in the morning tomorrow, and we'll go over everything." He then retreated from Tom's office with a look of disgust on his face.

After Trey exited, Winston looked at Tom and said, "Are you sure he's our guy? He is not happy at all about being involved in this. My son can't go to prison for something he didn't do. Are you sure, Tom?"

"Relax. Trey is the best damned trial attorney I have ever seen, and I've seen some of the best. He'll do what I ask him to do. You're in good hands—the best hands."

Trey detested Marshall from the time of their first meeting. He was a smug, arrogant man who had not accomplished anything on his own. He was living off of his father's money. He was the polar opposite of Trey and the antithesis of everything Trey believed in. In addition, Trey suspected from the outset that he indeed had raped the girl.

Trey begrudgingly labored through the discovery process involving the depositions of everyone who had seen the two that night and the experts. He reasoned that everyone, even a piece of trash like Marshall, deserved to be represented by an attorney in court, and he was just doing his job. He forced himself not to become emotionally involved in the case.

One late afternoon in November as the trial was nearing, Trey had just finished meeting with Marshall to go over the trial strategy. As Marshall got up, something fell to the ground behind his chair. As Marshall walked out of his office, Trey got up from behind his desk and retrieved the object. It was a Swiss Army knife. As he began to run out his door to chase down Marshall to return the knife to him, he stopped dead in his tracks and stared at the knife, remembering that the girl testified in her deposition that Marshall had used a small pocket knife while raping her. He opened it, and a long blond hair unfurled from the inside of the knife. Trey immediately wiped his prints from the knife, carefully closed the blade, and placed it in a Ziploc bag he obtained from the firm's kitchen. He then placed the bag containing the knife in his drawer and reclined in his chair in deep reflection. "He did it; the bastard did it," he mumbled to himself. What would he do with the knife? That was the question.

At the trial, Trey was on his A game, shredding with ease the credibility of every one of the state's witnesses. He almost appeared to be toying with the state's expert witnesses, getting them to stumble over their words as they attempted to explain themselves out of the boxes in which he had cleverly entrapped them.

After five days of testimony, the state rested its case against Marshall. That evening, Trey met with Tom, Winston, and Marshall in Tom's office. Tom and Winston congratulated him on his fine trial work. Trey knew that the state's case was fraught with reasonable doubt.

"Well, gentlemen, we're almost done. They have no case. We'll call a couple of witnesses to the stand tomorrow just to put the final nails in the coffin; then we'll rest our defense and make a motion for dismissal. There's no way the judge will even let this go to the jury."

"Wait a minute," exclaimed Marshall. "I don't get to testify to tell everyone what a lying bitch she is?"

"No you don't," responded Trey angrily. "There's no need for it. It's an unnecessary risk. The case is over." Trey paused for a moment in reflection before intentionally goading Marshall by saying, "The prosecutor is much smarter than you are, Marshall. You may just talk yourself into a guilty verdict."

Marshall stood defiantly and said, "Screw you, Trey. You think you're so damned smart. It's my case, my life, and I'm going to testify."

As Marshall neared the end of his testimony, he sat as smug as ever, figuring that he had showed the packed courtroom and his father how smart he was and that he had clearly proven his innocence. As he confidently stared around the courthouse, the prosecutor briefly ceased her questions and walked to her table. She then approached him and held up a bag containing the Swiss Army knife.

"Do you recognize this?"

A stunned Marshall gulped heavily before saying, "Yes, it's my Swiss Army knife."

As the prosecutor continued to grill Marshall, he slumped farther into the witness stand and the cocky arrogance he had displayed before receded from his body. Trey could show no emotion as he said to himself, "Dumbass."

After the prosecutor called DNA experts to identify the hair in the pocket knife as that of the raped girl, the case was over. Marshall was found guilty.

Later that night, Trey had a bottle of wine with Tara at dinner. He was ebullient.

Tara looked at Trey with a confused look on her face and said, "Why are you so happy? You just lost your first case."

"No, Tara," responded Trey with a devilish smile on his face. "I am still undefeated."

14

Although the entire experience with Toby and the disciples had been a harrowing one, it did have the benefit of making Trey a better man. Prior to it, he had been driven to succeed at work, make money, have material possessions, and impress others. He had a win-at-all-costs attitude. He now understood that the measure of his success in life was based upon the happiness of his wife and children, that they knew they were loved and what kind of a husband and father he was.

Trey and Tara had a second son, Alec, who was born on March 28, 1996. They would have two birthdays within eight days of each other.

One Saturday, as Christmas neared in 1996, Tara was on her way out the door with Alec to have lunch and go shopping with her girlfriends when she instructed Trey that he would need to take Trey III, who had turned two back in April, and two of the neighborhood boys to a birthday party. As Trey pulled into the drive in his $80,000 Porsche to drop the boys off, Trey III looked at him from the cramped backseat and said sullenly, "Dad, can Mom pick us up?" Trey, understanding that his son had no idea that his father's car was a nice one and appreciating the fact that his car was no longer practical, went to a Ford dealership and traded his Porsche in for a new F-150 four-door pickup truck. He didn't even mind that he had to take a bath on his trade. The Porsche represented his past priorities, the truck his current ones.

When Trey entered the house to pick up his son and two friends, Trey III exclaimed, "Dad, I thought I told you to have Mom pick us up." As they walked outside, Trey III marveled at the shiny new black truck in the driveway, and Trey beamed as he opened the front passenger door and instructed him to get in. "Yes, Dad!" Trey III yelled. "You got a good car."

As they drove the short distance from the birthday party to drop off the other kids, the three boys marveled at the truck and all the gadgets. Trey smiled as he thought of how impressed the boys were at the truck, which cost a third of what he had paid for his Porsche.

A few days later, Trey left the office for a few days off for Christmas. As he got home and entered the kitchen, he stopped suddenly and looked forward with a large smile on his face. At the kitchen table sat Tara speaking with his mother, whom he had only seen a couple of times since Trey III was born.

Trey III ran excitedly into the kitchen, jumped into Trey's arms, and shouted, "Look, Dad, Gramma's here for Christmas."

"So she is." He then walked to his mother, and as she stood, he hugged her and looked over her shoulder at a smiling Tara, and mouthed, "Thank you."

That night, Trey sat in his office for an hour speaking with his mother. Later in the conversation, he asked her about his father. She had little information to share. One day she awakened when Trey was two and found her husband gone, and she never saw or heard from him again. She told Trey that she was sure that his father loved him, but that he left because he had a lot of problems. Other than this aspect of his life, knowing little about his father, his life was complete.

It was early January of 1997, and Trey had been contemplating making a big change in his life. Tara was five months pregnant with their third child. Although she didn't speak about it, he knew how much she missed her family in Charleston. He also thought that it would be ideal for his children to grow up around their cousins. He was also growing weary of the big law firm environment. When a big case came in, he had little discretion over whether to be involved. If it was agreed among the other partners that he should take the case, he had little choice other than to comply.

Trey considered some of his personal injury clients to be exaggerating their complaints, or in some cases, to be outright frauds. It didn't matter to his partners. If there was money to be made, the firm took the case. Trey yearned to be in a smaller firm where he would have the authority to select which cases he would handle and which ones he would reject. He had secretly studied for and passed the South Carolina bar exam, and nothing was standing in the way of his moving the family to Charleston and opening up his own law firm.

One Friday after work, Trey came home and told Tara that they needed to talk. He told her that he wanted to put the house up for sale.

"Why? We have many good neighbors who are our friends. Trey III has playmates on the street. We don't need a bigger home. I am happy here. Why would you want to move?"

"I quit my job today. I just figured it was time for a change."

"You did what? Why would you quit your job? Why do we need a change? Everything is great in our lives."

"We're moving to Charleston. I have passed the South Carolina bar exam, and I am going to open my own firm there. What do you think?"

Tara ran to him screaming and threw her arms around him. She then spent the next couple of hours on the phone breaking the news to her parents, sisters, and old friends. She was elated, and Trey was proud that he could make her so happy.

The family settled in Charleston in February, and Trey opened his law firm in a small building in downtown Charleston in the middle of May, a few days after Amanda was born on May the tenth. Tara's family, although overjoyed to have Tara and the kids in town, were still displeased with Trey regarding his behavior when he and Tara split up for two and a half months over three years earlier. Trey understood this, and he knew it would take time to regain their acceptance of him, especially with regard to Richard, Tara's father.

Trey went to Richard's office one day to speak with him. After sitting down, he looked across the desk at Richard, who stared at him with a menacing look on his face. Trey said, "I know how much she means to you, and I know how you must feel about me, knowing that I have hurt her. If you didn't despise me right now, I wouldn't respect you. I can only say that I am truly sorry. I'm not here to make excuses or to ask you for your forgiveness. I'm here to merely promise you that I will spend the rest of my life doing everything in my power to make her happy and to earn back some degree of respect from you. Thank you for your time." He then got up and walked out. Although Richard was still pissed off at him, he felt much better about the situation, and there was something about Trey that he could not help liking and respecting.

At dinner that night, Tara, with a smirk on her face, asked Trey, "So how did your meeting with my father go?" As Trey looked at her with a look of disbelief at how she already knew of their meeting, Tara just smiled and said, "I heard it went well."

In June, Trey moved his mother into a small duplex a couple of blocks from them. Everything in his life was coming together, and he was determined not to screw it up again. Although he was making far less money, he had never been happier in his life. His relationship with Tara had never been better. They had the newborn, Trey III had turned three in April, and Alec had turned one in March. Trey looked forward to getting home from work every day.

There was a horse stable a couple of miles from the house. When Trey got home, Trey III and Alec would run to him as fast as they could, jumping into his arms. This was the most awesome feeling he had ever had, and he received this incredible love every day. Alec, upon jumping into his arms, would say over and over, "Horkies, Daddy, horkies." Trey and Tara would gather their bag of carrots and take the kids to the horse stable where they would feed the horses. Trey glowed as he watched his boys feed the horses the carrots. The innocence and look of wonderment in their eyes were priceless, and when they giggled upon the horses taking the carrots from their hands, Trey knew that there just had to be a God. What other explanation was there for such beauty and perfection in the world.

A little over a year after moving to Charleston, Trey received a postcard at his office from Stacey depicting the beach in California; it was accompanied by a graduation notice. She had done it. She was graduating from college. He smiled widely as he looked over the postcard and graduation notice. He was immensely happy for Stacey, but he also relished what this symbolized. With faith and a little luck, anyone could go from the bottom to the top, realize great happiness, and accomplish awesome things. Also, this was further confirmation that if one had patience and a resolve to never quit, eventually things would come full circle and fairness and justice would prevail in the end. This, to Trey, was the best evidence that God in fact existed, he was actively working in the world, and he rewarded those who deserved it.

A few days later, Trey was preparing to leave for home early one evening. It had been a long day, and he couldn't wait to get home to Tara and the kids. It was after 5:00 p.m., and he was the only one in the office. He heard the front door to the office open and yelled that he would be right out. As he finished the letter he was writing, he looked up and much to his consternation saw Marshall standing in the doorway.

"Marshall," said Trey, doing his best not to look concerned. "How are you? You're out of jail already. I figured you had a few more years."

"I got out early. Jail overcrowding and time off for good behavior."

"Well, that's certainly good news. What do plan to do now?"

"The first item on my agenda is dealing with you, Trey. You know, I had nothing but time to think about things while in jail. I couldn't figure out how the prosecutor got a hold of my knife, and as you know, without it, they had no chance of convicting me. I had it in my hand up by the girl's face and head while I was raping her, but I knew I didn't leave it at the scene. In fact, the more I thought about it, I remembered having it in my back pocket when I went to your office to speak with you just before the trial. That was the last time I saw it. I figured it fell out of my pocket somewhere. But I kept thinking, how did the prosecutor get it, and how did she know it was mine or involved in the crime? The only explanation was that it fell out of my pocket when I was in your office and you turned it over to the prosecutor.

You screwed me, Trey, and I spent over three years in prison because of it. My father has disowned me, and I have nothing left. I can, however, make things right between me and you. You ruined my life, and now I am going to ruin yours. That's fair, right?"

As Marshall pulled a gun from his jacket, Trey exclaimed, "What a minute, Marshall. Why would I do that? That case ended my undefeated streak, and I strongly encouraged you not to testify. You do remember that, don't you?"

"Because you hated me," responded Marshall with a deeply chagrined look on his face. "You thought I was guilty, and you coaxed me into testifying by saying I wasn't as smart as the prosecutor; then you somehow got the knife to her."

"Well, you were, after all, guilty, and what you did to that young girl was horrible. Look at the bright side: you only spent over three years in prison for scaring that young girl emotionally for the rest of her life."

Marshall then ordered Trey outside and instructed him to get in the car.

"Where are we going, Marshall?"

"We're going back to Asheville."

"Asheville? Look, Marshall, if you're going to shoot me, just do it now. Why in hell are we going back to Asheville?"

"That would be too easy," responded Marshall with a demonic smile on his face. "I have something much better in store for you, Trey."

When Trey didn't return home at his customary time, Tara became concerned. She couldn't reach him at the office or on his cell phone. This was not like him, and she became increasingly distressed as the evening progressed.

Four hours after the car departed Charleston, they entered the Asheville city limits, and Trey soon became familiar with the surroundings. They were on the road on the outskirts of town where the Bikers and Babes bar was located. As they approached the bar and he could see the neon sign, he asked Marshall for one last favor.

"Marshall, you're right. I set you up at the trial, and believe it or not, I'm sorry. I deserve whatever you have planned for me. I would ask just one favor of you. It looks as if we are coming up on a bar. Let's go inside. You can keep your gun on me. I won't try anything funny. I just want to have a couple of shots and a beer before your dispose of me."

"A dying man's last request. Okay, I'll grant you that, Trey, but I swear, you try anything, and I'll shoot you dead on the spot."

"Thank you, Marshall," said Trey as they pulled into the bar.

There were several bikes parked outside the bar, but it was not overly crowded. The two sat at the bar as about ten bikers stopped and looked at them.

Jack walked over from behind the bar, took one look at Trey, and said, "Well, well, my old friend, what brings you here?"

"I don't believe I know you. Just bring us a few shots and a couple of beers."

Jack took a look at Marshall, walked to the other side of the bar, poured the shots, and grabbed two beers. He came back, put the shots down, and as he began to put the beers on the bar hit Marshall in the side of the head with one of the beer bottles, knocking him to the ground. Trey jumped on him, grabbing his gun before several bikers surrounded Marshall, who was writhing in pain on the floor.

Trey looked at Jack, handed him the gun, and said, "Old friend, how many times have you saved my ass?"

"No matter; it's always my pleasure." Jack instructed one of the bikers to give Trey a ride to a car rental place. He gave Trey a big hug and said, "Go, my friend. We'll take care of this gentleman. Trust me; you'll never see him again."

After getting in the rental car at 10:30 p.m. and proceeding back home to Charleston, Trey called Tara and explained everything. Tara wanted to call the police, but Trey emphatically demanded that she not.

"But what if he comes back and tries to kill you again, Trey?" declared a clearly distraught Tara with her voice trembling badly. "We can't take that chance."

"No, Tara, that won't happen. The Dreadnaughts will see to that. We'll never see him again. No one will ever see him again. The son of a bitch has dug his own grave."

15

It was the summer of '98, and Trey III was four. Trey was coaching his T-ball team. As the game neared its end, he looked up at the bleachers at Tara and was astonished to see a familiar face sitting next to her, Alec, and their one-year-old, Amanda. As Trey III hit a ball off the tee and ran around the bases, Toby cheered loudly.

After the game, Trey approached Toby and said firmly, "What are you doing here? You promised Tara that we would not have any more problems from you."

"Relax, counselor. I just wanted to see the five of you. You will never see me again after this."

He hugged Trey and Tara. As Trey III ran up, Toby asked if he could hug him. Trey was aghast when Tara said yes.

As Toby held him, Trey III asked, "Who are you?"

"Let's just say I am a friend of your mom and dad."

Toby then turned to Trey, looked him in the eyes, told him good-bye, and said that he left something with Tara that would explain everything. He then patted Amanda on the back gently before looking at Alec and then Tara. She nodded her approval, and he picked up Alec and hugged him and then put him down and walked off.

When Trey got home, Tara handed him a dirty envelope. He went into the study and opened it. There was a copy of Toby's driver's license. The name on it was Trey T. Jackson. With it was a small note that read: "I don't even understand the choices that I have made in my life, but I understand one thing and one thing only—I love you, son." Trey put the note down and stared blankly with a shocked look in his eyes for a minute. This explained everything.

Trey had thought that he would never see his father again, but now he felt as though his life was totally complete. He knew his father, and he knew that his father loved him. Although his father was an outlaw and a killer, he had risked his life to save Trey's life, he had put Trey over himself, and he had made sure that he was back with Tara and happy before he left. He obviously also cared for and loved Tara and their children. In a strange way, Trey always felt that Toby would be there if he really needed him and that at times he would be there watching his family from a distance.

As the children grew older, Trey and Tara were not without their disagreements. She had grown up with a silver spoon in her mouth, whereas he had grown up eating bologna sandwiches. Her tendency was to spoil their children. He wanted his kids to have the things in life that he didn't have as a kid, and he wanted them to have easier lives. He did not, however, want to spoil them, and he wanted them to have to earn the things they wanted.

This resulted in some periodic minor disagreements, but it flared up when Trey III was getting ready to turn sixteen. Trey had made an agreement with all of his kids. He would give them $100 for every straight A report card, meaning they could earn $400 a year that would be deposited in their bank account. When it came time to buy a car, he would match whatever amount there was in the account. Trey III had never made a B, and he had $4,000 in his account. Trey added a matching $4,000, resulting in him having $8,000 for a car.

One Saturday morning, Trey and Tara went to look for a car for Trey III. She was driving, which was unusual as he did not consider her to be the best of drivers. But he had strained his back on Friday working out, so he let her drive. As they drove down the road, he searched the glove department for an Advil as she pulled into a BMW dealership.

Trey looked up, turned, looked at Tara, and said, "What are we doing here? You can't be serious. He doesn't have the money for a BMW. The Ford dealer is down the road. We can get him a decent used pickup truck for $8,000."

"Trey, he's made straight A's his whole life, he's worked hard to be an excellent basketball player, he's been a model child, and he's done everything you've ever asked of him."

"That's why he's getting a nice pickup truck."

Tara responded, more than a little peeved, "No, Trey. *You* can't be serious. All his friends received nice cars when they turned sixteen, and if any kid has earned a nice car, it's Trey III."

"But we've had a deal since he was six. Don't you remember, Tara? He gets straight A's and he gets $100. We match whatever he has in his account.

That gives him $8,000 for his car. Why did we even make that deal if we weren't going to stick to it?"

"That was your deal with him. I thought it was just incentive for him to make good grades. I didn't think you were serious. I don't want to argue with you. We're just looking right now. We're not going to buy anything today anyway."

As they walked around the lot, Trey had a noticeably disinterested look on his face, as he considered this to be a total waste of time. They went into the showroom, and Tara immediately spotted a smoke-colored M3. As she excitedly looked it over, a salesman joined them. She sat in the driver's seat as Trey glanced at the $60,000 price tag on the window. The salesman indicated that the car went from 0 to 50 in five seconds, with a top speed of 140 miles per hour.

Trey remarked, "Oh, that's great, Tara. Did you hear that? It goes 140 miles an hour. Just what every sixteen-year-old needs to kill himself."

Tara climbed out of the car and began taking pictures of it with her cell phone. The salesman looked at Trey and stated, "Well, sir, would you like to drive it home today?"

"Yeah, sure. If you'll take $8,000 for it, we've got a deal."

Tara interrupted. "Trey, you need to relax. He's a very responsible child. He's not going to be going 140 miles per hour."

"You're damn right he's not; the pickup doesn't go over 90."

They drove down the road to the Ford dealership where Trey located several trucks in their price range. "Now these are fine vehicles, and they're safe," he said as Tara looked on with a clearly disturbed look on her face.

When they got home, they argued over the car situation. Tara said, "Well, Daddy was going to get him something, and Mommy as well. Why don't we pool all of our money and just get him one big gift? A nice car he can be proud of."

"We were going to give him individual gifts totaling $60,000?" Trey made Tara promise him twice that she wouldn't purchase a vehicle until they had come to an agreement.

A few days prior to the birthday, they sat down to discuss the car. They stated their respective positions. When they realized they were not going to come to an agreement, Trey decided that they would give the $8,000 to Trey III and let him choose his own vehicle. Tara, realizing that he was not going to acquiesce, stormed off.

On the day of Trey III's birthday, several of his friends came over. He opened his gifts from his friends, and they all stood waiting to see what kind of car he was going to get. As Trey was getting ready to announce that he and Tara were going to give him $8,000 to buy his own car, Tara's cell phone rang. She hung up and said, "Wait, Trey. Daddy and Mommy just pulled up, and they want everyone to come outside and help carry Trey III's gift." As they walked outside, Richard and Edith were standing next to the BMW M3. Richard said, "Happy birthday, Trey III. Come check out your new ride." Trey III and his friends rushed to the car to inspect it.

As they were inspecting the car, Tara was overwhelmingly happy at Trey III's reaction to it; then she remembered how much trouble she was in with Trey. She turned to look at him as he stood on the front porch. He looked at her with a feigned smile on his face as he slowly tore up the check.

When Tara went to him, she tried to explain that her father had insisted on buying the car for Trey III. Trey stared at her expressionlessly and said, "Oh, stop the bullshit, Tara. I know exactly what happened here."

Trey III yelled up at Trey, "Dad, come check it out. It's awesome."

With Tara still by his side, he said softly so that Trey III couldn't hear him, "I know. It goes 140 miles per hour." He then went out and went for a drive with him.

As Trey lectured Trey III on driving such a high-performance car responsibly, Trey III said, "Dad, I know you didn't want me to have a car this nice at sixteen. I know this is Mom's idea, and I'm not sure how she pulled it off, but I promise you that I'll drive it according to any rules you make, and I'll take care of it. And one more thing, Dad, please don't be mad at Mom on my birthday. I love you two."

"Well, son, you're right about all that, but you need not worry. Every time I have been upset with your mother since I met her, I never have been able to be mad at her long, because she always acts out of love and a good heart." He paused briefly before saying, "Happy birthday, son. You know, you really have earned this car, nice as it is. You're the best son a man could ever ask for. But can you do me one favor?"

"What's that?"

"It's your birthday, but would you at least let me act as though I am upset with your mom for an hour?"

They looked at each other and laughed as Trey III said, "Sure, that's fair."

Trey III and Alec were both very good high school basketball players. Trey III had started since he was a freshman and had been the best player on the team since he was a sophomore. Trey III as a senior was the starting point guard, and Alec, a sophomore, was the starting shooting guard. It made Trey happy to see them playing together for one year.

West Charleston High was undefeated, and they were playing their long-time cross-town rival, East Charleston High, for the district championship. This rivalry had been a very fierce and heated one for as long as anybody could remember. There was always a lot of trash talking on the court, and in the stands as well. The game was played on West Charleston's home court, which gave them a slight advantage.

West Charleston did not play well in the first half, and East Charleston was up by twelve points at half time. The East Charleston fans were boisterous and obnoxious throughout the first half, basking in the thrashing they were giving West Charleston. Trey and Tara sat in the stands with Richard and Edith. Tara made several comments throughout the first half about how crass the East Charleston fans were behaving. When West Charleston's cheerleaders, including Amanda, went out to perform at half time, the East Charleston fans booed them loudly. Tara, Richard, and Edith were very upset that the opposition's fans would treat even the cheerleaders so badly.

Trey told them to relax. He said, "This is the district basketball championship; it is not a cheerleading competition."

Richard responded, "That doesn't mean the kids can't compete with dignity and the parents can't control themselves and set a good example for the kids."

Trey, already agitated that West Charleston was playing so poorly in its biggest game, turned to Richard and said, "Richard, you were on your high school's chess team. What would you know about athletic competition?"

Tara stared down Trey with a disturbed look on her face before saying, "Trey, that was totally unnecessary. All these kids need to learn sportsmanship and respect for their opponents."

West Charleston came to life in the second half. It was down by only two points at the end of the third quarter. As the fourth quarter began, the game was going back and forth, and it was getting very animated. At one point, Alec began getting into it verbally with an opposing player. As their verbal back and forth escalated, Trey, who was so engrossed in the game that he had not even noticed Tara get up from her seat, saw her walking toward the West Charleston bench. He was horrified as he watched her walk over to West Charleston's coach and start talking to him. The coach called a time out, and Tara took Trey III and Alec off the court and out the gym door into the hall.

With West Charleston's best players out of the game, East Charleston quickly jumped out to an eight-point lead with just a few minutes left in the game. Just as Trey was about to get up and go get them, Tara came back through the door with Trey III and Alec. The coach immediately got them back in the game. They didn't say a word to the opposing team the last few minutes of the game, despite the East Charleston players continuing to talk trash to them. They led West Charleston back with a furious rally in the last two minutes, with Alec talking a pass from Trey III on a fast break for a driving lay-up with three seconds left to win the game.

Tara and Trey stood in the kitchen waiting for the boys to come home. He said, "Tara, did you see the kids from the two teams hug each other and show respect for each other after the game? That's how it works, but during the game, it is a war."

"I don't care how it works. My kids will not act like that during the game. If they can't keep their mouths shut and just play without disrespecting their opponents, they will not play anymore."

When the boys pulled into the drive, Trey met them at the door and hugged them both with a large smile on his face. He whispered, "Great game, guys. You two were warriors. I'm very proud of you, but you need to go into the kitchen and say the right things to your mother if you want to go out and celebrate." The boys went into the kitchen and apologized to Tara. She lectured them on sportsmanship and integrity for ten minutes before turning to Trey and asking him if he had anything he wanted to add. He said, "Yes. Boys, I agree with your mother, and if you want to continue to play, no more trash talking, no matter how much trash your opponents talk. Do we understand each other?"

Alec said, "Yes, Dad, we get it. No more trash talking. I promise."

Trey III added, "Sorry, Mom. I promise it won't happen again. Thank you for letting us go back and finish the game."

"You two may go out and celebrate your victory," said Tara.

As the boys walked out the front door, Trey followed them out. He said, "Guys, great job with Mom. Again, awesome game." He handed them each a twenty and told them to go have a good time. As he turned to go back inside, Tara stood in the doorway with her arms crossed. "Oh, hey babe," he said as she looked at him crossly, "I was just making sure the boys got the point regarding sportsmanship."

Trey took Tara's hand and led her upstairs to the bedroom. He sat her on the bed and stood before her.

Before he could say a word, she said, "If you think we're going to fool around now, you're crazy. I'm still very upset with you."

"No, babe, that's not what this is about. I'm just going to try to show you in another way how a basketball game works. See, during the game, the two teams are enemies, and they go after each other."

He then began to try to engage her in some playful wrestling on the bed. She wasn't having any part of it initially, continuing to have a miffed look on her face. He pulled her down onto the bed and began tickling her. She began to laugh and wrestle back. After a couple of minutes, he had her on her back with her hands pinned down above her head. They both stopped, staring deeply into each other's eyes. Trey said, "Then, when the game's over, they become friends again." He kissed her softly and began caressing her body slowly and delicately. He made love to her in the truest sense of the word.

When they were done, Trey stared into her eyes and asked, "Do you get it now?"

"No," responded Tara softly, "but I'm willing to continue to try to learn."

Raising the boys proved easy for Trey, but the youngest, Amanda, was a challenge for him. The same year the boys won the district basketball championship, Amanda, a freshman in high school, came home from school one evening after cheerleading practice in an exceptionally good mood. At dinner, she smiled widely as she ate. Trey looked at Tara with a quizzical look on his face, and she looked back as if to say she had no idea. Amanda said, "Oh, Mom and Dad, I've got some great news." Her two older brothers elbowed each other and looked on with the utmost interest, as they obviously knew what was coming next and couldn't wait to get Trey's reaction.

Amanda said, "Josh Miller asked me to the homecoming dance. Isn't that great?"

"Josh Miller," said Trey. "Isn't he a junior?"

"Yes, he plays football, and he's a really cool kid. All the girls like him, and he chose me."

As the boys continued to look on with great anticipation, Trey said, "Absolutely not. It violates the one-year rule."

"The one-year rule. What is that?"

"Boys, would you please explain to Amanda the one-year rule."

Trey III said, "Sure, I'd be happy to. It's real simple. You don't date or go out with anyone in high school who is more than a year older or a grade ahead of you."

Amanda looked at Tara, seeking her help, and yelled, "Mom, that's so unfair. Dad is so unreasonable sometimes. Josh is a great kid."

"Honey, that rule applies to your brothers as well. It's always been the rule." A visibly upset Amanda threw her napkin on the table and ran upstairs.

Trey looked at Tara and said, "The rules are the rules."

"Trey, I get where you're coming from, but she was so excited. You could have been more sympathetic." She then went upstairs to talk to Amanda.

Trey looked at the boys and said, "What is Mom talking about, being more sympathetic? Did I handle it poorly?"

Alec said, "Oh no, Dad. You handled it perfectly. You know how women get all emotional."

Trey III chipped in, "Amanda just needs to understand that the rules are the rules, no exceptions. You know, Dad, just like you lay down the law to Mom and she follows all of your rules, right?"

As Alec laughed, Trey took a drink of his water, set it down, stared at Trey III, and said, "That's not funny."

The following evening, the doorbell rang. "Trey," said Tara, "why don't you get the door?" He opened the door, and the young man standing before him said, "Mr. Jackson, my name is Josh Miller, and I would like to speak with you for fifteen minutes if you have time." Trey invited him in.

As they made their way to the billiards room, Trey passed Tara and gave her a look that clearly indicated that he knew that this was her doing and he was not pleased. Josh made a good impression, and he said all the right things. Trey was also impressed that he had the courage to come over and speak with him and assure him that his intentions were good.

Toward the end of their conversation, Trey said, "Josh, you seem sincere, and I really hope that you're shooting straight with me and not just telling me what you think I want to hear. Do you go to church, Josh?"

"Yes, sir, Mr. Jackson."

"Then you know what happens to young men who lie or who aren't completely honest with other kid's parents, right?"

"They go to hell?" asked Josh with a disconcerted look on his face.

"Yes, that's exactly right, Josh. They go to hell. But let me make sure that you are perfectly clear on something. If you don't treat my daughter well, if you disrespect her in any way, you are going to wish you were in hell when I get done with you. Are you clear on all this, Josh?"

Josh, with a great deal of trepidation, responded, "Yes, Mr. Jackson. I understand very clearly what you are saying. I promise you that you have nothing to worry about."

"Do you still want to take Amanda? Because if you don't, I won't be upset with you, we'll still be friends, and I'll break the news to her myself."

"Yes, Mr. Jackson, I still want to take her."

Before Josh had reached the front door, Tara was upstairs breaking the good news to Amanda. As Trey returned to the billiards room, Trey III and Alec were waiting for him.

Trey III said, "So, Dad, you set Josh straight, right? You know, about the one-year rule."

Alec added, "Yeah, who does that kid think he is coming over here and thinking he could get Dad to change his mind? What the hell was that kid thinking, Dad?" Trey stared at the television as if he didn't hear them before they began walking out of the room laughing.

As they exited the room, Alec quipped, "Nobody messes with Dad."

"Yeah," Trey III said, "the rules are the rules."

Trey murmured to himself, "Smartasses."

Amanda ran into the room and sat on Trey's lap, saying, "Daddy, I love you. You are the greatest."

"I just hope I'm not making a mistake, baby, but I do trust you. I know you understand the difference between right and wrong, and I know you respect your body and your reputation."

"You can trust me, Dad. It will be fine; I promise."

Later that night, as Trey and Tara lay in bed, he stared at her without saying a word for a several seconds before she laughed and said, "What, Trey?"

"I know you told Amanda last night that Josh needed to come speak with me. Did you tell her what the kid needed to say as well?"

Tara smirked and said in an exaggerated southern accent, "Why no, Trey, I would never do that."

"You know what happens to people who lie, Tara?"

"Why of course I do. They go to hell, or worse yet, they have to deal with you." Tara then smiled and kissed Trey good night before turning off the light.

16

It was the middle of June in 2012. Trey III had just completed his senior year of high school, Alec his sophomore year, and Amanda her freshman year. They were all on summer break. Trey called Edith and Missy to make arrangements for them to stay at the house for a week and watch the kids. Tara's forty-fifth birthday was a few days away, and he had a surprise for her.

Trey arrived home from work early and told Tara to pack her bags. When she inquired as to where they were going and for how many days, he told her one week, and that's all he was revealing. She stated that she needed more information so that she would know what to pack. He told her they were going on a summer vacation and to pack beachwear, nothing nice.

They arrived at the airport, and as they were checking their luggage in, Tara realized that they were going to San Francisco. She let out a restrained scream and jumped into Trey's arms. She had indicated to him for years that she had always wanted to go to San Francisco and then make the drive in a convertible down the Pacific Coast Highway to Los Angeles.

They arrived in San Francisco, rented a convertible, and checked into a quaint little bed and breakfast in the hills overlooking the ocean. As Tara stood on the balcony, she remarked, "It's so beautiful. It's just like I imagined it would be. Thank you, Trey. This is such a wonderful surprise. You're the best."

They went to Fisherman's Wharf for a casual dinner and then walked the beach at dusk holding hands. Tara said, "This is so wonderful. I feel like I did when we first started dating." They sat on the beach and watched the sunset with their arms wrapped around each other.

The following day, they slept late and checked out of the bed and breakfast. They ate lunch at a different restaurant at Fisherman's Wharf, as Tara loved it there. Trey loved to see the glow on her face. It was obvious that she was having a great time. After lunch, they got into the convertible and began the drive down the Pacific Coast Highway.

For the next three days they would drive two to three hours and stop at a hotel or bed and breakfast overlooking the ocean about noon. They were having the time of their lives, acting like kids for the first time in years.

They arrived at Santa Monica Beach, just outside Hollywood, on the fifth day. The following morning, Tara wanted to go into Hollywood and shop on Hollywood Boulevard. They hit all the stores, with Tara making a few purchases. Trey despised shopping; however, she was trying on outfits and coming out of the dressing room and modeling them for him, so he didn't mind.

While Tara was in the dressing room and Trey anxiously waited to see her in the next outfit, a voice uttered, "Trey, is that really you?" Trey, not expecting to see anyone he knew in this area, turned with a perplexed look on his face. It was Erin, whom he had known in the past as Stacey. It had been almost twenty years since he had seen her, but she looked much the same, just older and more professional and refined. Tara walked out in her outfit, and he turned to her, at a loss for words. He had confessed to Tara his episode with Erin when they got back together eighteen years ago, but she had never met her.

Erin broke the ice by looking at Tara and saying, "What a gorgeous outfit. You look sensational, and very sexy. Hi, I'm Erin, an old friend of Trey's." She motioned for her husband to come over, and she introduced him as well.

"How do you know Trey?" asked Tara as Trey's stomach sank.

"I was a secretary in his law firm in Asheville before moving to Los Angeles. He spoke of you often, and after all these years, I finally meet you."

"Well, it is a small world after all. How would you two like to have dinner with us tonight?" Trey began to feel ill as Erin and her husband accepted the invitation and selected a restaurant they thought Trey and Tara would enjoy.

When they got back to the hotel, Tara stated that they needed to get ready for dinner. Trey got a dejected look on his face and said, "Tara, you need to sit down. We're not going to dinner with them." She sat on the bed looking confused as she stared at him. He looked as if he was in pain as he fumbled with his words trying to find the way to tell her who Erin was. After letting him twist in the wind for a minute, she abruptly smiled and said, "Trey, I know who she is. You told me her name—Erin—and she was supposedly kidnapped by the Dreadnaughts and went by some other name. It was almost twenty years ago, but a girl doesn't forget a thing like that. I was 90 percent sure based upon the way you were acting before I invited her to dinner. I now am 100 percent sure. She is very pretty."

Trey looked at Tara incredulously and asked, "Then why did you invite them out to dinner?"

"Two reasons. One, she was young, and she got sucked into the Dreadnaughts and their games. I don't blame her for what happened between the two of you. Second, I want to make sure that I'm the one you want to go home with tonight." She then got up and walked to the shower as Trey looked at her with a profound look of disbelief on his face.

Trey dressed casually, consistent with the restaurant to which they were going. After sitting on the bed and waiting for thirty minutes, he yelled, "Tara, what are you doing in there? We need to go." Ten minutes later she walked out in the little black dress wearing black high heels. She had on red lipstick and was all made up. Trey had not seen her dressed up like this in a few years, and he was awestruck by her beauty.

"Tara, this is a casual restaurant, and you're all dressed up. I didn't bring any nice clothes, and I didn't buy any today. I don't look like I even belong with you."

"Oh, you're just now realizing that you married up. Let's go."

The restaurant was on the beach. Patrons were dressed in all modes of attire. Tara looked like a movie star. Trey looked like an unshaven beach bum, albeit a good-looking one. They didn't see Erin and her husband immediately, so Trey took Tara's hand and led her straight to the bar. He badly needed a drink. He ordered a double rum and Coke and a glass of wine for her. He knocked his down rapidly and ordered another.

Tara looked at him and said, "Take it easy, big boy. You've got an important decision to make tonight."

"Very funny."

Erin and her husband arrived, and they grabbed a table. Erin, although not as dressed up as Tara, was dressed very nicely, while her husband was, as Trey, dressed down. They had a nice dinner. Everyone relaxed, and the conversation was very pleasant. Trey was pleased, although he tried not to show it much, that Erin had done very well. She had graduated from UCLA with a degree in architecture. She got her contractor's license and had taken over her father's construction company. She expanded the business and was building many high-end homes in the area. She had been married for eleven years and had two girls, who were eight and ten. Her husband was a stay-at-home husband. He took care of the home and kids, and she built her business, working long hours. She was very happy, and Tara seemed to like her very much. They laughed and had a good time.

When the check arrived, Trey was relieved that the evening was drawing to a close, and he couldn't wait to get back to the hotel. Tara and Erin had consumed a few glasses of wine, and Trey had a displeased look on his face as Erin said, "You know what would be fun? It's only ten o'clock. There's a great nightclub right down the road. Great dancing. What do you think?"

Before Trey could say no, Tara responded, "That's a great idea."

When they arrived at the nightclub, Tara and Erin walked right past the bouncer, but he stopped the men and said they weren't wearing the proper attire. The girls came back, each hanging on one of the bouncer's shoulders and saying, "Please, Mr. Bouncer. If you let them in, we'll do anything. My, what big muscles you have."

The bouncer laughed and said, "Anything, huh? You gents may enter."

They stood at the bar and ordered drinks. Trey was not much of a dancer, and apparently neither was Erin's husband. The girls decided to dance together. As they danced, Trey wondered if Erin's husband was getting as turned on as he was.

The women returned to the bar, and they all finished their drinks. The women then coaxed the men out on the dance floor. The bar wasn't too crowded, as it was a weeknight, and Tara danced as sexily as she could around Trey. He wasn't sure if he had ever been this excited, and he would have done anything Tara wanted him to do. She backed him into the far corner of the bar and danced around him until her back was to the corner. She straddled his thigh, grabbing his hands and putting them under the back of her dress. He caressed her butt and ran his hands through her thong. Tara then took his hands away and danced him back to the middle of the dance floor.

As a new song began, Tara grabbed Erin and pulled her over to Trey. She then switched over to Erin's husband and began dancing with him.

As Trey danced with Erin, she whispered to him, "She's great. I'm so happy to see you still together with her. It's great we can all go out and have an awesome time together. Fortunately, she doesn't know what happened between us twenty years ago."

"Oh, she knows."

"What?"

After the song was over, Tara took Trey by the hand and led him over by the restrooms. "Well, what's it going to be? You got to dance with both of us. Whom do you want to take home now?"

"Tara, this is stupid."

She covered his mouth and said, "Choose."

125

Trey put his arms around Tara and said, "You are the sexiest woman I have ever seen. I choose you today, tomorrow, and every day for the rest of my life." They all walked outside and hugged each other good-bye.

On the short cab ride back to the hotel, Trey and Tara kissed passionately, and she climbed up on him and straddled him. They pulled up to the hotel, and the cabbie asked, "Do you want me to take a couple of laps around the block?"

"No," Trey laughed, "we're good."

Trey had not seen Tara quite like this since they were in their twenties, but who was he to complain? He was loving it, and he knew with complete clarity that he had the best girl in the world.

They entered the hotel, and Tara ran giddily toward the elevator as Trey ran behind her, not much caring that they were making somewhat of a scene. They got into the elevator, and she attacked him as if she wanted to do it then and there. Trey got her off the elevator and struggled to get her the thirty feet to the room as she was all over him.

The next morning, Tara, not accustomed to drinking in excess, was not feeling very well. They made it to the airport, and she slept the entire flight home. As for Trey, he smiled the majority of the flight, periodically looking at Tara and stroking her hair.

When they got home, Tara embraced Trey lovingly and said, "Thank you so much. That was one of the best weeks of my life. I had such a good time."

Trey held her hands, looked her in the eyes and winked, saying, "Yeah, me too."

"I love you."

"And I love you."

17

Trey's forty-ninth birthday was a week off. It was early August of 2016, and all the kids had gone back to school the week before. Trey III was in his first year of law school, and Alec and Amanda were in college. Trey made it clear to Tara that he wanted no surprise parties or gifts. He wanted to load up the car on Saturday morning, including the surfboard he had kept since his youth, go to the beach, spend time with her relaxing, and try to relive his youth by surfing, which he had not done in over twenty years.

He said, "Tara, that's all I want to do, and I want you to promise me that you will honor that. No parties. No gifts."

"That sounds like fun. Let's do it. I could use some work on my tan anyway."

The Friday night before his birthday, Trey and Tara went out for pizza. Her tastes were a little more refined than his, and she wasn't particularly fond of pizza joints, but this was his weekend, and she agreed to go without complaint. They ate pizza and had a few beers. They talked about their children and how well they were all doing in school.

Upon arriving home, Tara asked Trey to wait for her in the living room while she went upstairs for a few minutes. He walked into the living room and saw a six-foot long box in wrapping paper with a bow on it. Although he had made it clear that he didn't want any presents, and his birthday was not until the next day, he was anxious to see what was in the box. He dug into the box and found inside wrapped in plastic a new surfboard. Tara had it specially made. It was a white board, trimmed in black, with his name in large red capital letters in the middle. Near the bottom of the board, in smaller capital letters, was her name with the silhouette of a sexy girl wearing a bikini.

Trey laughed as he looked at the silhouette of Tara etched on the board, and he heard her voice, "So, how do you like it?"

"It's awesome."

He turned toward her and froze and just stared at her as she stood there wearing red lingerie and red pumps. She may have been in her late forties, but she had the same body she had when he met her, and he totally forgot about the new surfboard as he stared at her, not saying a word. She came to him and said, "What's wrong, surfer boy, cat got your tongue?" She grabbed his hand and led him upstairs. Once upstairs, she playfully said to him, "You know, surfers have always turned me on. What did you say your name is?"

It was the best night Trey could have imagined. Pizza, beer, a new surfboard, and the hottest woman on the planet dressed in lingerie and giving herself to him. He dozed off with a smile on his face.

Tara awakened the next morning and made her way downstairs. Trey had already packed the car and was ready to go. "Hey, pretty girl, put on your sexiest bikini and let's hit the road," he said.

As they drove the short distance to the beach, Tara leaned over, kissed him, and whispered, "Who was that surfer boy in my bedroom last night? He was an animal."

"That was me, ma'am. I hope I satisfied your needs."

"And then some," said Tara as she ran her hands through his graying hair.

Once at the beach, Trey helped Tara unload the car and find a spot to put their cooler and towels. He anxiously grabbed his new board and began to put wax on the surface for traction. "Before your leave me here all by myself," said Tara, "will you rub some suntan lotion on my back?" As she lay on her stomach while he put the lotion on, he was overwhelmed with her beauty and more than a little bit turned on, which is what she wanted. When he finished with the lotion, she sat up, and he kissed her passionately before grabbing his new board and running toward the ocean. She laughed as she watched him run with the board covering his front midsection.

Trey surfed for three straight hours. Tara watched in amazement as he maneuvered the board on the waves. She had never seen him surf before, and although she knew little about it, she thought he was very good. As he came out of the water, two young and very fit looking girls stopped him to talk. Trey had salt-and-pepper hair, and although he was not as ripped as he was in his younger days, he exercised regularly, as did Tara; he was still a very good-looking man.

As he returned to Tara, she said, "So, you have the young ones hitting on you, huh? I don't know if I can let you go surfing by yourself."

"I haven't lost a thing, have I? But the thing is, I already have the hottest chick on the beach."

Trey ate the lunch that Tara had packed the day before. He then went back out and surfed for a couple more hours. It was about 4:00 p.m., and he was exhausted. He sat on his towel talking to Tara and admiring her bikini and suggested that they pack it up and head home. Just then, he heard several voices behind him. As he turned, they yelled in unison, "Happy birthday, Trey."

Initially, Trey was not pleased with Tara, because he was tired and had specifically told her that he did not want a party. It made it easier that Charles, who had become one his best friends since the bachelor party debacle, was there with his wife and a cooler full of beer. There were only two other couples. One was an attorney friend of Trey's and his wife, and the other was Tara's best friend and her husband, with whom Trey got along well on the occasions when they were together. At least, he thought, it was a good group and a small gathering.

They drank beer, told stories, and laughed for a couple of hours before Charles convinced Trey, as the sun was going down, to show them what he could do with the new surfboard. Tara had already proudly shown off the board, making sure to point out her name and silhouette on the bottom of it. Trey, reenergized after a few beers, surfed for thirty additional minutes before it became too dark.

By the time he returned, the others had gathered together some wood for a bonfire, and Trey rolled his eyes when he saw a couple of guitar cases. He had heard Charles play before, and he knew he was terrible. The bonfire kicked up, and they drank more beer. Trey was having a great time. Tara had a knack for making things perfect, even when she was going against his wishes.

As the night wore on, the guitar playing started, and although Charles was as bad as Trey remembered, the other fellow was pretty good. They sang songs from their youth, laughed, and drank beer until midnight. Trey, having had too much to drink, relinquished the keys to Tara. Exhausted from the day's events, he fell asleep on the drive home.

The following morning, Sunday, Trey thanked Tara, telling her that was the best birthday he had ever had, the best weekend he had ever had. They then went on a long run, which was their custom on Sunday mornings after attending church. They had gotten up later than usual, and he had talked her out of going to church that morning. They then rented some movies and rested the remainder of the day.

When Trey went to work on Monday morning, he could not get his mind off of the new surfboard, his fun weekend, and Tara in that red lingerie with the pumps. He called her and asked her to take a picture of the surfboard and send it to him on his phone. After he received it, he called her back, thanked her, and asked if she wouldn't mind sending him a picture of her in the lingerie so that he would have a picture of the other vivid memory of his birthday.

"I can't get it out of my mind."

"Get over it, pal. It ain't your birthday anymore."

Later that day, Trey was meeting with a client when his phone buzzed. As he looked at it, he laughed as a picture of Tara with her lingerie on appeared on the phone with the text message: "Your birthday celebration is now officially over. Have a great day. Tara." He loved that about her. She was as tough as anyone when she needed to be, but she always went out of her way to make him happy and laugh. He couldn't believe that there was a time in his life when he nearly lost her. He couldn't imagine what life would be like without her.

Trey took off work early on Monday so that he could pick up something special for Tara in appreciation for all she had done to make his birthday perfect. He went to an antique jewelry store that always had some unusual heirlooms, some of which dated back to the Civil War era. She loved that stuff. As he perused the counter, looking at the jewelry, a woman asked him if she could be of assistance. He explained that he was looking for something unique for his wife. "If you really want something one of a kind, I have something you may want to look at over here," said the woman.

She handed him a gold necklace with a large gold heart attached to it. Trey could tell that it was very old, but it was not overly pleasing to the eye. He looked at the sales lady quizzically, and she told him to open up the heart. He opened it, and in tiny letters, somewhat faded, but still readable, was the inscription: "My love. If fate should not bring me back to you, know without hesitation that you are the love of my life and I will be with you always, in heart, mind, and spirit." "That's real sweet," said Trey, "but what's so special about it?" The woman explained that it was given by a Confederate soldier to his wife before he went off to fight the Union. He was a prominent member of the Charleston community, and it came with a certificate of authenticity.

"Did he come back?"

"The story comes with the certificate. You'll have to read it, but no, he did not."

"This is perfect. I'll take it."

Trey couldn't wait to get home to give the gift to Tara. He found her in the kitchen taking their dinner out of the oven. "Perfect timing; it's time to eat," she said. He said that he wanted to talk to her first in the living room. Once they sat down, he gave her the gift-wrapped present.

"Trey, what is this? You didn't have to get me anything. Why did you do that?"

"Why did you send me the picture this afternoon of you in your lingerie?"

"Because I love you," responded Tara, realizing that she had answered her own question.

Tara unwrapped the box and opened it. She inspected the necklace before opening the large gold heart and reading it. She then read the certificate of authenticity and the story of the necklace that came with it.

She looked at Trey as he waited anxiously for her response and said, "I love it Trey, but it's so sad. He never came back to her."

"But, Tara, that's the same way I feel about you. If something ever happened to me, I wouldn't want to leave without the opportunity to say those things to you. With this, you'll always know. Every day I walk out that door, every minute I am away from you, you'll know how I feel." Tears began to form in her eyes as she ran to him and held him, telling him how much she loved him.

After dinner, Trey and Tara watched television as she held the necklace, periodically opening the heart and reading the inscription to herself. Although the knowledge that he may leave one day and not come back was a sad and sobering one for her, she was overwhelmed with the feeling of the love he had for her. Although their marriage had had gotten off to a rocky start, there was nobody with whom she would rather be than him, and she understood the thought that he had put into the gift, and that made it all the more special.

Later that night, as they were preparing to go to bed, Trey went into the garage and retrieved his new surfboard. As he carried it into the bedroom, Tara looked at him with a stunned look on her face and asked sternly, "Trey, what in heaven's name are you doing?"

"I like to look at it. I'm going to put it in the corner where I can see it. Maybe I'll hang it from the ceiling when I have time. I knew that you wouldn't let me put it in any other room in the house, where company can see it."

Tara got out of bed and got Trey's phone from the dresser top. She clicked the phone a few times and then gave it to him, saying, "When you want to look at something from your birthday, look at that."

"But, Tara, it's too good for the garage, and I hardly ever see it when it's there."

"One week; then it's back in the garage."

As Trey climbed into bed, Tara started laughing. He stared at her, puzzled at her laughter, and she said, "That's why I love you. Every day is an unpredictable and entertaining journey with you. Good night, baby."

18

Trey's law practice had been very successful over the years. He had just turned fifty, his once sandy blond hair had turned mostly gray, he had a receding hairline, and his once chiseled body was not so chiseled anymore. He reflected back upon his life and was proud of the life he had lived. He continued to be madly in love with Tara. Trey III was in law school and doing very well, Alec was a senior in college playing basketball, and Amanda was a junior in college hoping to go to medical school. He had a great family and a great life.

Trey had periodically thought of his father and wondered where he was and what he was doing. Every time he saw a motorcycle on the road, he looked closely to see if the driver just might be Toby. He figured that Toby would be close to seventy years old, and he desired to know what had happened to him.

Trey enjoyed going to the local high school basketball games, although his kids were no longer playing. He didn't really watch the NBA games or college games on television, but he loved sitting in the bleachers and watching the kids play. It was basketball in its purest form. It was mostly about pride, not money or show. Tara sometimes would go to the games, but she wasn't a true basketball fan. She had never missed a game in which one of her boys played or her daughter cheered, but they had been out of high school for years, and she couldn't get excited about a game unless one of her two boys was playing or her daughter was cheerleading.

West Charleston High usually had a pretty good basketball team. The school district was comprised of about 75 percent from a well-to-do area and about 25 percent from a downtrodden area of town. Trey loved to watch the kids from the two areas come together as a team. He knew from his own experience that on the basketball court, it didn't matter how big your parents' house was, how much money they had, or what kind of car you drove. Everyone was equal, and the kids from the vastly different areas of town would come together as a team, develop friendships with each other, and most importantly, cultivate a trust and respect for each other.

Trey had become friends with the high school coach when his kids played, and he would regularly give a kid, always from the bad area of town, a summer job at his office to help him and his family out. The job consisted primarily of filing, running errands, or delivering documents to other law firms. He had a great ability for developing a sense of pride in these kids, and by the end of the summer, he had them doing research and believing that they could go to college and accomplish anything they wanted. He frequently talked to them about their dreams and goals. They respected him, and he was their friend as well as mentor.

The coach, Mike, had been at the school for thirty years, and the alumni were having a retirement party for him. At the party, Trey asked him who was going to replace him.

"I'm glad you asked me that question, Trey. I'm recommending you for the job."

"What?" said Trey, obviously being caught off guard.

"Oh, come on, Trey. You give these kids summer jobs, they respect and love you, and I know you care about them. You're obviously qualified. You were the star of a state championship team, and you played in college. Frankly, you should see some of the other candidates. I spent thirty years building this program, and you are the only one I trust to turn it over to. You are by far the best candidate. So what do you say?"

Trey had already made up his mind. "Yes, I'll do it. It's an honor. I only hope I can live up to the lofty standards you have set for this program."

"It's not all about winning and losing and state championships. It's about turning kids into responsible men, and that's what you're good at."

"Yeah, and winning too," said Trey as the men laughed.

Various persons gave speeches about Mike and what he had meant to the basketball program, the school, the kids, and the community. He approached the podium last. After thanking everyone for their support, kind words, and the party, he announced, "I have some very good news, great news. Trey Jackson has agreed to take over as coach. The program will be in good hands." As everyone stood and cheered in approval, Tara looked at Trey with a bemused look on her face. It didn't surprise her that he would want to take this on, and she knew he would be a great coach, but she had no idea he was even being considered for the job. He looked at her, smiled, and whispered in her ear that he had no idea that Mike was going to make the announcement tonight.

"I was going to discuss it with you first, babe."

"Oh, bullshit, Trey. You had already accepted it. You're going to make a great coach and really be a positive influence on the kids. I think it's a great idea."

It was the first week of practice, and Kwan, who was supposed to be the best player and team leader, was in a funk. He wasn't playing well, and his attitude toward his teammates was less than stellar. Trey called one of Kwan's friends into his office in the gym and asked him what was going on with Kwan. The kid shook his head and said, "He has a really bad deal right now. His mother left the family a few months ago, and his dad is a really bad drunk who can't hold a job. They got evicted from their apartment a month ago. As far as I know, he is still living over behind the Piggly Wiggly. I went to see him a few nights ago and offered to let him stay at my place for a while. Although my family isn't doing so well either, he at least would have a roof over his head and a mattress on the floor, but he said no, he would work out his own problems. It's really sad, coach. I don't know how he is eating dinner, and when it rains, he turns a dumpster upside down and props the front of it up with pieces of wood so he can get fresh air and see outside. There are some really bad people in that area, and I don't know how much longer he can make it living there."

Trey called Tara, telling her that he had some work to do on the team's schedule and would be an hour or more late for dinner. He then got in his car and headed for the Piggly Wiggly. It was dark outside. He parked his car in front of the store, grabbing a flashlight he kept in the glove department. There was a light drizzle, and as he got to the back side of the grocery store, on the far side of the pavement he saw an upside-down dumpster in a barely lighted area.

He approached the dumpster and knocked on it while saying, "Kwan, are you in there, son?"

"Coach, is that you?"

"Yes, Kwan, come on out here. I just want to talk to you."

"No, coach, I'm not coming out. It's my problem, not yours."

"Well, if you're not coming out, then I'm coming in."

Once inside, Trey took a seat on the asphalt next to Kwan and said, "You're wrong, Kwan; it is my problem when my star player isn't performing at practice and providing the leadership this team needs."

"Coach, look at me. I'm living under a dumpster because my parents left me. I'm only eating lunch. I'm sorry about the basketball, but my head's not right now."

"I get it. It's not about basketball. Your health and education are far more important. I don't care if you never play basketball again, but I do care about your future."

"So what am I going to do?"

"Well, I have a proposition for you, but it's not going to be easy. I'm not offering you a free ride. You live with me as long as you need to, but you must study at least two hours every day, including the weekends. You will have a list of chores to do. Also, you will stay out of trouble in and out of school. You will let me or my wife know where you are at all times. Your attitude will be good, and you will show me, and especially my wife, respect at all times."

"You mean it, coach? You would really do that for me? I can stay as long as I need to as long as I live by those rules?"

"Let's get out of this dumpster."

Trey and Kwan walked through the front door, and just before Tara was going to get on Trey for being so late, she saw Kwan, who was standing behind him. "Tara," said Trey, "this is Kwan, and he's going to be staying with us for a while."

"Hi, Kwan. Come with me, and I'll show you your room." She showed him his room and told him to join them for dinner whenever he was ready.

Tara and Trey were fifteen minutes into dinner when she went to check on Kwan. She came and got Trey to follow her. They peeked into Kwan's room and saw him passed out in bed.

The following day after practice, Trey and Kwan walked into the house. Tara said, "Guys, dinner's in fifteen minutes. Oh, Kwan, I got you a few things today. Look in your drawers and closet. If you need anything else, just let me know." He went into his room and found new jeans, shorts, shirts, socks, shoes, and underwear. He couldn't believe it.

Kwan came to dinner in a new outfit Tara had purchased for him. He had a wide grin on his face as he sat down.

With tears in his eyes, he said, "Miss Jackson, I don't know what to say. Nobody's ever done anything like that for me, not even for Christmas. But I promise, I'll do any chores or work you want around the house to pay you back."

"You can pay me back by being a kid and making good grades in school."

"And leading us to a state championship," joked Trey.

Kwan laughed and said, "Don't worry, Miss Jackson. I'm going to make really good grades, and when I graduate from college, I'm inviting you to my graduation. Coach, I've got you covered too. We're going to win that state championship this year."

"So long as we understand each other," said Trey sarcastically as Tara slapped him in the arm.

As they ate, Trey and Tara noticed that Kwan seemed as if he hadn't eaten in a week. Trey looked at her as he saw that Kwan had mashed potatoes dripping from his face and mouthed, "Thank you. I love you."

After dinner, Kwan had his first opportunity to survey his new surroundings. He had never been in a house like this. It seemed like a mansion to him. He had never seen so many rooms in one house. He loved the billiards room and the flat-screen television. He felt as if he was having a dream, and he feared that he would wake up under that damned dumpster. When he returned to his room for his two hours of studying, he couldn't believe that his bedroom even had a television.

As he turned it on, Trey stuck his head in and said, "No television during study time, Kwan."

"Yes, sir, coach," said Kwan as he turned it off.

A couple of weeks later, as the three were eating dinner, there was a knock on the door. It was Kwan's dad, and he was very drunk. Trey opened the door, and the man began to berate him, yelling, "Who the hell do you think you are, stealing my kid? Just because you're a rich attorney gives you no right to steal my boy from me."

As Kwan heard the yelling and realized that it was his father, he ran to the door with Tara following behind him. He yelled, "Dad, what are you doing?"

His father yelled back, slurring his words badly, "Don't you see, son? They just want you because he's using you to win a state championship. Then when you get drafted out of high school into the NBA, he's going to use you for all the money you're going to make. He probably wants to be your agent."

"Dad, I was living under a dumpster, and I would still be had it not been for coach and his wife. They're just trying to help me. Besides, I'm going to college. I'm not good enough to go directly into the pros from high school."

Trey told Tara to take Kwan back into the house. He then grabbed Kwan's father by the arm and took him out to the end of the drive. He got on his cell phone and called a cab before grabbing Kwan's father by the shirt and saying sternly, "Listen, you sorry son of a bitch. You get your son back when you become a father. That means you quit drinking and hold a steady job for at least six months. Until then, he stays here where he is safe, and if you show up here again drunk, I'll give you an ass whipping that you'll never forget. Do you understand me?"

"Yes," said the man as the cab pulled up. "Tell Kwan I'm sorry. I'm going to change." Trey gave the cabbie a twenty and instructed him to take the man wherever he wanted but not to give him any change.

Trey went inside, where he found Tara in the billiards room comforting Kwan. He said, "Kwan, let's play a game of pool." As they played, Trey said, "Kwan, I don't want you to worry about anything. You're not going anywhere until I'm positive that he's ready to be a good father to you. You can stay here as long as you want."

Kwan stayed with Trey and Tara for the remainder of his senior year. The team didn't win that state championship, but they fought hard for it, making it to the state semifinals before losing. Kwan played well enough to get a college scholarship to the University of South Carolina, and he graduated with a 3.2 grade point average. As he left for college, Trey and Tara hugged him, and she cried just like she did when her own kids left home to go to college.

Kwan looked at Trey and said, "Sorry I didn't get that state championship for you, coach."

"Kwan, what you gave me is worth far more than any championship. If you ever need me or Tara for anything, you call us. We'll come up to visit you and watch you play a couple of times this year. You make good decisions and you'll be just fine. If you don't make good decisions, you can be sure I'll be there to kick your butt, and I'll bring Tara with me. You don't want to deal with her, trust me." Kwan laughed, hugged them again, and went off in the used pickup truck Trey had bought him.

19

It was 2018, and Trey was fifty-one. He had to go to Asheville for a deposition. It concluded at 6:00 p.m., and he, tired and not wanting to make the four-hour drive home, decided to stay the night. He drove by the Bikers and Babes bar, and much to his surprise, it was still there and had a good crowd. Maybe, he thought, the Dreadnaughts were still around, and so was his father. He thought better of going in the bar. He was older now and not much of a risk taker anymore. The twenty-four years following his experiences with the Dreadnaughts had mellowed him. The biggest adventure for him these days was going out to dinner with Tara and having a beer.

The following morning, Trey called Tara and let her know that he was on his way back. He couldn't resist. The night before, he lay in bed for hours staring at the ceiling and reliving his encounters with Toby, Jimmy, and the Dreadnaughts. He embarked on the forty-five-minute trip up the mountain.

As he entered the field he could see that the old farmhouse was still there. There wasn't any activity, but as he neared the house, he saw a handful of bikes outside. Against his better judgment, he pulled up and got out of his car. As he walked up to the house, he heard several voices. Five bikers exited the house and looked at Trey, and one of them said, "Who the hell are you?" Before he had an opportunity to answer, four of them grabbed him aggressively and started to ask questions. Just before it got ugly, the fifth biker said, "Whoa, wait a minute." He strolled up to Trey and closely inspected his face for a few seconds before saying, "Trey, is that you?" He then instructed the others to get away from him before giving him a hug. "By God," he said. "Fellas, this is Trey, the son of Animal." The other bikers immediately warmed up to him and shook his hand. Skinny introduced himself to Trey as Toby's best friend.

Trey and Skinny then went back inside the house and sat down. The interior had not changed much over twenty-four years, except that there were no longer any jugs on the mantle containing heads or other body parts. Trey asked him if Toby was still around or if he knew what had become of him. Skinny explained that Toby had disappeared for two years after Skinny had taken over the gang. "He showed up again one day out of nowhere," said Skinny. "I think he tried to make an honest living out in the real world, but being a biker was in his blood."

Skinny explained that several years ago a rival biker gang had formed, and the last few years saw a violent war between the gangs. He then got up, grabbed a bottle of whiskey, two glasses, and said, "C'mon, Trey. Take a walk with me."

They walked about thirty yards to a back edge of the field. There were several tombstones, and Skinny pointed to one of them. It was Toby's. After Trey knelt down and viewed the stone for a couple of minutes, Skinny said, "He went down in a blaze of glory a year ago. He was our fiercest warrior. They attacked us here in the field. We were greatly outnumbered. Some rode off out the back. Not your dad. He took out about a dozen of them before they finally got him."

Skinny poured two quarter-full glasses of whiskey and handed one to Trey. Skinny raised his glass and said, "To Toby: A great biker, a great warrior, the best of friends, and a great man."

Trey raised his glass and said, "All of those things, and a great dad. I love you, Dad." The two men guzzled their whiskey, leaving their glasses on his tombstone.

As Trey got into his car, Skinny halted him and ran into the farmhouse. He came out and handed him a crumpled piece of paper and what looked to be a ragged book explaining that Toby had instructed him to see that Trey got them if anything happened to him. As Trey drove from the field, he unfurled the paper, which contained the word "Fishcatcher" and just below that "Murrell's Inlet." He had no idea what this meant, but he chuckled at the thought that Toby, although dead, had left him one more mystery to experience.

Trey returned to Charleston, and on Sunday afternoon, he retreated to his study and began to read the journal. There were various writings about Toby's life. He had an extremely difficult childhood. His father was an alcoholic, and his mother was addicted to a variety of drugs. His mother, as troubled as she was, at times showed him love, whereas his father never did. His father would come home drunk and, on a good day, would yell at him and tell him he was no good. On a bad day, the treatment was much worse. His real name was Trey, but his father called him Toby because he viewed this as a derogatory name to which blacks were referred in the old South. On occasion, he was tethered to a tree in the yard, where he was sometimes left in the hot sun for hours without water. In his early teens, he tried to run away a few times, but his father always found him, and the consequences were not pretty.

Trey sat in his home office for a couple of hours reading the journal, weeping at times as he began to understand the events in Toby's life that created the adult he ultimately became. There was not one mention in the journal of a fond memory of his childhood or of an encouraging act or loving word from his father. Trey gained a renewed respect for him, and he wished he had known these things and tried harder to allow him to be a part of his life and family while he was still alive.

There was one particular entry that was unimaginable to Trey. Toby grew up in Boston. When he turned thirteen, his father opened a beer, handed it to him, and told him that it was time he became a man. Initially, Toby thought that maybe he was finally bonding with his dad, until his dad instructed him to get into the car and took him to the loading docks where he was made to fight men who were several years older than he was. This routine was repeated a couple of times a week. Toby, although a tough kid, usually got far worse from the encounters with the much older and more mature opponents he was forced to fight. He would come home a bruised, battered, and bloody mess. On the ride home, his father would tell him that he made him do this for his own good and that one day he would thank him. Once home, his mother would tend to him and fix him up the best she could. The couple of times she tried to scold her husband, he would just knock her around.

Trey came to an excerpt that was very interesting and even more disturbing. When Toby was sixteen, there was a carnival in town, and one night he was climbing out of his window to sneak out of the house to go to the carnival. As he hit the ground and looked up, he saw his father standing there with a belt in his hand. As his father raised the belt to strike him, Toby yelled at him to stop. He told his father that if he struck him, it would be the last thing that he ever did. His father, apparently very intoxicated, laughed as he drew the belt back to hit him. His father hit him with one lash of the belt. As he fell to the ground as his father mocked him, his hand felt a rock the size of a softball. Toby rose up, and with all the fury that had been building up inside him for years, he struck his father in the head.

As his father lay on the ground mumbling and bleeding badly from his head, Toby dragged him the thirty feet to the tree to which he had been so frequently tied. He took off his belt and tied his father to the tree. He went to the shed and retrieved a canister of gasoline. He returned to his father, and as he began pouring the gasoline over him, his father began begging for his life. He apologized for the father he had been and promised to never hurt Toby again. Toby stated that this wasn't for him and that his father had already ruined his childhood. This was for his mother. His father would never hit her again.

As his father, the tough old man who had put Toby and his mother through hell, continued to cry and plead for his life while drenched in gasoline, Toby lit a match and stood over him, disgusted at what a coward his father was. He couldn't even die like a man. Toby pitied him so much that he walked away.

Toby walked into the house to say good-bye to his mother, as he was leaving and would never be back. As he entered the bedroom, he found his mother weeping in bed with her back to him. As he explained to her that he loved her and that he was leaving for good, she rolled over and begged him to stay. She had a badly blackened eye and a swollen lip. Toby, like a man possessed, walked out of the house and back out to his father. He called his father a cowardly bastard before he was engulfed in flames.

Toby went to the carnival and, after wandering aimlessly, came across an Indian woman who appeared to be in her midthirties who was reading palms and telling fortunes. He watched for an hour as she read palm after palm, and then she motioned him over. The carnival was ending, and she asked him to come inside her tent area. She looked at him, telling him that she could tell that he was deeply troubled. He stated that he had done something very bad and was probably going to be going to jail for the rest of his life.

The lady grabbed Toby's hands, stared deeply into his blue eyes, and responded that he was just a boy and his father deserved it. Toby, amazed that the lady could know what had happened, began to stammer as a huge commotion began outside. The woman peered outside and saw that the grounds were swarming with police officers. She took him and hid him inside a trunk, where he remained until the officers were gone.

Toby spent the ensuing couple of years traveling from small town to small town with the carnival. They put him to work, paid him a small salary, and fed him. The Indian woman became his second mother. With the exception of his real mother, who had futilely attempted to protect him a few times, the woman was the only one who had cared about him and protected him.

The carnies had known that Toby had always been fascinated with motorcycles, especially choppers, and on his eighteenth birthday they all chipped in to buy him one. It wasn't nice, but to Toby it was the most beautiful thing he had ever seen.

Shortly thereafter, Toby set out on his own. The Indian woman cried when he told her he was leaving, and he promised her that he was going to make something of himself and be back for her some day.

Toby eventually made his way to Myrtle Beach. He was nineteen when he met Trey's mother. She was tending bar, and she was the most gorgeous woman he had ever seen.

He found a job working on choppers, and every day after work he would go to the bar, drink beer, and stare at her, not saying much. After about a month of this ritual, she asked him his name. She then asked him if he was going to stare at her for the rest of his life or ask her out.

The two eventually settled in a little town named Marion about forty-five miles inland. Again, Toby found a job working on choppers. He also found that he was very good at air-brushing graphic designs on them. Trey was born, and for the first couple of years, things were pretty good. Toby worked, stayed out of the bars, came home after work, and gave Trey and his mother all of his attention.

At work, Toby began hearing about a motorcycle gang in the Asheville area. He also was making friends with the wrong people. He began using drugs heavily and drinking whiskey. He was also more irritable, and his marriage was suffering. One morning, he woke up, looked in the mirror, and he saw his father. He left his wife what cash he had, and he got on his bike and headed off toward Asheville, never to be seen or heard from by Trey's mother again. He anguished over leaving Trey. He loved him, but he knew that Trey would be better off without him as a father. He expressed his hope that Trey's mother would marry a man who could give him a normal upbringing.

Toby, who was twenty-two, rode into the Asheville area not knowing where he would find the motorcycle gang. He found a job at a small garage air-brushing designs and elaborate portraits onto choppers. He figured he would encounter some of the gang members through his work, and he was right. A good portion of his work was performed for those with the Dreadnaught insignia on their jackets. He was exceptionally good at his job, and the Dreadnaught members were thrilled with the graphics he created on their bikes. He would strike up conversations with them and began to learn information on the gang. He had heard many references to the Bikers and Babes bar on the outskirts of town, but he knew better than to go there without a specific invitation.

Three or four nights a week, Toby would go to another small local bar where Dreadnaught members would periodically hang out. When the Dreadnaughts entered, the bar became quiet for a few seconds as everybody took notice of their presence. If a member asked you to buy him a drink, you did. If he told the bartender that you were picking up their tab, you did.

There was no arguing with them or questioning them. If they picked your girl to hang out with them and leave with them, you had no choice but to accept it. They were all-powerful, and nobody messed with them.

On one particular night, there was a small skinny man appearing to be in his young twenties at the bar bragging about being a Dreadnaught. This seemed highly unusual to Toby, because the gang almost always traveled in numbers, and this man had no jacket with the Dreadnaught insignia on it. As time passed and the man consumed more alcohol, he became more boisterous and obnoxious. He even bragged that the leader of the Dreadnaughts was his cousin. He stated that his name was Skinny.

Eventually, three burly men, clearly tired of the skinny man's excessive bragging, stood from their barstools and towered over him. They asked why he wasn't wearing his colors or vest. Skinny responded that he would have his vest soon and be a full-fledged member. He also told the men that he strongly recommended that they leave him alone and that they pick up his bar tab. The three men erupted in laughter, obviously not buying a word of the man's story.

Although the skinny man's story did not make much sense to Toby, if it was true, and he was the cousin of the Dreadnaughts' leader, Toby understood that this was his window of opportunity to get in with them. As the three large men were about to pummel the slight man, Toby jumped up with a beer bottle in each hand. He struck one in the back of the head with a bottle and then another. He then proceeded to beat the remaining man until he begged him to stop.

Skinny looked at Toby with his mouth wide open and told him that he was an animal. He told Toby to follow him, as he had some people he wanted him to meet. The two men exited the bar, and Toby instructed the bartender that the three groaning on the floor would pay their tabs. The skinny fellow, who would have certainly sustained serious bodily harm had it not been for Toby's intervention, told the bartender to let him know if they didn't.

They got on their choppers and rode up a mountain, beside a small town where they turned up a dirt road, and eventually into a field. The journey took about forty-five minutes, and Toby nearly turned around a couple of times as he had no idea where they were going and why it was so far away.

They drove to the far end of the field where a farmhouse was located. As they entered, several Dreadnaughts froze and stared at the two men. One of the men angrily asked Skinny who he had brought to the headquarters without the permission of any of the disciples. The man, who was obviously the leader, was thirty-one, eight years older than Toby. He advised Skinny that they would have to kill his friend because he did not have permission to bring him there. He was upset with Skinny for disrupting his party. The leader had been telling stories, getting drunk, and groping his bitch for the night. He suggested that maybe he should kill Skinny, too, for his act of disrespect.

A clearly nervous Skinny protested and stated that his friend was an animal. He explained what Toby had done to the three big men at the bar and stated that the Dreadnaughts wanted to have him on their side.

The leader then declared that he was in a very good mood and would give Skinny's animal friend a chance. He introduced Toby to Reapor, who was sitting across the room. He stated that Reapor was the biggest, baddest, and most sadistic son of a bitch he had ever known. Reapor stood, stared at Toby, and cracked his knuckles. He was a beast of a man. He looked to be six feet, six inches tall and three hundred pounds of mostly muscle. The leader told Toby that if he took Reapor, he would be welcomed into the gang, but if Reapor took him, he would kill him and Toby's head would end up in a jar on the mantle. Toby's first thought was to make a run for it, but he knew that he would be caught and killed anyway. The leader only made matters worse when he explained that Reapor had never lost a fight.

As the two men stood outside about twenty feet from each other surrounded by a loose circle of ten Dreadnaughts, a few of their women, and Skinny, Toby, at five feet, eight inches tall and 160 pounds, contemplated his strategy. The leader, not at all concerned about the outcome of the altercation and considering it to be merely a form of entertainment, held a whiskey bottle in one hand as he groped his bitch with the other. Toby charged Reapor wildly and cocked his right arm to strike him. As he threw the punch, Reapor caught his clenched fist in his left hand. He then picked Toby up over his head and threw him ten feet as if he were a little kid. The leader and the others laughed as they disparaged Toby. One asked Skinny what kind of animal his friend was, and he suggested that he was a pussy cat as the others laughed robustly. Toby made it to one knee as Reapor approached him and the others screamed and yelled merrily. He looked like a Roman soldier waiting to be beheaded. Before anyone realized what was happening, Toby threw a right uppercut into Reapor's crotch. Reapor dropped to both knees as he groaned in pain, holding his groin area.

Suddenly there was dead silence as the onlookers watched in shock as Toby stood and, with both fists clenched together, struck Reapor in the face, knocking him onto his back. He then jumped on him and pummeled him with both fists until he was unconscious. He then looked at the leader and asked if he should kill him. The leader pushed his woman to the side as he looked at Toby in disbelief. He then laughed and gave him the thumbs up, saying that Reapor was no animal, but they still needed him. The leader then approached Toby, introduced himself as Jimmy, slapped him on the back, and instructed him to come back inside.

As they all walked back toward the door, Skinny ran to Toby and hugged him as he yelled to Jimmy that he had told him that his animal friend was the real deal. As Jimmy held the door open before walking in, he turned toward Skinny and indicated that his head would end up on the mantle if he said one more word. They all went into the house and resumed partying until the wee hours of the following morning. Toby would thereafter be known as Animal, and he and Skinny would be best friends.

After a couple of days of nearly nonstop partying, Jimmy and the two other disciples called Animal and Skinny upstairs into a room where the disciples met to make all the decisions regarding matters concerning the group. A cowboy was also present. Jimmy explained that there was a bad apple in the group who had been supplying marijuana in a nearby town. He had been selling the dope but not giving the Dreadnaughts the agreed-upon amount of money. In addition, he was receiving and selling the dope of a smaller rival group whom the Dreadnaughts had nearly eliminated. He had been warned twice, and this was his third strike. Jimmy told Animal and Skinny that they would accompany the cowboy to take him out, and Animal must shoot him. Upon successful completion of the mission, Animal and Skinny would be formally inducted into the group and presented with their jackets.

As a precondition to membership into the gang, the disciples always required the one seeking to be admitted to kill someone. This assured that he was not FBI or associated with any government agencies or authorities. If he was, he would not commit murder.

Skinny, always cursed with a big mouth, spoke up and said that Animal had already become an official member of the gang by kicking Reapor's ass. Jimmy looked at Animal, testing him more than anything, and asked if he had any problems with this. He responded that he didn't.

Jimmy, liking Animal but needing to make sure that he was not undercover law enforcement sent to infiltrate the gang, told him that if he successfully completed this assignment he would be inducted into the gang with cowboy status, which was unprecedented. It usually took many years of loyalty and proving yourself before being considered for that honor.

That night the three embarked on their journey in a van driven by the cowboy. Fortunately, the mark resided on a dimly lit street with only a few houses on it. They arrived about 11:00 p.m. and parked across the street. They passed around a whiskey bottle and smoked a couple of joints. Toby, now Animal, had been hitting the whiskey bottle hard. Although he had been in his fair share of altercations in his life and had injured many people, he had never taken a life, other than his father's, not even in self-defense. By 1:00 a.m., the lights to the house had been out for about an hour, and the cowboy said that it was time.

They approached the house, and the cowboy picked the lock to the front door. The three crept into the house with guns with silencers attached in their hands. They entered the bedroom and flipped on the light. Lying in the bed were the mark, his woman, and in between them, a young girl appearing to be one or two years old. Animal immediately instructed Skinny to take the woman and the little girl into another room.

As the mark begged for his life, the cowboy looked at Animal and said to do it. Animal, his hand shaking slightly, fired four shots into the man. The cowboy waited a moment before inspecting the man to make sure that he was dead. They then left the room and found Skinny in another room with the woman balled up in a corner crying hysterically and cradling the young child, who was also crying profusely. Animal told Skinny that they needed to leave immediately. The cowboy stopped them and said that Animal needed to kill the woman and the child also; they could leave no witnesses. Animal responded that he could go screw himself. They were not killing women and children.

The cowboy then pointed his gun at Animal's head and said that it was either him or them. As Animal's face turned red and he began yelling at the cowboy that he was a sick bastard and a coward, a shot rang out. Animal fully thought that he was dead for a few seconds but then watched with a relieved look on his face as the cowboy dropped to the floor. He looked at Skinny, and Skinny declared that they were best friends for life. Skinny would watch his back, and he would have his. Animal looked at the woman and asked her if she knew how close that she and her daughter came to dying. The woman cried that she did, and she thanked them for not killing her and her daughter.

Animal then put the cowboy in the bedroom with the mark. He put his gun in the cowboy's hand and Skinny's gun in the mark's hand. He then took from the cowboy anything that may link him to the Dreadnaughts. He and Skinny returned to the woman, and Animal explained to her the story that she needed to tell the police. She would tell them that she was sleeping in her daughter's room because the kid could not sleep. She heard several shots, and after waiting several minutes to make sure that the coast was clear, she went to the bedroom and found the two of them. She never saw anyone else. He instructed her to wait thirty minutes before calling the police. The woman stated that she understood, and she promised that was the story she would tell. Animal advised her that if he ever heard another version of the story, they would be back to get her and her daughter. The woman swore that they wouldn't have to.

146

Animal and Skinny returned to the farmhouse, and Jimmy immediately asked where the cowboy was. Skinny explained that the mark was ready for them. He was hiding behind the bedroom door, and when the cowboy entered, the mark shot him in the head. Animal jumped into the door, knocking the mark to the floor. He then shot him several times. Skinny said they made sure he was dead before leaving, and they staged the scene to make it look as if it was a drug deal gone bad. They also took everything off the cowboy that may connect the Dreadnaughts to the scene.

The following day, a ceremony was held at which Toby was officially inducted into the Dreadnaughts as "Animal" with the designation of cowboy. Skinny was inducted as, well, "Skinny."

As Trey read on, he was shocked that Toby had followed his life from afar. He was at his state championship basketball game and his high school graduation. He had been to many of his college basketball games and his college graduation. Much to Trey's amazement, Toby even knew he went to Yale Law School, and, yes, he went to Trey's graduation. He knew of his relationship with Tara while at Yale, and he even considered contriving a way to get into their wedding, though he thought better of it. The best part was Toby's description of how he and Reapor killed the Polo Killers. Trey was dumbfounded at this revelation and amazed that he would go to such lengths to protect Tara, his fiancée at the time.

Trey wasn't sure why Toby wanted him to have this journal and know this information, but as unpleasant as the details were, he felt good knowing what his father had been through. This went a long way toward explaining who he ended up being and why he left Trey. It also made him more thrilled than he would ever admit that Toby cared about him and loved him enough that he had followed his life and attended important events. His father was clearly proud of him, and he protected Tara.

As Trey flipped through the journal, he came upon some additional entries. Toby, after riding with the Dreadnaughts for several years, took a bitch, the Dreadnaughts' not-so-seemly name for girlfriend. Although the couple of pages were sparse on details, it looked as though she at one point got pregnant and gave birth to a baby named Samantha, who he surmised would be about eight years younger than him. He was at once happy and apprehensive that he had a younger sister out there.

Trey was pleased to see that upon her birth, which was kept hidden from the Dreadnaughts, Toby had secreted the baby and mother away from the gang and set them up in an apartment far away. He periodically sent financial contributions to them. Trey, although dismayed and hurt that Toby never financially supported him and his mother, was glad to see that he at least tried to do what was right by his younger sister and her mother.

It was evident from the general tone of Toby's writings about Samantha that he was not all too impressed with her. He expressed deep sorrow that she had dropped out of high school and didn't have much going for her. Toby had left the Dreadnaughts in March of 1994 after helping Trey extricate himself from them. He tried to make an honest living, but after tiring of it, he returned to the Dreadnaughts in March of 1996. He and Skinny ran the gang upon his return.

On Samantha's twenty-first birthday on November 2, 1996, Toby went to visit her. As she began to explain to him that she wanted to ride with her father and become associated with the Dreadnaughts, he stopped her and told her that there was no way in hell that was going to happen. She was going to be a respectable citizen and business owner. He then handed her a briefcase with $100,000 in it, drug money from the Dreadnaughts' operations, and told her to open a small business.

There were no more writings in the journal. Toby had left him with one more surprise—he had a younger sister.

Trey was changing to go to the club to work out when Tara got home. He handed her the journal and told her to read it while he was gone. She asked what it was, and he responded simply, "Read it."

When Trey returned from his workout a couple of hours later, Tara grilled him about where and when he got the journal. He explained that after his deposition in Asheville earlier in the week, before he came home he just had to go see the old farmhouse. He also wanted to see if Toby was still around. He explained what had happened. Toby was dead, and he and Skinny, Toby's best friend, had toasted over his grave. Trey had said his good-byes, but before he left, Skinny had gone into the house and come out with the journal. He had promised Toby that he would get it to Trey if anything happened to him.

Tara said, "Oh my God, Trey, you have a sister named Samantha." She told him that they needed to find her.

"How? We have no idea where she is. We don't even know if she's still alive at this point."

"We can hire an investigator." She then thought better of her suggestion to send someone to question members of the Dreadnaughts. "We can do something."

"Tara, I'm too old to go on a wild goose chase. We don't even know where to start. That's it. I don't want to hear another word about it."

Trey did not tell Tara about the note he had stuck at the bottom of his sock drawer. His life had been serene and stable for nearly twenty-five years, and he was highly suspicious that this journey would come with some form of high drama, some additional piece of a puzzle to solve, or some price. He resolved himself to leave the paper in his sock drawer and not think about it, but he couldn't bring himself to throw it away either.

A few months passed, and Trey had not thought much of the note he had placed in his sock drawer upon returning home from the farmhouse. One Sunday morning he opened the note, glanced at it, and knew that eventually he would have to go see if he could find his sister on Murrell's Inlet. Besides, Murrell's Inlet was only an hour and a half drive away.

Trey dressed in his typical weekend attire, basketball shorts and a sleeveless T-shirt. He went downstairs and, upon seeing Tara in the kitchen, handed her the note. She looked at it and then stared at him with a confused look on her face. He simply smiled at her and said, "It's from Toby. I have no idea what it means." She looked at him with an uneasy look on her face. Although she liked Toby, she knew that he could not be involved in anything without major drama enveloping the situation. After trying unsuccessfully to persuade him not to go, she said she was going with him.

Upon arriving at Murrell's Inlet, they ate lunch at a quaint little restaurant where they had eaten a couple of times before. Tara liked it, not so much for the food but because you could see the boats coming in and going out. As they ate lunch and watched the boats, they reminisced about Toby and the events that transpired almost twenty-five years before. Toby, observed Tara, was an amalgam of good and evil. Trey mostly listened, as that was a time in his life when he did things he was not proud of.

Tara stopped talking in the middle of a sentence and stared out into the water. Trey looked, and they both stared for what seemed like minutes at the large white fishing boat with the word "FISHCATCHER" written in black across the bow. After the boat disappeared into the inlet, they looked at each other anxiously. They were equal parts excited and apprehensive, as neither knew exactly what they were getting ready to walk into. Trey assumed that the note revealed the location of his sister, but he wasn't sure, so he hadn't shared the possible connection to his sister with Tara.

They drove to the location in the inlet where the boats were docked. After finding the *Fishcatcher,* they were disappointed that nobody was aboard the boat. They eventually spoke to a man who told them that the boat was owned and operated by a woman named Sam, and that she had probably left for the day. Tara thought for a few seconds before screaming, "Trey, she is the sister that Toby wrote about in the journal."

On Monday, Trey left for work. Tara quickly got dressed and ran out the door. She sat on a bench and waited patiently at the inlet where she had seen the boat docked the day before. As noon approached, Trey called her on her cell phone and asked her what she was doing. Trey, sitting in a chair on the porch of a bait and tackle shop no more than a hundred feet from her, chuckled as she made up a story about being in downtown Charleston with a girlfriend. Shortly after, the *Fishcatcher* rounded the corner and made its way toward its docking point in front of Tara.

As the boat docked, several people disembarked happily. They were carrying large coolers containing the catch of the day. Tara approached the boat and called to a man who was cleaning the deck. She asked the man if Sam was aboard. Sam walked out of the door and asked her if she could help her with anything. Tara stood speechless as she stared at the woman, as if she were looking at a ghost. "Are you okay, ma'am?" asked Sam. Again, Tara could not talk. Sam looked as if she was the female version of Trey. Tara was totally convinced that this was his sister, but she didn't know what to say. Finally, after having mustered some degree of composure, she told Sam that she had someone whom she wanted her to meet. "What is this about?" asked Sam, at which time Trey put his hands on Tara's shoulders from behind, startling her. She was surprised and relieved that he was there. Trey and Sam stared at each other for several seconds before he said, "Hi, Samantha. If you had a father named Toby, then I'm Trey, your brother."

Sam walked slowly to him, studying his face closely, before hugging him and saying, "I didn't know if I'd ever meet you. It's so awesome to see you."

20

Samantha, Tara, and Trey became fast friends. Sam was only an hour and a half from them, and she would come over for cookouts on the weekends. Also, she and Tara would get together a couple of times a month to have lunch and go shopping. She became one of the family.

One Friday, Trey took off from work at noon and picked up Tara, and they made their way to Murrell's Inlet. They waited for Sam's boat to come in so that they could have an early dinner with her. Her boat came in, and after the customers deboarded, she began to help her two-man crew clean the boat. Tara and Trey approached and asked her to have dinner with them. Her crew encouraged her to go, indicating that they would clean the boat.

Sam went home and showered prior to meeting Tara and Trey at Drunken Jack's, a popular restaurant on the inlet. As they ate, laughed, and discussed various matters, Sam looked at Trey and stated that she had the following week off. She revealed her intention to sail her boat to Alice Town in Bimini, an island in the northern Bahamas, which she had been doing a few times a year for many years. "Why don't the two of you come with me?" she asked. Tara said that she would love to, but she had some prior engagements and things that she needed to do the following week.

Tara looked at Trey and said, "Go—it will be fun. Just you and your sister spending a week getting to know each other better."

He took a large drink from his rum and Coke, leaned back in his chair, and said, "Why not? I could use a little adventure in my life."

"Not too much. Remember, you're fifty-two and not a young pup anymore."

"No worries," said Sam. "I've made the trip dozens of times, and I'll take good care of him. I promise."

The following morning, Trey showed up at the marina at 9:00 a.m. He had his good-luck black Adidas gym bag from college packed, and he was ready to go. Sam walked off of the boat and greeted him with a big hug, and Trey got on the boat. She gave him a quick tour of the vessel.

"Damn," said Trey, "this sure is an incredible boat, or should I say yacht?"

"I've been doing this for over twenty years. I did well enough over the years to allow me to buy this boat a couple of years ago."

"Tell me about the boat."

"It's fifty-three feet long, powered by twin diesel engines, and has a comfortable cruising speed of twenty knots. It will take us about twenty-four hours to get to Alice Town in Bimini."

They departed at 10:00 a.m. Most of the day was consumed talking about their father. Sam revealed that she saw him once or twice a year when she was a kid and that he had given her the money to buy her first boat when she was twenty-one, refusing to let her have anything to do with the Dreadnaughts. In fact, Skinny was the only gang member who ever knew of her existence. Trey recounted in great detail his ordeal with Toby and the Dreadnaughts. Sam was his sister, and he trusted her implicitly, so he left out nothing, including the affairs.

"Tara's incredible," stated Sam. "It takes a strong woman to understand what you went through and forgive you. You couldn't have done any better. I love her like a sister."

"No question. Although the good Lord had seen fit to put me through hell twenty-five years ago, he blessed me with Tara. Without her, I truly don't know if I would have walked out the other side of that fire. Even if I had, my life would not have been near as fulfilling without her." At 11:00 p.m., they went below to get some sleep.

It was 10:00 the following morning as they approached Alice Town. They anchored the boat at a little marina as the man who ran the marina approached the boat and yelled, "Sam, how are you? I haven't seen you in a couple of months."

As they walked down the deck, Trey looked at Sam and said, "How often did you say you come here? He acted as if you two were old friends."

"A few times a year. They treat visitors really well here. That's what I like about it."

They checked into a local hotel. At noon, they dressed casually for lunch and took a five-minute cab drive to their destination. As the cab came to a stop, Trey stared out the window at the sign with bright pink letters: "Toby and Sam's." He turned and looked at Sam with a bewildered look on his face, and she said, "Don't ask any questions. They'll be answered soon enough; just follow me."

As they entered the restaurant, Trey's mind raced wildly as he attempted to understand the situation. The restaurant, which was on the beach, was impeccable. It was an upscale restaurant with the booths and bar area trimmed in dark mahogany. As they made their way through the restaurant, everybody who worked there, and many who were dining on fine seafood, stopped Sam to give her a hug and speak with her for a few minutes. It seemed as if an hour passed before they made their way to an outdoor bar area.

As Trey grabbed Sam by the arm to ask her what was going on, her eyes became affixed on a figure sitting at the far side of the bar. As she smiled at him and the man beside him, Trey turned, looked at them, and just stared for several seconds as if he were in shock. Trey thought that he had to be in an episode of *The Twilight Zone* as he looked at Skinny and Toby. They raised their beers and motioned him over.

He looked at Sam and said firmly, "Sam, assuming that is really your name and you are really my sister, there had better be a very good explanation for this. You had better not got me into something dubious."

"Well, I'm not sure what you mean by dubious, but I assure you that I am your sister and that everything is fine."

Trey approached Toby and stood before him studying his face to make sure it was in fact he. "Quit looking at me like you're looking at a ghost," said Toby. "Give me a hug, son." Although he was seventy-one years old and looked like the old man that he was, there was no question that it was Toby at whom Trey was looking. He could only shake his head and embrace him.

Trey then looked at Skinny and said, "You son of a bitch. What was that ceremony we had ten months ago at the farmhouse in the mountains? There was a tombstone with his name on it. He went down with guns blazing. You remember that shit, Skinny? What the hell was that all about?"

"I thought he was dead, Trey. The bastard conned me too. A few months ago I went to visit Sam. I didn't know what I was going to do. The Dreadnaughts had been decimated by the rival gang and the FBI. There were only a few of us left, and we all went our own ways. A couple joined the rival gang. I knew Sam had a boat, so I went to find her to see if I could get some work there. I ended up here. Believe me, I was as surprised as you are to see Toby."

The four then went inside and up some stairs to a room to speak privately. Toby explained that after Trey's involvement with the Dreadnaughts, he had left the gang for two years. Upon his return, he was welcomed back as a legend, and he and Skinny ran the gang. Their drug business thrived, and the gang made more money than they ever thought possible.

The Dreadnaughts made so much money over the twenty-one years following Toby's return that he and Skinny filtered $100,000 or more a year to Sam the first few years and then $200,000 or more every year thereafter. There was so much money that nobody even missed it. Toby's plan was to provide Sam with enough money initially to open a small business and ultimately her own restaurant and live a good, easy life. He didn't need to worry about Trey. He knew that Trey didn't need money and that he was okay.

The rival gang emerged and began moving in on the Dreadnaughts' territory, and the FBI was all over them, jailing a good portion of its membership. Toby saw the writing on the wall. He would soon end up dead or in jail for the rest of his life, so when the opportunity arose, he seized it and fabricated his death. He couldn't just leave and run away. Eventually the FBI would catch up to him. He was also the number-one mark of the rival gang, and if they didn't track him down, the remaining Dreadnaughts would for running away in a time of war.

Almost two years ago, the rival gang had stormed the field up in the mountains where the farmhouse was located. Toby, thinking he was about to die and not seeing any way out, figured that he would die with honor, with guns blazing. He ran out into one side of the field and rushed the rival gang, shooting wildly as he was struck many times and badly wounded. In the midst of the ongoing gun battle, he dragged himself several feet into the woods. There at the edge of the woods he came across a dead rival gang member who looked nothing like him, but he did have red hair and looked to be about the same size. Toby, although bleeding profusely and in bad shape, somehow managed to change clothes with the man. He then picked up a large rock with both hands and hit him in the face several times until his face was unrecognizable. He then crawled a half mile through the woods to the roadway below.

The next thing he knew, he was in a hospital bed. He had serious gunshot wounds and was only given a 25 percent chance of surviving. "Wouldn't you know it?" said Toby. "I was in there for two months, but I walked out with a new life."

"We barely held the rival gang off that time," said Skinny. "After the battle, we found him. We had no reason to believe that it wasn't him, so we gave him a hero's farewell and buried him in his vest out back in the Dreadnaughts' burial hall of fame. I mourned the bastard for months. Hell, he was the best friend I ever had."

"I had my out," said Toby. "Everybody, the FBI, the Dreadnaughts, and the rival gang, thought I was dead. When I got out of the hospital I found Sam, and we were looking for a location to open the restaurant with all the money Skinny and I had funneled to her over the years. Well, this is it. It was finished six months ago. What do you think?"

"So you and Skinny have gone legit? You're business owners?"

"Totally legit."

"No drug dealing out of the restaurant, no killings, no crime of any kind, totally legit?"

"One hundred percent legit. No illegal activity of any kind."

Trey raised a shot of whiskey and announced, "To my dad, his best friend Skinny, and my beautiful sister Samantha, and to being legit." The four downed the shots, paused for a few seconds looking at each other, and then simultaneously burst out into laughter.

As the afternoon progressed and the four continued to drink upstairs, Trey stood and pointed at the other three, calling them by name as he pointed at them. He then declared, "Are there any more secrets of which I am not aware? This is the night to clear the air and get everything out in the open. I don't want to find out later that something wasn't true. No more surprises in the future. Is there anything else that I need to know? I want to make sure that when I leave this room, I know everything accurately."

"No, that's about it," responded Toby. "Oh, Stacey was the girl from the town that we supposedly kidnapped. She had been repeatedly raped by her stepfather. We didn't take her. She came to us, and we helped her out."

"She told her cousin what happened," said Trey, "and her stepfather was found hung in the woods. She's doing well and living in California close to her biological father."

"Well, well, you seem to know more than we do," stated Toby.

"Seriously, is there anything else I need to know? Is Sam really my sister?"

"You know everything, son. You've got my word. As to Sam, she is without question your blood sister."

Trey returned home, extremely happy with how everything had evolved. He wasn't sure how he would tell Tara the story. He sat down with her for thirty minutes and told her the story of what had transpired with Toby and Sam over the last twenty-five years.

After he was done, Tara looked at him and said, "So Toby is still alive, and he, Skinny, and Samantha own an upscale restaurant and bar in Bimini. Why am I not surprised? We could tell this whole story from the beginning to one hundred people, and not one would believe that it is nonfiction. This is crazy."

Trey shrugged his shoulders and said, "That's my family! The family you married into. Maybe you're the one who married up."

Tara sat quietly for a couple of minutes reflecting about the past and trying to fully absorb what Trey had told her before looking up at him and saying, "I want to see him. I want to go to Bimini to see him."

"Are you sure, Tara? Are you sure that's a good idea?"

"He's my friend, and my father-in-law."

21

Tara called Sam to speak about their girls-only trip to Bimini to see Toby and Skinny. Trey came home from work and walked into the kitchen. He popped open a beer and sat down at the table, listening to her conversation. She was extremely excited as she spoke with Sam about the upcoming trip. He was thrilled that she was so happy about the trip and seeing Toby. He was also anxious, since trouble seemed to follow Toby like that black cloud that always followed Pig Pen in the Charlie Brown specials.

As Trey listened to her conversation, Tara stated that she had spoken to Missy, Trey's mother, and she was up for the trip as well. Trey looked at her incredulously as she covered the mouthpiece of the phone and whispered that she would tell him about it later. She then looked at him as though she was curious as to what his reaction would be as she told Sam that her mother, Edith, would also be joining them. He nearly choked on his beer as he heard this. Edith was the last person whom he would expect to want to go on this excursion.

After Tara got off the phone, she looked at Trey with a wide smile on her face and yelled, "Can you believe it? Sam, Missy, Edith, and I are going to Bimini to visit Toby and Skinny. Isn't that incredible?"

"Incredible is the appropriate word. Now please tell me how this all came to be. How in the world did my mother and your mother get brought into this? Wait a minute; let me grab another beer first. This should be interesting."

Tara sat down across the table from Trey and looked at him with a touch of anxiety in her eyes as she said, "I know you're going to kill me for this, but I gave Toby's journal to your mother a few days ago."

"You did what?"

157

"Hear me out, Trey. Missy had no idea why Toby left her, and she didn't know about his childhood. The horrors he endured at the hands of his father. She deserved some answers."

"Tara, you had no right to make that decision on your own. I probably should not have let you read it. It contained the most personal of matters. It was a bearing of the very soul from a father to his son. He didn't authorize anyone else to see it. You had no right." He then put his beer down as he stared contemptuously at Tara and walked away from the table.

Tara let Trey cool down for a few minutes before going upstairs. She found him sitting in a chair in their bedroom. She walked to him, got on her knees before him, and held his hands, saying nothing but looking at him in a way that said, "Please forgive me." As she began to speak, he put his index and middle fingers over her mouth and said, "I know why you did it, Tara. You did it for what you thought were the right reasons. Your heart is always in the right place." He then looked at her, and to her great relief, he smiled, kissed her on the forehead, and asked, "Now, please tell me how Edith got involved. Surely Richard has not signed off on this."

Tara explained to Trey things he had not known. She told him that Edith's family had been the one with the money and that Richard was from much more modest circumstances. "Edith's father got him his first job and helped him advance in the company," said Tara. As he listened with the utmost interest and a restrained smile on his face, she continued, "You don't know my mother. She to a large extent let my father run the show when we were kids, but when it came to an important issue or a matter about which she felt passionately, she put her foot down, and he fell in line quickly. He may look like he's the boss, and she goes along with it publicly, but make no mistake, privately she calls the shots. She said she needs an adventure in her life, so she's going. I'm sure Dad is not happy about it."

Trey laughed heartily as Tara playfully slapped at him. She said, "Shut up. Don't you dare make a smart-aleck comment to my dad." As they tussled playfully, Trey wrestled Tara onto the bed. As they lay side by side, Trey stroked her hair and stared lovingly into her eyes for several seconds before smiling devilishly at her and saying, "Now, you've been a very bad girl. You're going to do everything I tell you to do, without saying a word."

Trey labored to fit all of Tara's luggage into the trunk of the Range Rover. He picked up Missy, who had only one suitcase, which he easily placed into the backseat. He looked at Tara and quipped, "Now tell me again why you need three large suitcases for a one-week trip?"

Trey, Tara, and Missy pulled up to the marina at Murrell's Inlet at 4:30 p.m., the same time that Richard and Edith were arriving. Trey reveled in the miserable look on Richard's face. As he unloaded Tara's very heavy and packed-to-the-hilt suitcases, he looked at Richard, who was unpacking Edith's suitcases several feet away with a pissed-off look on his face, and as he turned to Tara with a big smile on his face, she said sternly, "Not a word, Trey; not a word."

As the boat set sail, the two men stood on the dock and watched for several minutes as the boat made its way out of the inlet. Trey said, "Not to worry, Richard; she's in good hands. My father and his friend have killed many people. I don't think anybody is going to mess with the girls. My dad's friend is missing a hand, although he is a good-looking fella. On second thought, you may be in trouble." He then slapped a disgusted-looking Richard on the back before walking to his vehicle laughing to himself.

After the boat got out of the inlet, Sam opened a cooler full of wine and beer and announced that it was time to party. The girls drank and told stories. They laughed and had a great time. Tara and Sam were their usual outgoing selves, and Missy and Edith even opened up after a couple of glasses of wine. Edith told stories about Richard that Tara had never heard before. At midnight, the women tired and turned in below for the night.

As the sun rose the following morning, Tara went up top where she found Sam. "We'll be there at about five, just in time for dinner," uttered Sam.

"I think Missy and Edith will be out for a while longer." They looked at each other and laughed, both thinking of all the hysterical stories that were told the night before.

By the time Edith and Missy arose at 10:00 a.m., they were about seven hours from their destination. Several hours later, as they saw the coast of Alice Town in Bimini, Tara could sense that Missy was becoming very nervous. "It will be fine," said Tara as she put her arms around Missy in an attempt to comfort her. "It's just two old friends getting together who haven't seen each other in fifty years. I am sure he'll be very happy to see you."

"I don't know. I hope you're right."

What Missy had never acknowledged to anyone was that Toby had always been the love of her life. Although she had dated several men over the years, none of them made her feel the way he had. She had no expectations that they would get back together after all those years, but she held out hope that he would at least be happy to see her and that maybe they could be friends. She didn't know what to expect, however, and she was very anxious as to how he would react upon seeing her.

Missy had read Toby's journal, which Tara had given to her. She understood much better why he had made the decisions in life he had made, and she felt as if she knew him better than she did when they were married, as perverse as that seemed. Trey had also at various times told her the stories of his experiences with Toby and the Dreadnaughts. Tara had told her that Toby had funneled large amounts of Dreadnaught money to Sam over the years to buy the boat and open the bar in Bimini and how he had faked his death. She didn't know everything about his life over the last fifty years, but she knew his upbringing for the first time, and she understood a lot.

The women were greeted at the dock by several men. As always, Sam and her guests were treated as royalty by the locals. Their luggage was painstakingly placed into a cab, and they were taken to their hotel, where they checked into adjoining rooms, Tara and Sam in one, Missy and Edith in the other. After they unpacked it was 6:00 p.m., and the women then took the five-minute cab ride to Toby and Sam's.

Toby was expecting Sam, but he had no idea that Tara, Missy, and Edith were coming. As they entered the restaurant, Sam knew where to find Toby. He and Skinny had a predictable routine. They would meet between 11:00 a.m. and 11:30 a.m., eat lunch in the main restaurant, and then go to the outdoor bar by 1:00 p.m. to start drinking.

As the four women walked through the door to the outdoor bar, Sam spotted Toby and Skinny in their customary seats at the far end of the bar. They spotted Sam right away and got off their barstools, walking toward her. "Hey, how's my baby doing?" asked Toby as he gave Sam a big bear hug. As he hugged her, he looked at the woman standing behind her and got a huge smile on his face. "Tara," he said softly, "you're as beautiful as ever. How's life been treating my daughter-in-law?" He then let go of Sam and gave Tara the most heartfelt hug she had ever received. After embracing her for several seconds, he looked at the women behind her, and he said, "Who are these two foxes you brought with you?" Just as he finished the question, his face turned pale as he stared at Missy. "My God," he uttered softly, "is that really you, Missy?" She was visibly shaking as she shook her head affirmatively. He then approached her, standing before her while studying her face intensely. Without saying another word, he embraced her with everything he had and held her for what seemed like minutes. As he held her, Missy felt at ease and all of her anxiety disappeared. He then backed away slightly, held her hand, and said, "It's good to see you. I'm glad you came."

Tara then introduced Toby to her mother, who was uncharacteristically dressed casually. He said, "Edith, I see where Tara gets her good looks. You're family, and I'm very happy you came as well."

Tara introduced Skinny to the ladies, and he hugged them also. Toby grabbed Missy, looked at Skinny, and said, "Skinny, this is my ex-wife." Skinny looked at Missy and said, "So you're Trey's mother. You did one hell of a job raising that boy. You should be very proud. I must say, though, that you have very poor taste in men." He looked at Toby, and they all laughed.

The six of them grabbed a table, and the women ate dinner as Toby and Skinny continued to drink. They ate, drank, and laughed for an hour. At 7:30 p.m., Toby stood up and announced, "You're going to have to excuse me. I have to go home and clean up. I have a date tonight." Tara looked at him with a scowl on her face, thinking how insensitive he was being, and heard him say, "Missy, what time shall I pick you up? Say about eight thirty?"

Missy looked up, beaming, and said, "That would be fine."

A few minutes later, Sam suggested that the women return to the hotel before turning to Skinny and saying, "Skinny, you're one lucky man. You have the pleasure of going out with three hot babes. Pick us up at eight thirty as well."

"Yes, ma'am," responded Skinny with a sly smile on his face.

Skinny and his dates went out to a mellow bar on the beach and had a few drinks. He spent the evening hitting on Edith as Tara and Sam laughed loudly every time she slapped his hand. Edith could not remember the last time she had this much fun.

Toby and Missy went to a cliff on the island where they could look out over the ocean for miles under the stars. After they sat down, he said, "Missy, there are so many things I could say to you, but I don't know where to start. My past hasn't been pretty, and I have done so many things I'm not proud of, but the thing that has always bothered me the most is the way I left you. I was so confused, so messed up. It took me a long time to figure it out and escape the mess of a life I had created for myself."

"Toby, one thing I know is that it is not important where you have been in life; what matters is where you are and where you're going. Besides, you have two awesome kids. You should feel blessed."

The six spent the following four days together, having a great time. When it was time for the women to leave, Toby and Skinny came to the dock to see them off.

As the women were getting on the boat, Toby grabbed Missy by the hand and said, "Whoa, Missy, where are you going? I'd very much like you to stay awhile if that's okay with you."

"Yes, I think I'd like that."

When the boat pulled back into the marina at Murrell's Inlet, Richard and Trey were waiting for the women. As they stepped off the boat, Trey looked at Tara with a puzzled look on his face and said, "Wait a minute—where's my mom?"

Tara, smiling from ear to ear and in all her glory, said, "She's with your father," before breaking into her gloating dance.

Trey rolled his eyes before looking at Richard and saying, "You're just damned lucky that Edith came back. You've never seen Skinny. He has quite a way with the ladies."

22

It was April of 2022, and Trey was fifty-four. One Saturday afternoon he went out to the mail box to get the mail. He returned to his study to open it. When he got to the last piece of mail, he saw that it was from Kwan. He opened it and sat with a wide smile on his face as he read the graduation notice. He exuberantly pumped his fist in the air.

Trey tucked the notice back into the envelope and excitedly called Tara into his study and handed it to her. She opened it, paused for a moment as she read it, and screamed, "We got an invitation to Kwan's graduation. He did it. He kept his promise to me. I can't believe it."

"He made it. He escaped some pretty dire circumstances to achieve something really great, a college degree from a good school."

"Trey, this must make you feel really good about yourself. He probably couldn't have done this without your help a few years ago."

"You helped him too, Tara. You showed him that you cared about him, and you made sure that he took his academics seriously."

"This is just awesome."

"Kwan's the one who should feel proud of himself. We gave him a break in life, but it would have meant nothing had he not taken advantage of it."

"I know. He should be very proud of himself."

Trey still hadn't won that state basketball championship, but his success as a coach he measured in terms of the lives of young kids he influenced for the better, not by championships.

In May, Trey and Tara made the drive to the University of South Carolina in Columbia. At the end of Kwan's graduation ceremony, they spoke to him, telling him how proud they were of him and asking about his future plans. As he stated that he hoped to get picked in the NBA draft, a man came up and hugged him.

"You remember my dad, I'm sure," Kwan said.

"I want to apologize for my conduct that night," said the man. "I also can never repay you for what you did for my son back then. I took what you said to heart. It took me a little while, but I quit drinking three years ago, and I have had a steady job since then as well. I have become a father to Kwan. Would you two like to join us for a celebration lunch? I'm buying."

Tara responded, "That's very nice of you to ask, but this is a very special occasion to be shared between a son and his father."

"Tara and I would like to take you and your father out to dinner tonight if you can fit us into your plans," said Trey.

"Fit you into my plans?" emphatically stated Kwan. "Coach, I wouldn't even be here if it were not for you and Mrs. Jackson. I love you two. I will fit dinner with you two into my plans."

Tara and Trey spent the next couple of hours walking around the school. They eventually walked into the arena where Kwan had played basketball for four years. Trey marveled at how magnificent the arena was.

"I played against them here at the old arena over thirty years ago," remarked Trey. "Of course, it wasn't even close to this big, or this nice."

"Really, how did you do?"

"Well, I scored about twenty points, but we lost by about thirty. The Gamecock cheerleaders loved me. They flirted with me after the game."

"Oh yeah? How did that work out for you? Did you score with one of them?"

"No, our coach chewed me out in the locker room for being friendly with their cheerleaders after we had just got our asses kicked. In any event, I met you about eight months later, and not one of those cheerleaders was anywhere near as hot as you were when I met you."

"Yeah, I bet."

They met Kwan and his father at dinner. After they had eaten, Trey wanted to have a serious conversation with Kwan.

"Kwan, about your future plans. We really didn't have an opportunity to discuss them after your graduation ceremony. What are you going to do?"

Kwan's father, Archie, interjected, "He's going to get drafted and play in the NBA."

"Oh, that's great," said Tara.

Trey glared at Tara before saying, "Kwan, I think it's great that you are going to pursue your dream of playing professional basketball, but what is your back-up plan in the event that it doesn't work out?"

Archie once again interjected. "He doesn't need a backup plan. He is a surefire first- or second-round pick."

Kwan said sternly, "Dad, coach is right. I was a pretty good college player, but the pros is a whole different story. I need to start thinking about what I am going to do if I don't get drafted or get cut. I highly doubt that I am a first- or second-round pick. If I do get drafted, it will probably be in the later rounds, where I am not guaranteed a spot on the team, and I could get cut."

"But, son, you averaged almost twenty points a game playing division-one basketball."

"Putting twenty points on college teams is not the same as putting twenty on the Los Angeles Lakers. We're talking apples and oranges, Dad. I am a six-foot point guard. There are six-six point guards in the NBA who can do the same things I can do."

Trey, distraught at the direction in which the conversation was going, said, "Kwan, don't count yourself out. I've seen you play, and I sincerely believe that you've got a shot. Do you have any workouts scheduled with any teams for them to evaluate you prior to the draft?"

"Yes, I have my first one in a month."

"Then you're coming with me and Tara back to Charleston, and I am going to get you ready. It's not going to be easy. I am going to work your ass off. We're going to see how much you want this. If it doesn't work out, however, we'll sit down after the draft and discuss your future plans."

"That makes sense to me," said Archie. "Coach, you get Kwan ready. I know you two can do it."

Tara and Trey returned to their hotel room. She could tell that he was upset.

"What's wrong, baby?"

"I'll tell you what's wrong. That son of a bitch Archie is dreaming of his big house and his Cadillac with a personalized license plate. He views Kwan as his meal ticket, not his son."

"Trey, you've got to give Archie some credit. He has quit drinking, and he does have a job."

"Yeah, he did those things when he started to see the dollar signs. I don't want to talk about it anymore."

The following morning, Trey, Tara, and Kwan headed back to Charleston. On the drive back, Kwan said, "I'm sorry about last night at dinner, coach. My dad just wants to be proud of me." Trey slammed on the brakes and pulled off the side of the road.

"Proud of you? You just got a college degree despite being left in a dumpster when you were seventeen, you are a very bright and good kid, and you are a good enough basketball player to have even a chance of playing professionally. How much prouder could he be? Let me tell you something, son. Your job is not to make your dad proud, or for that matter, to make me and Tara proud. You job is to be able to look in the mirror every day and be proud of yourself. It doesn't matter what anyone else thinks. Having said that, Tara and I are extremely proud of the young man you have become."

"Thank you, coach. You're right."

The draft was sixty days off, and Kwan had workouts scheduled with five teams. Trey worked him harder than he had ever worked a kid, including his own.

One Saturday morning, Alec, who was twenty-six and last played competitively over four years ago in college, walked into the West Charleston High gym dressed ready to help Trey work with Kwan. As Trey worked out Kwan, he was pushing him hard and yelling a lot.

"Damn," said Alec. "Are you trying to kill him, Dad?"

"I've got to get him as ready as he can be. The people to whom I've spoken tell me that he is borderline between getting drafted in the last round or two and not getting drafted at all. I have to give him his best chance."

Upon hearing this, Alec jumped in and got on Kwan as well. Alec worked so hard in two-man drills with him that he nearly collapsed from exhaustion at the conclusion of the workout.

As they left the gym, Alec looked at Kwan and said, "Kwan, you're ready. You look really good. I'm just glad that Dad wasn't my high school coach. Coach Mike took it a lot easier on us."

Trey looked at Alec and said, "Listen, smartass. If you could have run a 4.6 forty and had a thirty-inch vertical leap in college, we would have been doing the same thing. Those were the only two things that you were lacking to have had a chance."

It made Alec feel good that his father believed that he was that close to playing professionally himself. His father obviously had a great deal of respect for his game.

Kwan said, "I know why coach is working me so hard. I have no complaints. I get it."

Alec responded, "Kwan, you've got a tremendous work ethic, and your head's on straight. Even if you don't make it, you're going to be successful at whatever you do in life."

The draft was on early Sunday afternoon, and Trey and Tara discussed whom they would invite over to watch it. Alec and a few of Kwan's high school teammates were coming. When she stated that they needed to invite Kwan's father as well, Trey grimaced.

"Trey, we have to invite him."

"I know, but as the rounds pass by without him being picked, Archie's house keeps getting smaller, his new Cadillac turns into a used Honda, and the personalized license plate falls off; I'm not sure how he's going to react."

"It will be fine."

"I hope you're right, because if he shows the slightest bit of disappointment in Kwan, I'll throw him out of this house just like I did over four years ago."

The draft started, and as Trey had feared, the rounds were passing Kwan by. In the seventh round of the draft, late in the evening, the mood had become extremely somber.

Kwan looked at Trey and said, "It's okay, coach. We did the best we could, and you've always taught me that is what counts. I appreciate everything you've done for me. Maybe tomorrow we'll sit down and go over the backup plan."

As Kwan finished his statement, the basketball commissioner stood at the podium and announced, "With the next pick in the NBA draft, the Los Angeles Lakers select Kwan Murphy out of the University of South Carolina." Everyone, including Archie, began jumping up and down and yelling and screaming.

A few days later, Kwan was packing his bags and getting ready to fly to Los Angeles to begin playing in the preseason rookie league. Trey walked into his room and asked him to come downstairs into the study so that he could have a few words with him. They sat in the study and began to talk.

"Coach, I am very excited about this opportunity, but I understand that my chances of making the final team are slim. If I get cut, can I come back here to speak with you about the best direction for my future?"

"Kwan, you know that you are always welcome in this house, and I'm always here for you, no matter what. Kwan, you have more courage than any kid I have ever met. You go out to Los Angeles, trust your game, and act like you belong. Don't you back down to anyone. You play with more heart than anyone on the court, and you work harder. You do those things and we won't need to have that talk about a backup plan."

On the car ride to the airport, Tara said to Kwan, "Good luck, Kwan. I'll miss you very much." Tears began rolling down her face as she said, "Kwan, I want you to know that I love you just like you were one of my own kids."

Kwan, with tears rolling down his face as well, responded, "I know you do, Mrs. Jackson, and I want you to know something as well. I love you and coach just like you were my parents. Actually, you two are the closest thing to parents I've ever had."

Trey interceded and said, "Kwan, you remember what I said in the study. Oh, by the way, I want you to send me some tickets for one of the games with seats close to Jack Nicholson. I've always wanted to meet him."

Kwan laughed and said, "I'll see what I can do, coach."

23

It was September of 2022, a couple of months after Kwan had left for Los Angeles. Trey and Tara had recently turned fifty-five. Trey had been working largely on a part-time basis for the last couple of years. Three years had passed since he first made the journey to Bimini with Sam. He and Tara would go to Alice Town with Sam three or four times a year. Tara, Sam, and Edith had their annual girls-only trip to visit with Toby, Missy, and Skinny. As it turned out, Toby and Missy had never been divorced.

Trey and Tara's three children were doing very well. Trey III was twenty-eight and Alec was twenty-six, and they both had good jobs and were happily married. Amanda was twenty-five and had begun her fourth year of medical school. Life was good, and Trey would often reflect on how amazing it was that everyone's life had turned out so well, when at various times long ago circumstances had seemed so abysmal. Trey and Tara thanked God for their good fortune every Sunday at church. He knew that in the past he had escaped what seemed to be certain death, the grips of a deadly and violent motorcycle gang and the brief loss of Tara. There was a God, and he had been very good indeed to him and to those for whom he truly cared.

One Saturday morning, Trey and Tara sat in the kitchen drinking coffee as he read the paper and she did the crossword puzzle. The phone rang, and she answered it. She stood in silence for a few seconds before she began to cry. As he looked at her with a very concerned look on his face, she said, "Okay, Sam, we'll see you there at noon." She then hung up the phone and began bawling. He hugged her and did his best to comfort her as he desperately tried to get her to tell him what had happened. She was trembling and could barely get the words out as she said, "Toby died last night."

After Trey had calmed her sufficiently, he asked her how Toby had died. "He was drunk and fell off a cliff into the ocean," she replied. "That's all Sam told me. We need to meet her at the airport at noon to fly to Bimini." They spent the next hour packing for the trip as Tara wept. Trey was either taking his father's death much better than she or he was too worried about her to get emotional himself. He knew how much Toby meant to her. He had become like a second father to her.

As Tara got on the phone with her mother, Edith, to give her the news and ask if she wanted to go, Trey had a couple of minutes to reflect on the situation for the first time. He thought how ironic it was that Toby, a man who had surely cheated death on numerous occasions in the past, had died falling off a cliff out of drunkenness. He was like a cat that had just used up its ninth life.

As Tara got off the phone, she said, "We need to hurry, Trey. We need to pick up my mom; she wants to go. How are you taking this so well, Trey? I know you loved him."

Trey went to Tara, grabbed her hand, and sat her down on the bed. As she continued to sniffle and wipe the tears from her face, he said, "Tara, I'm going to miss him too, but he lived a full life. Hell, he probably lived more life than any ten men combined. The beginning and middle of his life were not so great, but I take great comfort in knowing that the last part of his journey was so good. He was so happy, so content. He had many people who cared about him and loved him so much, and he loved them just as much. Let's face it. I know this sounds perverse, but he died doing what he enjoyed, hanging out and drinking whiskey and beer."

"I know, but it's still so sad to me."

When they arrived at Edith's house they found her waiting in the driveway with her bags, and much to Trey's surprise, Richard announced that he was going as well. He had never been to Bimini, nor had he met Toby. In fact, his relationship with Trey had been a mostly cold one for over thirty years. Tara ran to Edith, and the two hugged as they cried hysterically.

As Richard and Trey stood at the back of the Range Rover loading the bags, Trey looked at him and said, "So, Richard, why have you decided to grace us with your presence?"

Richard looked stoically straight ahead as he placed a bag into the back of the truck, and he said simply, "Respect."

Although Trey had been initially aggravated at Richard's presence in the driveway with his bags packed when he had always taken a condescending attitude toward Trey's family, he decided to accept his answer, whether or not sincere. In any event, he had more important matters than being pissed off at him on his mind. He knew that he had two women to comfort on the trip, and he knew that Skinny and Missy had to be crushed. Skinny had played Robin to Toby's Batman since their early twenties, and Missy was Toby's soul mate, like Tara was his, and Toby was being taken from her once again. He knew he had to be the strong one, and quite candidly, he didn't give a damn about Richard anyway.

As they walked into the Charleston airport, Sam ran to Trey and jumped into his arms crying. She whispered in his ear, "He loved you so much."

Trey, for the first time showing some emotion, with tears in his eyes said, "He loved you too, sis. You were his baby girl, and you always will be." Tara and Sam then held each other as they wept.

On the flight, Trey looked at Tara and noticed that she was writing in something. He saw that it was Toby's journal.

"What are you doing, baby?"

Tara, with tears rolling down her face, replied, "Only the bad part of his life was in here. I'm writing the rest of the story, the good parts. I'm going to bury it with him."

"That's a really good idea."

Tara continued to write in the journal the majority of the flight, periodically crying. Richard comforted Edith, and Trey and Sam said little, but they held each other's hand frequently.

Once in Bimini, they caught cabs and made their way to their hotel rooms. On the cab ride to the hotel, Trey noticed that the city's flag was at half mast and wondered if an important dignitary had died. *Certainly this isn't in honor of Dad,* he thought. They hurriedly checked in, and without unpacking, they jumped back in the cabs to go to Toby and Sam's, where they knew they would find Skinny and Missy.

It was 3:00 p.m. when they arrived at the restaurant, and without delay they made their way to the outdoor bar. Trey immediately went to Missy. They hugged for minutes, saying little. After all the hugging, consoling, and crying had subsided, they all sat at the bar to eat and have a beer. As Richard went to sit down, Skinny stopped him, telling him that was Toby's bar stool. Richard, on his best behavior, found another stool without comment.

After eating, Trey pulled Missy aside and they went to a table to talk. "Mom, what happened? How did he get so drunk that he fell off a cliff?"

"When he stuck to beer, which he usually did, he was fairly reasonable, but when he got going on that whiskey, he would get irrational at times. He insisted that he had to go to the cliff overlooking the ocean, as he had some people to talk to. He was very irrational. I begged him not to go, but you can't talk sense to him when he gets like that."

"He was going to talk to some people?" asked a newly concerned Trey.

"Oh, no, no. When he became drunk like that, he sometimes had conversations with people from his past, but not people who were physically there. Some were pleasant or loving conversations; some were bad and ugly conversations. There was no rhyme nor reason to them. He took off on his chopper and left. I waited for thirty minutes, and then I went to find him. I figured I would find him passed out on the rocks, but he wasn't there. I called our police friend, and an hour later they found him down below, dead at the bottom of the cliff with the waves beating on him. If only I had not let him go."

"Mom, there was nothing you could have done. Dad had a mind of his own, and if he was determined to do something, there was no stopping him."

The following day, they all dressed and went to the funeral. It was a simple proceeding, with the closed casket overhanging the hole in which it would be lowered at the funeral's conclusion. As they exited the limousine, an impeccably dressed man sought out Trey and asked if he could have a few words with him. They walked several yards away and began to talk as the others made their way to the burial site.

The man said, "I just wanted to let you know what your father has meant to this city. He has paid for a community center so that the poorer kids would have a place to go and stay out of trouble. He has paid to have a church built. If we ever needed anything, we always knew we could count on him. He was the greatest benefactor of this place, and his contributions were invaluable. He was the finest and most generous of men. I just thought you should know."

"So the flag at half mast?"

"Yes, that is in honor of him, and I as mayor have ordered it lowered for a full thirty days, the longest period in memory."

"Thank you. It means a lot that you shared that with me. I'll make sure his daughter Sam knows what you have told me."

At the funeral, after the priest's typical comments, everyone approached the casket and said their emotional last words. At the conclusion, Tara asked Trey to have the priest open the casket and place Toby's journal in it, which the priest did. The casket was then lowered slowly into the ground as everyone cried. As it was being lowered, Trey said softly to himself, "Good-bye, Dad. I love you. You never cease to amaze me."

After the casket was lowered into the ground, a gentleman dressed in a suit and tie said he had an announcement to make. He said, "Skinny, Trey, Samantha, Tara, and Missy, I need to speak with you." As they gathered, he explained that he was Toby's estate attorney and they all needed to meet for the reading of his will. He said they could bring their family members as well.

They followed the gentleman into the interior of town to a small block office that didn't look like much of an attorney's office. Once inside he invited them all to sit down. Richard and Edith had come as well.

He sat at his desk and announced, "I will now read Trey Jackson Senior's last will and testament: 'To the best friend a guy could ever ask for, Skinny, one half interest in the restaurant and bar, Toby and Sam's. Also, a 12.5 percent interest in the STM trust. To my beautiful baby girl, Samantha, one half interest in the restaurant and bar, Toby and Sam's. Also, a 25 percent interest in the STM trust. To the love of my life since I first laid eyes on her, Missy, a 25 percent interest in the STM trust. To my son, who has always made me proud, and whom I have always loved, Trey Jackson Jr., a 25 percent interest in the STM trust. To my second daughter, whom I love unconditionally, Tara Jackson, a 12.5 percent interest in the STM trust.' That's it. I'm sure you all have questions."

"What does STM stand for?" asked Missy.

"To the best of my recollection, it stands for Samantha, Trey, and Missy."

"How much is in the trust?" asked Skinny, unabashedly asking the question that was on everyone's mind.

"A little over ten million," responded the man as everybody sat dumbfounded.

"Damn," said Skinny. "I thought he may have had a mil or two stashed away, but ten? That's incredible."

"He was very smart, a genius when it came to investing," stated the man.

"I always wondered why he read the *Wall Street Journal* every day at lunch," said Skinny.

Trey broke out into laughter, stood, and walked out shaking his head in disbelief. When he got outside, he pointed toward the sky and yelled, "Old man, one last surprise. You couldn't leave without throwing one more at us."

The group then traveled to Toby and Sam's. They all sat at a long table and ordered drinks. There was an elaborate food buffet set up. As Trey took a large gulp of his drink, he noticed that the girls were in various stages of crying. He stood, banged his glass with his fork, and announced loudly, "I propose a toast to Toby, my father. He was a genius, a brilliant investor, a philanthropist, a great friend, a good husband, and an awesome father." They all stood, clanged their glasses together, and took a drink. "One last thing," said Trey. "Toby's looking down on us now. Do you think he wants us to be sad, or do you think he wants us to laugh merrily and celebrate his life?" With that, the mood changed and everyone had a great time, sharing their stories about Toby.

As they left the restaurant, Richard came up to Trey and said, "Trey, I don't know how much time I have left, but I would like to have a better relationship with you, if that's possible."

"Sure, if there's one thing I've learned, it's that anything is possible."

24

The following morning, Trey, Richard, and Edith flew out of the North Bimini Airport to return to Charleston. Sam and Tara stayed behind to comfort Missy and Skinny. Trey would have stayed, but he had some important work to do on a couple of cases in the next few days.

Skinny was acting, predictably, like a man who had lost his best friend. His routine of the last few years just wasn't the same without his sidekick. Although he now owned half the restaurant and bar, it was on automatic pilot, and he really didn't have to do anything. He knew any important decisions would be made by Sam. It gave him some degree of comfort that Sam, Tara, and Missy were there, but their routines were much different than the one he and Toby had perfected.

Missy was depressed, and Tara spent most of her time with her. Toby was the only man she had ever loved, and she had just lost him again. The last five years with him had been in many ways the best years of her life. They visited his gravesite daily, leaving flowers on many occasions.

On one particular early evening as the two were at the gravesite, it was beginning to get dark. Missy was not feeling well, so she stated that she wanted to go back to the home she had shared with Toby. She looked frail, as she had not been eating much in the last few days. The gravesite was within walking distance of her house, and Tara, who had been staying with Missy in the house, told her to go on ahead of her. She had some personal things that she wanted to say to Toby.

Missy walked the half mile home and lay on the couch and fell asleep. When she awakened on the couch early the next morning, she put on a pot of coffee and sat in a rocker waiting for Tara to arise. At 8:00 a.m., when she hadn't come out of the bedroom, Missy opened the door slightly to check on her. She was not in the bedroom. Missy thought maybe she had gotten up early and gone for a walk. By 9:00 a.m., she had not returned, and Missy began to become concerned. She called Skinny and woke him to ask if he knew where Tara was, thinking that maybe she had walked to his house. He hadn't seen her since she and Missy had left the restaurant after dinner the preceding evening. Skinny requested that she call him back if Tara did not return shortly, and he would come over to help look for her.

At 10:00 a.m., with no sign of Tara, Skinny pulled up in his truck. They drove to Toby's gravesite, but there was no sign of her. They then retrieved his binoculars from his house and went to the restaurant's outside bar balcony from which they could see the beach in both directions for miles. Again, no sign of Tara.

It was approaching 11:00 a.m. as Skinny and Missy pulled into the local police station. The chief, upon realizing who was missing, went on red alert. All officers were called in, and a massive search of the island began.

Missy was a nervous wreck, barely able to communicate. Skinny knew that he had to make the call to Trey, but it was the worst call he had ever had to make.

Trey flew in by late afternoon, and there was still no sign of Tara notwithstanding the tedious search that had been proceeding of the small island for several hours. Trey joined the search, first going to the burial site and then to the cliff overlooking the ocean where Toby had met his demise. Despite an extensive search, by nightfall she had not been located, and Trey, Sam, Skinny, and Missy returned to Missy's house. Tara's bed was undisturbed, and Trey speculated that she had never made it back the night before.

As Sam sat on the couch with Missy and Skinny theorized on where Tara may be, Trey paced the floor in deep thought. He abruptly turned, looked at Missy, and stated, "What did you say Dad said before he went to the cliff? He had to talk to some people. That's what he said, right?"

"Yes, but when he was on the whiskey he would talk to people who weren't there. Sometimes he would talk to you, but you weren't there. It was like he was talking to ghosts. I don't think that he was meeting actual people there."

"Let's go, Skinny." Trey grabbed a flashlight, and they ran out the door.

As Trey began searching around the cliff area, Skinny asked him what he was thinking, what they were looking for. Trey said, "Before the funeral, when Mom was explaining what happened, something didn't feel right, but I couldn't put my finger on it. I forgot about it until we got back to her house tonight and I started thinking." He reached down and pulled a shiny object the size of a silver dollar off of the ground. "What's this,

Skinny?" he asked. "Do you know what it is?" Skinny stared at the object for a few seconds, as it was difficult to see in the dark, even with the aid of a flashlight. His face suddenly became flushed, and his eyes nearly bulged from his head.

"Damn it, Skinny; what the hell is it?"

"Oh shit; it's the Pagans."

"The Pagans. Who in the hell are the Pagans?"

"I knew I should've killed that son of a bitch before he turned."

"Skinny, Tara's missing, and you'd better start making some sense right now or so help me God, I'll push you off the cliff."

"That's exactly what they did to Toby. He didn't fall off the cliff drunk; those bastards pushed him off. They killed him. The Pagans are the rival gang that destroyed the Dreadnaughts. A couple of the remaining Dreadnaughts turned and joined the Pagans, and a few of us walked away from it all. One who turned suspected that Toby and I had been siphoning off large amounts of money for years. He obviously told the Pagans, and it took them this long to find us. Toby wasn't going to the cliff to talk to any ghosts; he was going to meet some of the Pagans to try to work it out. When they kill a rival gang member, they leave their symbol, the one you are holding in your hand."

As Trey listened with a bewildered look on his face, he shouted, "What does this have to do with Tara?"

"When they didn't get what they wanted from Toby, they had the place staked out. My guess is they were watching the burial from afar, and they identified certain of us who were the closest to him. When Tara was alone at dusk at his gravesite, they took her, knowing we would have to come to them to get her. The good news is that they took her for a reason. They view her as a tool to get the money Toby and I took."

"Where do we find them? They can have the damn money. I just want Tara back safe."

"Of course, but they are long gone by now. They won't fight this battle here. They'll make us go to their home turf."

"Where is that? We need to go now. We're just wasting time."

"The old farmhouse. They took it over."

Trey and Skinny went to Missy's to explain the situation. They called the police chief in and made it clear that Sam and Missy were to be watched carefully twenty-four hours a day by heavily armed officers. Sam begged to go, but Trey and Skinny would not hear it. "This is our fight, not yours, sis, and we'll take care of it," said Trey. "We're not coming back without her, I promise," he said as they departed for the airport.

Upon flying into the Asheville airport, they checked into a hotel and began to discuss their strategy. Trey suggested that they go to the old farmhouse and reason with them, offering them a couple of million dollars in exchange for Tara. Skinny pointed out that they and Tara would be killed, even if the Pagans agreed and they delivered the money. They needed a game plan, and they needed it quick. Trey shuddered at the thought of what Tara was going through, what the Pagans may be doing to her. They stayed up all night thinking, but it was difficult to devise a plan to take down an entire gang with just the two of them. Skinny got on the phone and called an old buddy of his who had fought in 'Nam but who was never associated with a gang. They had stayed in touch periodically.

As the sun rose two hours later, there was a knock on the door. Skinny, after peering through the peephole, opened the door and said, "Mack, how the hell are you? Sit down; there's no time to waste."

Mack was a loner, not a people person. He looked as if he was one of those antigovernment guys who lived in the woods. He didn't say much as Skinny described the situation.

"Can you help us?" asked Trey.

"I can try. I'll be honest with you, our chances are not good, but I'm in. We need to go get the materials I need to line the outside of the house with dynamite."

"With dynamite? Tara's in that damn house. What are you going to do, blow her up? What kind of a freaking plan is that?"

Skinny held up his hand and said, "Hear him out, Trey; he's the best. You have no idea of the shit this dude pulled off in 'Nam. I've heard the stories from others who were there."

"Okay," said Trey, "what's on your mind?"

"We go tonight and line the back of the house with explosives. You and Skinny find a way to get their leaders, probably two or three, outside the house with Tara. I'll blow the whole thing down to the foundation. Make sure you're at least fifty yards away. Then you and Skinny take out the two or three leaders. That's a hell of a lot better than two against a hundred. That's the best I can do."

Trey and Skinny looked at each other and said, "Let's do it."

They purchased the materials Mack needed, and Trey and Skinny got the guns that slid down from the forearm underneath the sleeve into the hand. As they drove to the farmhouse, which Trey had never thought he would see again, his thoughts were mixed as his mind raced back and forth between thinking of what may be happening to Tara and focusing on their plan to save her life. He knew that there was a very good chance that neither he nor Tara would survive this ordeal. He wondered if they could actually pull this off or if he was testing fate at this despicable place one too many times.

They parked the truck in town with about forty-five minutes of daylight left. They slowly made their way up the narrow pathway that was the emergency escape route. They made it to the opening in the woods where Toby had killed the disciples and two cowboys almost thirty years ago and then proceeded down the narrow clearing leading to the back of the house. As the sun began to sink below the horizon, they neared the end of the clearing. Two Pagans were standing guard at the mouth of the clearing as they talked. Mack told Trey and Skinny to stay down; then he maneuvered to within twenty feet of the two Pagans. He whistled, and as they turned, he shot both with his gun with the silencer attached before motioning for Trey and Skinny to move forward and join him.

As they surveyed the situation from the opening of the clearing, they heard a large number of Pagans in front of the house, and it sounded as though many more were inside partying. The three slid on their bellies to the back corner of the house, and Mack went to work while Skinny held a small flashlight to assist him. As he worked slowly across the back of the house, a couple of Pagans stumbled toward the back on their way to relieve themselves. Mack motioned for Trey and Skinny to get down on their stomachs. As the Pagans approached, Mack sprang up, and before Trey could bat an eye, he had snapped both their necks and was back to the task at hand. Skinny, still lying on his stomach, as was Trey, looked at him and whispered, "See, I told you he was the best." Trey became invigorated with the belief that maybe they could just pull this off.

As they passed a window, Trey looked in and saw Tara tied to a chair with her mouth gagged. She had been stripped to her panties and bra, and he would have gone through the window after her had Skinny not grabbed him and sternly told him to keep his focus if he wanted to save her.

After Mack had finished lacing the back of the house with explosives, they slithered like snakes back to the opening of the clearing in the woods. "You're up," he said to Skinny and Trey. The sun had completely sunk below the horizon, and the only light came from the house. They made their way through the woods to a location where they could approach the house from the front. It was well lit with floodlights projecting light well out into the field. They paused for a moment, surveying the crowd one last time before Trey looked at Skinny and said, "Let's rock and roll." They walked slowly out into the middle of the field and neared the house before the seventy or so revelers noticed them.

"Hey," one said, "there they are."

"Stop right there," demanded another.

As they stood, Trey softly mumbled to Skinny, "I hope we're fifty yards away. Isn't that what he said?"

"Hell, I don't know. What difference does it make at this point?"

Three Pagans eventually came out and instructed the others to go inside. They then strolled cockily toward Trey and Skinny. The Pagan who seemed to be the leader said, "Well, well, if it isn't Trey, son of the legendary Carolina Animal."

"Watch him," said the second Pagan, "I hear he can do incredible things."

"He doesn't look like much to me," said the third as they stood ten feet before Trey and Skinny.

"Hey, guys, I'm just a lawyer, a sissy in a suit," said Trey. "I'm no match for you fellas. I just want to know how to get my wife back."

The Pagan leader then instructed one of the two others at his side to go retrieve Tara. A few minutes later he dragged a sobbing Tara out of the house and to the group as they stood before Trey and Skinny. Trey said, "Hey, baby, it's going to be okay." He then looked at the Pagan leader and stated emphatically, "If she was hurt, or anyone laid a hand on her, as God as my witness, you'll be dead before the night's over."

The three Pagans broke out into laughter, and the leader said defiantly, "You mean like this?" He began caressing Tara's breast. "What are you going to do about it? There's ninety more of us in there. What are an attorney and one-handed old man going to do?"

"We're going to kill all of you," responded Trey.

As the three Pagans once again broke out into heavy laughter, wham, the house exploded as debris and smoke filled the sky and the house became engulfed in flames. The three Pagans looked back at the house momentarily before turning back toward Skinny and Trey. Skinny and Trey immediately opened fire, dropping all three instantly. Some of the other Pagans began running out of the house, and although most were badly injured or engulfed in flames, many had guns in hand ready to fight. Trey knew they were still in deep trouble. Then Mack jumped out of the woods with his semiautomatic rifle blaring, taking out Pagans as if he were playing a video game. A couple of minutes later, when the dust had cleared, there was not a Pagan standing. The three had taken out the entire gang.

After Trey had hugged Tara for what seemed like an eternity and given her his shirt, he heard loud groans coming from the leader who had caressed her breast. Trey approached him, looking down on him as the man lay there in considerable pain.

"My name is Trey, the son of Animal. This is for my dad."

He reached into his pocket, pulling out the Pagan symbol he had found at the cliff in Bimini where Toby perished. He kneeled down and shoved it in the man's mouth. He stood and yelled at the man to say his father's name.

The man, with the symbol wrenched in his mouth, struggled to say "Animal, Animal."

"Louder, with more respect, more feeling."

The man struggled mightily to yell "Animal, Animal" as Trey shot him three times in the chest.

Trey returned to Skinny and Tara as Mack inspected the Pagans, one by one, finishing off the ones who were not dead. The old farmhouse was nearly leveled. "It's over," said Trey, and they walked off together through the field and then down the dirt road leading to the road just outside the small town below. As they walked, Trey looked at Mack and said, "Hey, Mack, you need a job?"

25

It was February of 2025, and Trey and Tara were fifty-seven. He had had a gated fortress built on a hill in Alice Town. Missy and Sam lived in the main house, and Mack lived in the guesthouse as the groundskeeper and bodyguard. He spent large parts of the day smoking pot, but Trey didn't care, as he had seen what Mack could do. He knew Mack could be trusted, and most importantly, he felt comfortable that he would keep his mother and sister safe.

After Toby's death and the destruction of the Pagans almost two and a half years earlier, Tara and Trey remained in Charleston, although they visited Sam, Skinny, and Missy frequently. On one such visit, Trey went to Toby's gravesite to speak to him. He knelt down and said, "We got them, Dad. We got every one of those Pagan scumbags."

Although it had been nearly two and a half years since the incident with the Pagans, Trey knew that there was still a chance that there were Pagans out there who may attempt to exact revenge on him and his family or may even know about the money and come after them again. He decided that he wasn't going to live in fear, and he felt reasonably comfortable that his mother and sister were protected. He also gave the police chief of Alice Town $25,000 a year to make sure that the fortress he had built for them was well watched, as were Missy and Sam.

Trey was working part-time, leaving at 1:00 p.m. most days. He would usually spend his afternoons at the health club with Tara working out.

Trey was getting ready to leave the office for the day when he heard the door open.

As he finished drafting a letter, his secretary stood in the doorway and said, "Excuse me, Trey, there's a man here to see you. He won't give me his name, but he says he is an old friend of yours."

"Send him back."

He opened his desk drawer where he kept his Smith and Wesson snub nose .48 loaded with hollow-tip bullets. He had learned from experience that caution was the best part of valor.

The man came in and, after sitting down, said, "How you doing, Trey?"

Trey looked at him stoically with his hand a mere few inches from his gun as he said, "I hope you don't think I'm being rude, but do I know you?"

"What happened up in those mountains two and a half years ago? I just retired from active duty, and I have to know. Nearly a hundred Pagans dead, with not one survivor to tell us what happened. That old farmhouse demolished. Not that I mind, since they used to hold KKK meetings there in the thirties and forties and they burned blacks on the cross there in the field or hung them in the woods. One was my great-grandfather. I'm glad that godforsaken place is gone, but how did you do it?"

"You're Demps's partner. I didn't recognize you initially. I'm sorry, but what is your name?"

The man seemed to ignore the question and said, "You know, the FBI started digging out there, and they found all kinds of bodies. They identified Jimmy and some of the other Dreadnaught leaders. How in the hell did you get out of that one? Come on, Trey. I've got all afternoon—tell me your story. I had written you off as dead when you left the station in Asheville over thirty years ago refusing to cooperate with us. You were a dead man walking. Yet here you sit before me, looking well, I might add."

"Well, officer or captain or whatever you are, I really wish I had a clue as to what you are talking about. I told you back then that the Dreadnaughts had agreed to leave me alone, and they did. End of story. Regarding—what did you call them, the Pagans?—I have no idea who they are, but I must tell you that I am happy to hear that the farmhouse was destroyed. That was an evil place, put there by the devil himself."

The man laughed and shook his head as he tossed Trey's Rolex watch, which he had lost that night two and a half years ago, onto his desk. It was a gift from Tara. "How many Pagans you reckon wore 18-carat-gold Rolex watches with the inscription 'Trey I love you—Tara' on the back? You must be a superhero or something." He then got up and began to walk out the door.

As he neared the door, Trey said, "Hey, Willie," and as the man turned around, Trey asked, "You surf?"

"Do I look like I surf?"

"Well, if you can sit on a surfboard in the ocean long enough, I'll tell you the whole story."

As the two left the office together, Willie laughed, slapped Trey on the back, and said, "Shit, you knew exactly who I was when I walked in your door. Do I know you? What's your name?"

As they drove to his house, Trey said, "So why didn't you tell anyone? Why didn't you give the FBI my watch?"

"I'm not sure. I was just glad the house was destroyed and the Pagans were dead. They were vicious sons a' bitches. They killed a few of my fellow officers, good men all. They were far worse than the Dreadnaughts, and as you know, the Dreadnaughts were ruthless. When I picked the watch up off the ground behind where the house used to be, I looked at the inscription on the back, just smiled, and slipped it in my pocket. I suppose I figured that you were forced to do what you did, and I didn't think you deserved any trouble. The FBI would have been all up your ass within hours."

They got to Trey's house and went upstairs, and Trey threw Willie a pair of surf shorts.

"You don't really expect me to wear these?"

"Yes, and I want you to change in front of me."

"Oh, you still don't trust me completely. You want to make sure I'm not wired."

"Well, it's not because I enjoy looking at naked black men."

The two men got to the beach, and Trey laughed heartily as Willie attempted to paddle through the waves on Trey's old surfboard. After reaching calm waters beyond the break of the waves, Willie struggled for several minutes before he got his balance and figured out how to sit on the board.

The two men sat on the boards for two hours as Trey related the entire story to Willie, whose expression alternated between great excitement and disbelief at what he was being told.

When Trey finished the story, Willie slapped the water, nearly falling off his board, and said, "Damn, that's the most incredible story I've ever heard. It's even much better than I imagined. I should write a book about it, but nobody would believe it."

"You have another problem, Willie. If you did, I'd have to kill you."

"No, no, I'm only kidding about the book. This story, no part of this story, will ever leave my lips. I just wanted to know for myself."

After they paddled in, it was late afternoon, and they sat on the beach drinking beer that Trey had stopped to purchase on the way to the beach. He called Tara, and she met them there thirty minutes later.

As she approached, Trey looked at her and held up his left hand, saying, "Look, honey, the watch you gave me that I lost at the farmhouse."

Tara looked at Trey and his friend. "What's going on, Trey?" She shuddered as he revealed that he had told Willie the whole story of the Dreadnaughts and the annihilation of the Pagans. "Trey, these matters are never discussed outside of our family, with the exception of Skinny and Mack, who lived through them."

"I know, but it's okay, Tara, I promise. He will never repeat it to anyone, nor will I again."

Tara invited Willie over for dinner. While eating, she looked at him and intensely said, "Willie, I want your word that you will never utter a word of this to anyone, never."

"Hey, I love you two, and I just wanted to know what happened for my own personal knowledge, but you've got my word, Tara, I promise."

"He could have given the FBI my watch and involved me in the Pagan massacre if he wanted to," said Trey.

At the conclusion of dinner, Trey asked Willie what his future plans were. "I really don't know. I haven't really thought much about it yet."

"Do you have any family?" asked Tara.

"No, nobody living. Investigating gangs was my life."

"Where will you go, back to Asheville?" asked Trey.

"No, I really don't know to tell you the truth.

"Need a job?" asked Tara.

"What kind of job?"

Tara looked at Trey and said, "There is plenty of room for him in the guesthouse in Bimini, and Sam and Missy can't have too much security."

"That's a great idea."

Willie pounced on the idea. He would spend his remaining days on Bimini, drinking beer and protecting the girls.

Tara, Trey, and Willie flew to Bimini a couple of days later. Willie and Mack hit it off almost immediately, and Willie quickly became a member of the family. Mack did not have the biker racist mentality, and he had served in 'Nam, where the courage of a man was the standard by which he was measured, not the color of his skin. Willie, although a retired officer, didn't even mind Mack's pot smoking much as he was just happy to be in a beautiful place and be a part of a good family, which he never really had been before.

As Tara, Trey, and Missy sat in the main house waiting for Sam to return from the restaurant, Missy was acting a little strangely. Sam walked in and was startled to find Trey and Tara there.

"Who is that guy hanging out by the guesthouse with Mack?" Sam asked.

"He's a new member of your grounds crew and security force," responded Trey.

"Well, I guess two are better than one. Now sit down. I need to talk to both of you." Sam looked at Trey and then Tara and announced, "I'm pregnant. I know forty-nine is a little old to have a baby, but I am so excited."

As she waited for their response, Trey said insensitively, "Please tell me the kid's not Mack's."

Tara screamed, ran to Sam, and threw her arms around her. "Don't listen to Trey. That's great news. I am so excited. I can't wait to help with the baby shower."

Sam explained that she had met a guy while managing the restaurant and bar and they started hanging out together. He was a business owner on the island. "He rents jet-skis, catamarans, and surfboards to tourists. I know you'll love him." She continued to look at Trey to gauge his reaction.

Tara spoke up. "That's wonderful, Sam. We can't wait to meet him, can we, Trey?"

"I guess not."

Later that evening, Sam's boyfriend, Austin, came over for dinner. He looked like a typical surfer who never grew up. Like Sam, he was in his late forties. As Tara, Missy, and Sam cooked dinner in the kitchen, Trey and Austin stepped out onto the front porch with a couple of beers. Trey called Mack and Willie up from the guesthouse.

Once they arrived, Trey looked at Austin grimly and said, "You see these two guys right here? You don't want to mess with them. They're very bad men. If you ever lay a hand on Sam or mistreat her in any way, they will be knocking on your door, and I promise you, you're not going to like what they will do to you. Do you understand?"

"Yes, sir, but you've got nothing to worry about. I love your sister." He then told Trey that he had planned to ask Sam to marry him, but he wanted to wait to meet Trey to ask for his permission.

"What a great guy," uttered Mack.

"Okay, Mack," said Trey, "you and Willie are excused."

"I'll tell you what," Trey said to Austin, "you and I will hang out tomorrow and do a little surfing; then I'll give you my answer."

"That's great."

Trey and Austin met at 11:00 a.m. at Toby and Sam's for an early lunch. The more they talked, the more Trey liked him. They then went surfing for a couple of hours, and they had a blast. Tara, Sam, and Skinny showed up to watch the boys surf. The men went in to say hi and inspect the girls in their bikinis. Trey, ever the competitor, told the girls that he and Austin were going to have a surfing contest and the girls and Skinny were going to be the judges. As they paddled out and waited for a set of waves to roll in, he looked at Austin and said, "If you beat me, you've got my permission."

The two went at it furiously for about thirty minutes before returning to Skinny and the girls. "What are the results?" asked Trey. "Who won?" Sam looked at Austin and declared him the winner as she gave him a kiss.

Trey looked at Skinny and said, "Well, my old friend Skinny, it looks as if you're going to be the deciding vote."

"Wait a minute," said Tara. "I haven't voted yet."

As Tara announced that she was voting for Austin, Trey looked at her, smiled, and said, "Now that just isn't right."

As Tara was running her hands through his hair and telling Trey that he was very good also and the competition was close, Skinny said, "Oh hell, Trey, he beat you by a good margin."

Trey, realizing that it was true and that he was going to give Austin his permission regardless of the outcome, laughed and said, "Let's go eat at the outdoor bar. I'm starving."

A couple of months later, everyone came for the wedding. All of Trey and Tara's children were there, and a great time was had by all. It made Trey extremely happy that Sam had found someone who made her so content, although he was not so sure about the wisdom of having a child at her age.

On the way to the reception, Sam had the limousine stop at the cemetery so that she could introduce her new husband to her father. "I'm so happy, Daddy," she said as she and Austin stood in front of Toby's grave.

Tara looked from the limo and remarked, "He's looking down on us a happy man."

"You hope he's looking down," said Trey sarcastically as Tara slapped him in the shoulder.

26

One summer Saturday night in July of 2026 at Toby and Sam's, Skinny and Mack were upstairs playing poker and drinking with the chief of police and a few regulars. Luck was not on Skinny's side this night, so he retreated downstairs and went to the outside bar. He sat down with his feet perched on the deck rail, and he was looking up at the stars hanging out over the ocean. He was thinking of his old buddy Toby and the times they had experienced together when he overheard some derogatory remarks being made behind him.

Three fairly large middle-aged men, obviously having had too much to drink, were hassling two gay men who were locals and frequented the bar a couple of nights a week. Skinny turned his head and yelled, "Leave them alone. They're welcome here, and they're good people."

One of the drunken men yelled back, "What are you going to do about it, old man? Hell, you've only got one hand."

"Yeah," said another as the three laughed heartily, "what the hell are two gay guys and a one-handed sissy going to do?"

Sam, standing at the door separating the back porch bar from the restaurant and overhearing the conversation as it escalated in the wrong direction, summoned one of the waitresses to go immediately to get Mack and the others from the poker room.

Skinny, still seated and very drunk, retorted, "You three think you're pretty bad, huh? You are damn lucky my friend Toby is not here. Your asses would have already been kicked."

One of the men walked over to Skinny, grabbed him by the shirt, picked him up, and threw him down as he said, "Where's your friend Toby now?" As he hit the deck, the police chief came through the door followed by Mack and a couple of others.

The chief showed his badge and said, "Gentlemen, what's going on here? Why are you picking on this man?" As Skinny struggled to his feet, the chief approached the men and asked if they had any weapons before frisking them and announcing, "They're clean." He then went and took a seat next to Skinny, looked at Mack, and said, "They're all yours." Mack looked at the three and got a big smile on his face.

One of the men said, "What kind of a police chief are you?"

"The kind that makes sure it's a fair fight."

Skinny laughed and said, "That ain't fair. These three wimps against Mack. Mack'll kill em."

One of the men approached Mack as he continued to smile at him. As the other two come up on each side of their friend, one said, "He doesn't look so tough." He barely got the words out before Mack shot a straight right into his nose. He buckled to his knees and then to the ground, completely knocked out as blood spurted from his nose.

The other two immediately backed off, looking to the police chief as one of them asked, "Aren't you going to do anything?"

"You apologize to Skinny, and I'll call him off."

Skinny said, "Oh hell, they don't need to apologize to me. I've been shot five times and stabbed at least ten. They need to apologize to the two gentlemen over there."

The two gay men got big smiles on their faces and waved at the two still standing. "Hey, fellas," they said.

"Oh, come on," complained Mack, "I was just starting to have fun."

The two men walked over and apologized. They then picked up their friend, still lying unconscious on the deck, and carried him out of the bar.

Skinny sat on the deck for a couple more hours and drank and laughed with the gay men. He had become friendly with them in the past, and they frequently had drinks together when they came to the restaurant. They were from different worlds, and he would laugh at their stories. They would listen in awe and amazement at Skinny's stories of his past adventures.

Skinny slipped out of the bar that night with a half-full bottle in his hand. He walked the half mile to Toby's gravesite and sat on the ground beside it. He took slugs from the bottle and laughed as he recounted out loud some of their past escapades together.

The following morning, Sam and Mack went looking for Skinny. It didn't take long to find him, as they had a good idea where he was. Mack picked him up off the ground, and they took him home and put him into his bed.

Trey, Tara, and Amanda flew in later in the morning. Once they arrived at the gated compound and unpacked, they sat down with Missy and Sam and asked how Skinny was doing. Sam said, "You know, he is lost without Toby. We found him passed out with an empty bottle in his hand this morning at Dad's gravesite. Although it's been almost four years since Dad died, he is clearly depressed. He just misses him so much." Tara decided that she and Amanda, who had finished her residency in neurosurgery a year ago and had a week off from her job at the hospital, would take Skinny out for lunch and try to cheer him up.

They knocked on Skinny's door around noon, and a still groggy Skinny immediately lit up when he saw them. They waited while he took a shower and got dressed. As they were leaving, he announced that he needed his medicine. He opened a pantry door and pulled out a bottle of Jack Daniels and took a hefty chug out of the bottle. He said as he put the cap back on the bottle, "I feel much better now; let's go." Tara looked at Amanda, who had a stunned look on her face, and just rolled her eyes.

They settled on a little bistro down the beach from Toby and Sam's. Tara knew that the bistro didn't serve alcohol, and she wanted to have a conversation with Skinny while he was sober so she could gauge how he was really doing. They ate and had a really good conversation. It was clear how much Skinny missed Toby, but she got the impression that he was doing relatively well.

Tara teased Skinny, "I heard you have a couple of new friends. Are they like Toby?"

Skinny laughed robustly and said, "Not exactly, but you know what, they're actually really good guys, and I like talking to them. They make me laugh."

As they exited the bistro, Skinny put his arms out to stop the girls walking on each side of him and said, "Oh no, this is not good."

"What's the problem?" asked Amanda.

The three men from the night before were standing about twenty feet before them, and their expressions made it clear that they were looking for revenge. If that wasn't bad enough, they had two more friends with them.

Skinny said, "Now, guys, I'm the one you have a problem with. Let the girls leave."

Tara said, "I'm not going anywhere. Why would you guys want to harm an old man like Skinny? Surely you can find a better fight somewhere else."

"Shut your mouth, missy," said one of the men.

Amanda said, "What are you guys trying to prove?"

The man with the disfigured black-and-blue nose struck her with the back of his hand, knocking her to the ground. As Tara went to Amanda and dropped to her knees, the men began pummeling Skinny.

As they punched and kicked him, Tara yelled, "You have no idea what you are doing. You are messing with the wrong guy."

Another man came to her and backhanded her, saying, "Shut up, you stupid bitch. You have no idea who you are messing with."

As the men left in a car, several people came to the aid of Skinny, Tara, and Amanda. The police chief was called, and he and an ambulance were there within minutes. A severely beaten Skinny was rushed to the hospital. The chief took Tara and Amanda back to the house. They were crying as they entered, and the sides of their faces were pink and swollen. As they explained to Trey and Austin what had happened, the look on Trey's face said it all.

Trey called Mack and Willie up from the guesthouse. He explained to them briefly what had happened, and they also got the look on their faces that clearly indicated that they were going to war. Trey looked at the chief and said, "I want you back here within one hour with two of your best men, and you need to know where we can find them. There is a big bonus in this for you. It's bad enough the cowards did this to Skinny, but nobody, and I mean nobody, hits my wife and daughter." He looked at Mack and Willie and said sternly, "Get ready. Lock and load. We won't be taking any prisoners today." Although Austin wanted to go, Trey said no, telling him that he needed to take the girls to the hospital to be with Skinny.

The chief came back in forty-five minutes with two of his men. The group of men was at a local dive bar drinking heavily and bragging about what they had done. A couple of the chief's undercover men were in the bar keeping an eye on them. The six jumped into a police van heavily armed and headed toward the bar. The two undercover officers inside had been secretly advising patrons to leave so that there would be as few people as possible inside the bar.

The van pulled up to the bar, and Trey led the men inside. The five men were having a chugging contest when Trey landed the butt of his semiautomatic rifle squarely on the already busted nose of one of the men. Glass and blood flew everywhere. The undercover officers drew their guns, and all of the remaining patrons and the bar's employees were quickly cleared from the bar, leaving only Trey's group and the five assailants.

The man with the bloody nose had a look of terror on his face as Trey handed his rifle to Mack and began beating the man as he yelled, "You hit my wife, you struck my daughter, and you beat an old man." As the man lay unconscious on the floor, Trey told his four friends to take a seat. He turned a chair backward and faced the men. He asked Willie for his pistol. "Which of you brave men hit the girls?" After a few seconds of silence passed, he shot each of the men in a knee. As they writhed in pain on the floor, he instructed the others to take all five of the men to the van.

The men were cuffed before being rushed out of the bar and thrown in the back of the van. The chief, his two officers who came with him, Trey, Mack, and Willie took off in the van.

Trey asked the police chief, "Do you have a remote area of the jail in which to stick these cowards where they will be in isolation and never see the light of day again?"

"Yes, we have an underground wing just for serious degenerates who will never get out."

"What kind of bullshit is that?" asked Mack emotionally. "I thought we were going to take them somewhere and kill them. They don't deserve to live. Remember, Trey, you said we were taking no prisoners."

"I know, Mack, but I don't feel right about killing them."

The chief said, "Believe me, Mack, it's dingy down there. They'll suffer a lot more than if we kill them."

"Mack, it's the right thing to do," stated Willy.

Trey looked at the chief and said, "Can you assure me that they will never get out? If they do, they'll come after my family again, and I can't risk that."

"You have my word. Once someone goes down there, he doesn't come back up until he is dead."

Trey, Mack, and Willie were dropped off at the hospital. As they arrived, the girls were all crying. Tara ran to Trey and informed him that Skinny was not doing well. His brain was hemorrhaging, and the doctors believed that he didn't have long to live. Trey looked at Amanda, and she confirmed that there was nothing that could be done to save him.

Trey went alone into Skinny's room. "Man, Skinny, you don't look so good."

Skinny's eyes were swollen shut. Trey fought back tears, as he considered Skinny to be a part of his family.

Skinny forced a smile and labored as he said, "Trey, I love you like you were my own son. Promise me two things."

"Anything."

"First, you get those bastards who did this to me and the girls."

"Already done."

Skinny strained to smile and said, "I figured as much. Second, you bury me next to your father."

Trey said as he held Skinny's hand, "Skinny, I wouldn't let it happen any other way. Batman and Robin, buried side by side. You make me two promises as well."

"What's that?"

"When you get to heaven, you give Dad a hug for me and tell him I love him."

"What's the second thing?" asked a rapidly fading Skinny.

"The two of you have a shot of whiskey for me."

Skinny smiled just before his hand went limp and he passed into the next life. Trey, with tears running down his face, said, "Good-bye, old friend. God speed."

After the funeral, Amanda came to Trey sobbing and said to him, "Daddy, I didn't know your dad or Skinny very well. I've heard some of the stories of course. Do you think they're in heaven?"

"Well, baby, that's a hard one to answer. Only God knows for sure. They did the best they could with what they had. I would like to think that's what God takes into consideration, but I don't know for sure. I suppose they were like most people. They did a lot of really good things, and they did some not-so-good things. I think the important thing is that they tried. They were flawed, but they tried. And they loved, and they were loved. I can tell you I believe that when we die, we will be reunited in heaven with the family members who went before us, and I believe that Toby and Skinny will be there."

Prior to departing the island, Trey visited the police chief, handed him an envelope, and stressed the importance that Sam and his mother be protected at all times. He then went alone to Toby and Skinny's burial site carrying a bottle of Jack Daniels and a shot glass. There were two men standing there weeping.

"Hi, who are you?" asked Trey.

"We were Skinny's friends," responded one.

The other said, "He was a fierce biker, but he accepted us for who we are, and he even protected us. He was the best of friends. The stories he told. You wouldn't believe some of them if I told you. He told us that he, Mack, and his boy Trey killed an entire motorcycle gang of more than a hundred bikers."

"Well," said Trey, "you can't believe everything you hear."

Trey looked at the headstones, poured himself a shot, and said, "To Batman and Robin, the warriors. I love you guys." After downing the shot, he looked at the two men and asked, "You two want one?"

"Hell yes we do," emphatically responded one of them. Trey poured him a shot. He said, "To Skinny, the best of friends," before gingerly downing the shot of whiskey. Trey then poured the second one, and the man said, "And the fiercest biker," before consuming his shot with a grimaced look on his face.

Trey said, "You two take care of yourselves," and began to walk away.

As he walked farther, one of the men yelled, "Hey, mister, what is your name?"

Trey laughed to himself, turned slowly, and said, "Trey." The two men were awestruck with their mouths wide open and eyes as big as saucers as he said, "You know, guys, there were closer to two hundred bikers in that motorcycle gang." He then turned and walked away chuckling as the two men just stared at him in amazement.

27

It was November of 2026, three months after Trey had turned fifty-nine in August and four months since Skinny passed in July. Trey was playing pool upstairs at Toby and Sam's with Mack, Willie, and a couple of the island's police officers one Wednesday evening. It was a slow night, and Tara, Sam, and Missy were downstairs drinking wine, telling stories, and laughing.

A large gruff-looking man entered the restaurant and asked the greeter for Trey. She went to the table where the girls were talking and told them that someone was looking for Trey. Sam went to the entrance and asked the man if she could help him.

"I need to speak to Trey, and Trey only."

"May I tell him who is asking for him?

"My name's Bob, and I need to speak with him right now."

Sam was getting concerned since the man was wearing a black leather vest and he did not seem as if he was there with good intentions. "Turn around," she said. The man slowly turned around, hesitated briefly, and then turned and faced her. She had an angry look on her face as she said, "The Pagans. You're not welcome here."

"I'm by myself, and I just want to talk to him. I'm here to make peace, and I mean him no harm."

Sam escorted the man to a seat at the bar and said, "I'll see what I can do."

Sam made her way back to the entryway and walked up the stairs. She went into the room and said, "Trey, a Pagan biker is here to talk to you. He's at the bar. He says his name is Bob." Trey's and Mack's faces turned white.

Mack said, "Go get Tara and Missy out of here. I'll take care of this."

"Is he alone?" asked Trey as he looked out the window overlooking the parking lot and didn't see anything unusual.

"I think so." Trey instructed her to bring him up.

The two officers drew their revolvers and stood on each side of the door. Mack and Willie, sitting on each side of Trey, held their revolvers on the table in front of them. As the man opened the door and entered the room, the two officers immediately put their guns to his head. Mack walked up and frisked him thoroughly. He then escorted the man to the front of the table before retaking his seat.

Trey looked at him for a few seconds before asking, "So what's your business with me?"

"That's easy. You took out almost our entire group over four years ago. There were only a few of us who were fortunate enough not to be at the farmhouse that night. There are about thirty of us now. Your father also took hundreds of thousands, if not millions, from the Dreadnaughts, and when we crushed the Dreadnaughts and took over their territory, that became our money Animal took."

Mack said, "Kiss my ass. You're not walking out of here alive, and you're damned sure not getting a penny."

"Sure, you can kill me now, but others will come and bring the war to you here, where you live. Also, we know where your kids are back in the states, and we'll go after them."

As Mack stood and said, "Bring it on," Trey told him to sit down.

Trey asked, "What do you want? What will it take to get you leeches out of our lives forever?"

"We built a new house where the farmhouse was before you blew it up. You know where it is. You come alone, Trey, with a million dollars in cash, and you walk away. You'll never hear from us again. Be there at noon this coming Saturday and this can all be over."

A furious Mack said, "You can't be seriously considering this, Trey. Let me take care of this one now, and I'll go to Asheville and hunt down the other cowards one by one." He then looked at the Pagan and said, "You should rename your tricycle gang the pussies."

Bob laughed disdainfully, looked at Trey, and said, "Noon Saturday. That gives you over two days. If you don't show, the war starts, and you can't want that." He got up and walked out of the room.

Sam and Tara joined the men upstairs, and they explained the matter to the women. "Where does this end?" asked a frustrated Tara. Sam told Trey to just give them the money. Willie said that wouldn't work.

"They'll be back for more, and we'll never get them out of our lives."

Trey looked ahead in deep thought, reflecting back upon the time when Jimmy broke his promise to him that the Dreadnaughts would leave him alone, before saying, "He's right. We don't negotiate with terrorists. We need to end this now."

"But how?" asked an exasperated Tara.

Trey said, "I'm leaving by myself. I've got an idea."

"Hell no, I'm going with you," exclaimed Mack.

"No, Mack. I'm going to handle this. You all are going to have to trust me. Mack and Willie, I need you to stay with the girls."

The following morning, Trey kissed Tara on the forehead and assured her that everything was going to be okay. He then flew out to New York and checked into a hotel. That evening he took a cab to a residential building in the city. He was met by security outside of the building, and they asked who he was there to see.

"Mr. Gambotti. My name's Trey Jackson, and I have some important information he wants to know." One of the security guards buzzed Mr. Gambotti and advised him that a Trey Jackson wanted to see him and that he had some important information for him.

"I don't know a Trey Jackson. Ask him what information he has."

The man looked at Trey and said, "Well, you heard him. What've you got that Mr. Gambotti needs to know?"

"Tell him it's highly personal, and I need to tell him to his face."

The man laughed and said, "Oh shit, he's going to love this." He buzzed Gambotti again and said, "He wants to tell you to your face. Do you want me to get rid of him?"

"Yes. I don't have time for this crap."

Trey pushed the large man to the side, pushed the call button, and said, "Mr. Gambotti, I know who killed your brother thirty-three years ago."

The two security guards grabbed Trey by the shirt, and one said, "You've done it now. Who in the hell do you think you are?"

One hit Trey in the face just before Gambotti's voice came through the intercom, "Send him up."

Trey looked at the man who hit him, smiled, and said, "Nice punch." The men grabbed him and threw him inside.

Once inside, he was handed over to two stoic men in nice black suits and led to an elevator. In the elevator, one of the men frisked him. Neither said a word to him.

"You guys ever say anything, like how are you doing?" asked Trey.

One of the men turned his head to the side, stared at Trey, and said, "Do you have any idea who you are going to see? How 'bout, 'Good luck, chump.'"

"Thank you," said Trey sarcastically as the two men shook their heads.

The elevator came to a stop and opened into what looked like a waiting room where they were met by two more men in black suits. They went through a door and into a large living room area where three men were seated. Mr. Gambotti, in his late sixties, instructed Trey to sit down. The four men who escorted Trey into the room remained standing, one on each side of his chair, with the other two on each side of the chair on which Gambotti sat. The other two men already in the room were seated on a sofa.

Gambotti looked at Trey and asked, "So what do you know about my brother? Over thirty years have passed, and the organization could never determine who the bastard was who killed him. We had our guesses, and a lot of blood was spilled between us and a couple of our rivals, but nobody ever knew for sure who did it."

"Mr. Gambotti, first let me tell you that I am sorry for your loss."

Gambotti interrupted him and said, "Stop the bullshit. If you know anything, I suggest that you get to the point, and you had better not be wasting my time."

"When I was twenty-five, I was messed up, and I wanted to be a part of a motorcycle gang called the Dreadnaughts. I would hang out with them, and I was basically their errand boy, if you know what I mean. A group called the Pagans formed, and initially they were friendly with the Dreadnaughts and stayed out of their territory, and they helped them with drug deals and their rivals. On a few occasions, the Dreadnaughts and Pagans would party together. The Pagans bragged excessively about how they assassinated your brother in a bathroom stall while he was taking a crap in a nightclub in Atlanta. They said this would cause a war between the crime families up north because it would appear as though another mob family did it. They said they did this as a favor to the Dreadnaughts because it would open up the Southeast for them to take over the cocaine trade in that area. Shortly after that, I got out and went in a different direction with my life. I heard that the Pagans wiped out the Dreadnaughts several years later and took the Southeast territory, your territory, for themselves."

"Why are you telling me this? Why should I believe you?"

"Because the Pagans killed my father, who was a Dreadnaught. He was high up in the Dreadnaught hierarchy, and somehow the Pagans have tracked me down. I have done reasonably well in business, and they want me to deliver a million dollars to them by noon sharp on Saturday or they're going to kill me and my family."

"What do you want from me?"

Trey stood and handed him a map he had drafted indicating the exact location of the farmhouse. He said, "The way I see it, I'll show up at noon on Saturday and give them the money, and then they'll probably kill me.

Even if they let me go, it's just a matter of time before they ask for more. Or, if you're a man of integrity who doesn't want to see the Pagans do this to a good family and you have the honor and character to avenge the death of your brother, you'll show up. It's your choice." Trey stood and walked out.

Trey flew to Asheville on Friday morning and spent the remainder of the day gathering the million dollars in cash and resting.

At 11:00 a.m. on Saturday, Trey got into his rental car and placed the suitcase in the passenger seat. He looked at himself in the rearview mirror and said, "God, this is my last battle. I am asking you to deliver me from harm one last time, but if it is my time to go, I ask only that you keep Missy, Sam, Tara, and my kids safe." He embarked on that dreadfully familiar drive up the mountain.

As Trey approached the small town just down the hill from the old farmhouse, he called Tara one last time. "Trey, what are you doing?" she said frantically. "Are you facing the Pagans by yourself? That's suicide. Please don't do it. I can't lose you now."

"Tara, grab the necklace I gave you ten years ago, read it, and if I don't call you in about an hour, be happy for the time we had together. I love you." He then hung up the phone.

Tara ran to Sam and Missy crying. After they calmed her down, Tara put the phone down on the table in front of her and retrieved the necklace. The three women sat silently, each with tears running down her face.

Trey pulled into the field and was immediately stopped by three Pagans. They ordered him out of his car. He was frisked for weapons and then instructed to walk in front of them to the new house the Pagans had built to replace the old farmhouse. As he walked through the field, he repeated to himself, "Even though I walk through the valley of the shadow of death, I will fear no evil, for thou art with me."

As Trey neared the house, he guessed that about twenty Pagans with automatic weapons surrounded it. Three more Pagans, including Bob, whom he had encountered in Bimini, walked out of the entryway and stood ten feet in front of him and the three Pagans who had escorted him through the field. "Hi, Trey," said Bob, who appeared to be the leader. "No explosives this time. The house has been heavily guarded all week. Throw the suitcase down in front of you." Trey threw the suitcase down and said to himself, *Come on, Gambotti, don't let me down. Where are you?* One of the three men surrounding Trey then went to the suitcase and opened it. He looked through the suitcase and announced, "It looks like it's all here, boss."

Bob smiled and said, "Now that's a smart boy, Trey."

"How do I know you'll leave us alone now?"

"You don't," said Bob as the six Pagans broke out into laughter.

"You killed my father, and I have given you a million dollars in cash. Isn't that enough?"

"Well, you throw in Amanda and maybe we'll have a deal. She's hot."

Trey responded loudly and angrily, "You jerkoffs have no honor."

Bob walked toward Trey, stopped five feet in front of him, and said quietly, "You blow up our headquarters and you take out 95 percent of our members. Honor to me is your million dollars and your head on a platter."

As Bob began to raise his handgun, Trey yelled, praying that he hadn't miscalculated Gambotti, "And the Pagans' killing of Mr. Gambotti thirty-three years ago in cold blood, that was honorable?" With his gun pointed at Trey's forehead, Bob got a confused look on his face, and before he could say anything, there was a zip in the air as he fell to the ground. Trey immediately dropped to the ground as the zips of sniper-fired bullets filled the air. The Pagans almost simultaneously dropped like flies. It was over within thirty seconds. When the zips stopped, Trey got up and walked over to Bob, who, with his last breath struggled to say, "Who the hell is Gambotti?"

As Trey looked up, the place was crawling with guys who looked like Navy Seals. Gambotti came limping across the field yelling, "Kill all the Pagan bastards. Make sure they're all dead." He approached Trey and said, "So were you nervous? Did you think we were going to show?"

"Never doubted you for a second, Mr. Gambotti."

"You're full of shit, but I admire your courage."

One of Gambotti's men came out of the house with a book. He told Gambotti that it had the names and addresses of all thirty of the gang's members. Gambotti instructed him to check all the deceaseds' names and check them off the list. About twenty minutes later, he came to Gambotti and said there were five Pagans unaccounted for.

"You know what to do. I want them all dead within twenty-four hours."

"Yes, Mr. Gambotti."

"Man, you guys are thorough," said Trey.

"Hey, we're professionals. We've got to take the entire membership out so that there's no chance for retaliation. Within twenty-four hours, there will not be a Pagan left on the face of this earth. You'll never hear from them again, I promise you that." Trey thanked him, and Gambotti said, "Get back to your family, and thank you for helping me settle this score. I can now finally have the satisfaction of knowing that I avenged my brother's death." Trey hesitated for a moment, looking at the suitcase filled with money on the ground. Gambotti laughed and said, "Oh hell, take it. It's your money. Now get out of here."

Trey got into his car, and as he turned onto the concrete road at the bottom of the hill, he called Tara. She answered the phone, and as he stated that he would be back in Bimini for dinner, she screamed and the girls began jumping up and down, hugging each other and crying tears of joy.

Trey said, "It's over, baby. All the Pagans are dead or will be dead within a day."

Tara screamed, "How did you do it, babe? If you're leaving, how are the ones alive going to be dead in the next day?"

Trey smiled and said, "Mr. Gambotti."

"Mr. Gambotti? Who's he?"

"Toby killed his brother thirty-three years ago. I'll explain it all when I get back."

As he drove down the mountain, Trey got a wide smile on his face, looked at himself in the mirror, and said, "Jackson, Trey Jackson." As he drove farther and the enormity of what he had just pulled off fully hit him, he yelled, "Even though I walk through the valley of the shadow of death, I will fear no evil, for you are with me, and I, I am the baddest son of a bitch in the valley."

Trey returned to Bimini where he was greeted by the whole crew at Sam and Missy's house. After sitting in the family room and recounting the entire story to everyone for thirty minutes, he got up, hugged everyone, grabbed a beer from the refrigerator, and went to the theater room. He reclined in one of the seats, and as he drank the beer, he became somewhat delirious since he hadn't slept much in the last few days. He attempted to have a conversation with God. "Lord," he said, "I apologize for the comment I made about being the baddest son of a bitch in the valley. That was all you. You have brought me through the valley of evil and almost certain death three times now. I would like to think that you are a kind and forgiving God and that my dad and Skinny are in heaven. I know it's a lot to ask, but is there any possible way that you can say something to me or give me a sign?"

After waiting several seconds, Trey clicked on the big movie screen wired to a large satellite dish outside, and he watched as the announcer said, "The Lakers trail by one with eight seconds left. Kwan steels the ball and goes the other way for a monstrous dunk. Oh my God—Lakers win! Lakers win!" Trey got a huge smile on his face and mumbled, "Thank you, God," before passing out.

As Trey fell into a deep sleep, he dreamed that he and Tara had decided to go back to the Grove Park Inn in Asheville to celebrate their upcoming thirty-fifth wedding anniversary. They had spent the last couple of weeks at Missy and Sam's house in Alice Town. When they told the others of their plans, Willie spoke up and asked if he could go with them on the flight to Asheville since he wanted to visit with some of his old police buddies.

They flew into Asheville, and Willie went his own way while Trey and Tara caught a cab to the Grove Park Inn. They were last there a few months after they got married, and they sat on the balcony overlooking the mountains and valleys below, sharing a bottle of wine and reminiscing about the last thirty-five years.

The following morning, they decided to take a cab to Antique Row to see how it had changed and eat some lunch. They ate lunch, and at the end of the meal, Tara suggested that they take a stroll down the second row where the Apache store had been located over thirty years ago. As they walked down the second row, they thought they saw Willie walking into a store about where Apache had been located. As they got closer, they were amazed that the Apache store was still there, and they were intrigued as to why Willie would be in there.

Tara and Trey made their way into the store, but nobody seemed to be tending it. The interior of the store had not changed much, including the merchandise. They walked toward the back of the store where Tara had met with the old Indian woman and Toby many years ago. As they neared the back office, they heard voices. They looked in the office and stood speechless for several seconds.

Willie said, "Trey and Tara, how are you? Come on in. We were just talking about you."

They walked in and stared at Willie, the old Indian woman, and Tom, Trey's old law partner. They had not aged at all. Tara continued to stare, flabbergasted, not knowing what to say.

Trey had a perplexed look on his face as he asked, in a low tone of voice, "Who are you three?"

Willie responded, "I am the father, Tom is the son, and the Indian woman is the Holy Spirit."

"No disrespect intended, Willie, but do you really expect us to believe that you three are the Holy Trinity and the Apache store is your office?"

"Well, you can believe what you want, but that is exactly right."

"Do you want us to leave?" asked Tara, still in shock from what she was seeing and hearing.

"Oh no," responded the Indian woman, "we were expecting you. Have a seat and relax, dear. You know, I've missed you very much."

Trey and Tara sat down, and he looked at Willie and said, "So God is a black man. You realize of course that a lot of people would have a hard time believing all this?"

Willie laughed and said, "I know. That's why we are who we are and all the rest of you are like children, not understanding much."

"What should we call you?" asked Trey with a hint of sarcasm in his voice. "God, Jesus, and Holy Spirit?"

"No," laughed Tom, "Willie, Tom, and Indian woman are fine. Just don't refer to us in derogatory terms. A little bit of reverence would be nice."

"Tom, how in the hell are you the son, or Jesus? You insisted that I represent Marshall, and you had to know that he was guilty. You are, after all, Jesus."

"It was a test, and the knife did fall out of his pocket in your office, didn't it?"

"And what about the southern mansion you lived in? Since when does Jesus live in the lap of luxury?"

"Why not? There are many misconceptions that you humans have about us."

Tara, still in shock, looked at the Indian woman and said, "I've missed you too."

The Indian woman smiled at her and responded, "You're so beautiful. You've always been my favorite."

"Thank you," said Tara timidly.

"Wait just a minute," exclaimed Trey, "this is bullshit. Are we getting punked or something? If we are, Willie, I promise you that you are fired."

Willie laughed and said, "You're firing me? Now that is funny. You haven't seen Tom in over thirty years; does he look any older? Tara, the Indian woman was in her midsixties when you spoke to her last. Does she look as if she is nearing a hundred? They haven't aged a day. Trey, do you really think that you could have got out of that situation with the Dreadnaughts and decimated the Pagans, twice, without our help?"

"The first time with the Pagans was because of Mack, and the second time was because of Gambotti. You three had nothing to do with those events, and my father saved me from the Dreadnaughts."

Willie responded, "Oh, come on, Trey. You, Skinny, and Mack took out a hundred bikers? As to Gambotti, he wasn't real thrilled about the idea, but we made sure he got there. Although I must admit, that was really creative on your part. Let's just say we did those things together."

"Okay, what do you want from us?"

"We want you to be the president of the United States," responded Tom. "We were just discussing how to accomplish this before you and Tara showed up."

"The president of the United States?" exclaimed Trey incredulously. "Again, no disrespect intended, but has the Holy Trinity been hitting the peace pipe a little too hard?"

"Trey!" exclaimed Tara with a look of disapproval on her face.

"Oh, come on, Tara, you can't be going along with this utter nonsense."

"The world is in disarray, Trey," said Willie. "Man's heart is as wicked and depraved as we've seen it since Sodom and Gomorrah. Nuclear arms, the divorce rate, children being raped and killed, people showing no concern for others, terrorist attacks, starving children, drug abuse, greed—shall I go on?"

"No, I get the picture, but why would you want me to be president? Kennedy had Marilyn and his other dalliances in the White House, Clinton had Monica and that cigar thing going, and Nixon was a crook. They had their shortcomings, but I have shot people in the knees. I have killed people. Why in the world would you choose me?"

"We don't ask that you are perfect, Trey," said Tom. "Besides, you were either saving Tara or protecting your family. Look what you did for Kwan. We know your heart."

Willie said, "When you walked through that field and repeated, 'Even though I walk through the valley of death, I will fear no evil, for thou art with me,' I was really with you. You weren't alone. That comment later about being the baddest son of a bitch in the valley was a bit much, but I kind of got a kick out of it."

"It was funny," laughed Tom.

"So just how do you propose that I become president?" asked Trey.

"You leave that up to us," responded Willie.

"You will make a beautiful first lady," the Indian woman interjected as she looked at Tara. "Just like Jackie."

"And assuming that I become president," said Trey, "how am I going to fix all of the world's problems?"

"Again, leave that up to us," responded Willie. "We'll be with you."

"Shit, I was looking forward to taking it easy and enjoying my retirement years."

"Your work here is not done, Trey," said Tom. "Think of the world that you are going to leave for your kids and grandchildren."

Willie said, "That reminds me of a part of one of my favorite poems by Robert Frost. He was a great guy. 'The woods are lovely, dark and deep. But I have promises to keep, and miles to go before I sleep, and miles to go before I sleep.' I love that poem."

"Yeah, my favorite Frost poem is 'The Road Not Taken,'" said Trey, "and this is not the road I am sure that I want to go down."

"You have a higher calling," responded Willie, "and I have faith that you'll accept the challenge and go down the right road, and that will make all the difference in this world."

Trey and Tara left, and he headed directly to a little bar on the first row of Antique Row. Tara didn't say a word on the walk to the bar, as she was still in a state of semishock. After they sat down and received their drinks, he belted his down and ordered another. As he put his glass down, Tara, still with a bewildered look on her face, asked him what he was thinking.

"I'll tell you what I'm thinking Tara. I'm thinking that was the most ridiculous conversation I've ever had. By the way, Jackie Kennedy was not anywhere near as good-looking as you are." He then smiled and said, "I guess I could send Mack to the Middle East to take out the Taliban and al-Qaida."

Trey heard someone repeating his name. Tara had her hand on his shoulder and was shaking him. "Why don't you come to bed, baby," she said. "You always wake up with a crick in your neck when you sleep all night in a recliner."

The following morning Trey awoke to Tara staring at him. "Good morning," she said. "How's my hero doing today? What were you dreaming about in the recliner last night? You were cussing at Willie while I was trying to wake you."

"It was nothing, just some crazy dream I had. Willie wanted me to be the president of the United States."

"What? By the way, our thirty-fifth anniversary is in six months, and I thought maybe we would go back to the Grove Park Inn in Asheville. What do you think?"

"As long as Willie doesn't go with us."

"Why would Willie go with us?"

"Never mind; just promise me that we will go nowhere near that damned Apache store."

28

It was June of 2028. Tara had just turned sixty-one, and Trey would be sixty-one in August. They spent half the year in Charleston and the other half in Bimini. He spent a good amount of his time in Bimini running on the beach or surfing with Austin. She would run on the beach with Trey sometimes, but most of her time was spent with Sam or lying on the beach and watching Trey surf. They were enjoying their later years.

Trey III was thirty-four and a very successful attorney in Los Angeles. He had become good friends with Kwan, and he had season tickets to the Lakers games so he could watch him play. Alec was thirty-two and had taken over the West Charleston High School basketball coaching job from Trey. Amanda was thirty-one and had her private practice in neurosurgery, although she continued to spend a large portion of her time at the hospital in Charleston performing surgery. All three were happily married, and Trey and Tara were very thankful for their good fortune.

Trey III had given Tara and Trey two grandchildren whom they saw three or four times a year. Alec had one child whom they saw frequently. Amanda was immersed in her job, and she and her husband, also a doctor, had decided to put off having kids for a few years.

Trey III flew in to the North Bimini airport with his family. When they arrived at Sam and Missy's house, Trey, Mack, Austin, and Willie were watching Kwan play in a playoff game in the theater room. Tara and Sam were in the kitchen. Trey III went to the theater room and watched the game with the boys. His wife, Kerry, and the two young children stood in the kitchen talking to Sam and Tara.

After the game was over, the boys joined the women and children in the family room. After a few minutes passed, Trey III stated that he had been approached by some influential people in Los Angeles about running for the US Senate. Willie, standing next to Trey, whispered in his ear, "We checked him out, and he's just like you. We decided to let you relax and enjoy the rest of your life." Trey stared at Willie with a blank look on his face as he processed what was happening. After several seconds, he said emphatically, "Follow me."

The two men went into the den, and Trey shut the door. "Just what the hell was that supposed to mean?" he asked.

"After our conversation at Apache a year and a half ago, we decided to let you enjoy what remaining time you have. You are sixty after all, and, Tom, the Indian woman and I discussed the situation. Your son is perfect."

"But that was just a dream."

"Not really. You asked me to speak to you or show you a sign. I did both. I gave you a sign, and then we all had a conversation. It's hard to explain. Don't try to understand it, but the conversation we had at Apache was in fact real."

"Then why didn't Tara know that it happened? She was there."

"Actually, no she wasn't. Again, don't try to understand it."

"Willie, I want you to promise me that you and your two friends will look after him and keep him safe."

"We did a pretty good job with you, didn't we? You got into a lot of shit, some of which was your own doing, and some of which you had no control over. We brought you through that valley every time."

"Yes, you did. Where will you be, here in Bimini with us, or with him?"

"Physically, I will be here at Missy and Sam's; however, I will be with Trey III at all times. It's hard to understand, Trey. Don't even try."

"If you are God, was there ever actually a Willie? I mean, a human Willie, I should say."

"Oh yes. He died many years ago at the hands of the Pagans. I just took his physical body. He's in heaven with Toby and Skinny."

"So over three years ago, when you showed up at my office in Charleston, that was you, not Willie."

"That's the best way of looking at it."

"Then all those questions you had for me, and the whole story I explained while we were sitting on surfboards in the ocean, you already knew all that."

"Oh yes, every bit of it."

Trey began laughing, and he said, "Do you mean to tell me that God can't surf?"

"I could if I had wanted to, but that would have blown my cover."

"One day when nobody is around, you and I are going to see who is the better surfer."

"Deal, but you do realize that I am going to whip your ass."

"We'll see about that."

Willie laughed and said, "You know, Trey, that is one of the things that I have always loved about you. No matter how overwhelming the odds against you, you sincerely believe that you can prevail."

"Willie, there is one thing that I would like to know about—The Holy Grail. I saw that movie, *The DaVinci Code*, about twenty years ago. Is the grail the golden chalice containing Jesus's blood at the last supper, or did Jesus actually have a baby with Mary Magdalene, and he has human descendants walking around here on earth? Is the Holy Grail the secret bloodline?"

Willie laughed loudly and responded, "That was a great movie, but I assure you that my son had no baby with Mary Magdalene, or any other woman for that matter. He was tempted, but he would have been grounded for centuries. There are no human descendants of Jesus."

"So the grail is the chalice."

"Yes, it is the object to which you humans refer in your mythology as the Holy Grail."

"Can you tell me where to find it? I assume that you know where it is."

"Yes, I do. I'll make a deal with you, Trey. You beat me in that surfing contest, and I'll tell you where to find it."

"But who will be the judges?"

"We won't need any. There will be no doubt in your mind as to who won."

Later that afternoon, Trey looked from the main house out of a window at the guesthouse and saw Willie and Mack sitting in chairs. Mack was smoking pot and talking, making wild gestures with his hands, as Willie laughed hysterically. Trey shook his head and mumbled to himself, "Missy and Sam are well protected. Mack and God. It doesn't get any better than that."

The following seven and a half years passed quickly. Tara and Trey were sixty-eight. Trey III had been elected to the US Senate seven years before and rose quickly through the ranks, becoming the bright young star of the Democratic Party.

It was January of 2036, and although only forty-one, Trey III was being persuaded to run for the presidency. Some thought that he was too young and should wait another four years, and he sought Trey's advice.

Trey met up with Willie out at the guesthouse and asked, "Is it time?"

"Yes. I can't wait any longer."

Trey advised Trey III to make his run and begin his campaign.

In January of 2037, Trey and Tara stood in the front row to watch Trey III's inaugural address. He began:

We have many issues to address, and we must do better. No longer will you get out of jail if you have intentionally harmed a child. No longer will executives on Wall Street get paid millions of dollars while the companies they lead lose money. No longer will the quality of our children's education be low on our priority list. No longer will our elderly citizens have to choose between paying for food or for badly needed medication. No longer will any of our citizens collect Social Security disability benefits if they are capable of being retrained to learn to do new jobs and contribute to our society. We will become a nation known for its fairness, empathy, and work ethic. We will strive together to make not only the United States but the world a better place for all. Collectively, we will accomplish great things, with contributions from all of our citizens commensurate with their ability to contribute.

To those in other countries who would do us harm, we will hunt you down. You can run, but you can't hide for long. To potential suicide bombers, I say to you to choose life and join us to make this world a better place for everyone rather than to pursue death and the killing of innocent civilians. To the terrorists, your time is nearing an end.

To the president of Iran, we will no longer play games with you, and we will not be lied to and played for fools. You have thirty days to allow the UN weapons inspectors unfettered access to your facilities to destroy your nuclear weapons. If you do not comply, we will consider this to be a declaration of war against the free world, and we will forcibly disarm you.

As the president of Iran, Bijamadean, watched Trey III's inaugural address at his palace with his bodyguards and high-ranking members of his party, he said, "Who does this new kid president think he is? I have stood up in defiance of American presidents for over three decades. Does the imbecile actually think that he can invade us?"

"He is an idiot," responded one of his party members.

Bijamadean had planned a full-scale nuclear attack to take place that summer on the United States, Britain, and Israel. However, the comments and threats being made by Trey III forced him to hasten the attack. "Get the missiles ready to launch," he declared.

"What is that noise?" asked one of his bodyguards just as the palace was destroyed and all within killed by a bomb deployed from a drone.

Many in the military and the people of Iran had been growing weary and disgruntled with the man who had ruled their country for so long with an iron fist. Neighboring countries had as well. Five days before his inauguration, Trey III had secretly met with the vice president of Iran, who was very popular with the military.

"If we take him out, will you dismantle your nuclear weapons?" asked Trey III.

"Yes."

"Where will he be during my inaugural address?"

"At his palace."

Trey III and the new president of Iran, Mohammed, came to be good friends, and peace in the Middle East began to become a reality. Israel gave the Palestinians their own country of Palestine in the West Bank for which they had fought for so long, and the Arab countries officially recognized Israel. Israel and its neighbors began to respect each other. The suicide bombings stopped, as did the terrorist attacks. The entire world came together as one and simply decided to live in peace and harmony with each other and not to tolerate acts of aggression or violence.

Trey and Tara were very proud of their son. He had been chosen, although he had no knowledge of this, and he had made and was continuing to make a real difference at home and in the world.

Trey and Tara were in Bimini for a month midway through Trey III's second term in office. One morning, Willie approached Trey and asked him to take a walk with him on the beach.

As they walked, Willie said, "Trey III has done a great job. He was the world's last hope. If he had not taken out Bijamadean, the world was months away from a cataclysmic nuclear war that would have begun the end of the world."

"Yes, it was a good idea that you chose him instead of me. He's better than I am, and I say that with pride."

"Don't underestimate yourself. You walked into that field three times facing overwhelming odds, and with a little help from me and my friends, you conquered evil and walked away. Those victories were major events. You will understand more when you get to heaven."

"When you are in heaven, are you in human form? What do you really look like?"

"What difference does it make?"

"Numerous religions have had so many differing beliefs and characterizations of you over the ages, and I want to know who is right. Are the ones who are wrong automatically going to hell?"

Willie laughed and said, "You humans miss the point entirely. First off, when I am in heaven, it doesn't matter whether I am in human form, spirit form, or the form of a dog for that matter. Second, the things that are important to me are what's in your heart, compassion, and respect for all living things, that you try to be the best that you can be, and that you try to make other's lives better and the world a better place."

"I've done that, right?"

"You certainly have."

"Am I the only one who knows about you, Tom, and the Indian woman?"

"Yes."

"I would like to do one really great thing in the time I have left. Any chance that you'll tell me where that grail is?"

"I gave you your chance many years ago. You do remember that surfing contest, don't you?"

"That was hardly fair. You were hovering in the air and doing double and triple front and back flips. I had no chance."

"A deal's a deal."

Trey turned to speak further to Willie, but he was gone. He had vanished into thin air.

Trey walked back to the house. He went into the kitchen and stopped abruptly and froze, staring at the table. Sitting on the middle of the table was the golden chalice with small particles of cement and rock debris surrounding it. Beside it was a small note that read, "Trey, I love you. I'll see you in heaven when you get here. Your mom and dad say hi and that they are proud of you. Enjoy your remaining journey. My work here is done."

Trey III, nearing the end of his second term, addressed the nation from his office. He was fifty, and Trey and Tara had recently turned seventy-seven.

As they watched Trey III on television, Tara looked at Trey and remarked, "What is that golden goblet on his desk?"

"It is a gift I gave him a couple of years ago."

"Where did you get it?"

"Don't ask."

Tara, now with her curiosity piqued, asked, "Trey, what is it?"

Trey smiled and responded, "It's the Holy Grail."

"You were right, baby," laughed Tara. "I shouldn't have asked."

After turning back to the television and staring at the golden goblet for a minute, Tara looked back over at a still smiling Trey. She again looked at the goblet sitting on Trey III's desk as he spoke with a contemplative look on her face, and she wondered whether this was in fact the grail that she and millions of others were seeing. Her life with Trey had led her to realize that anything was possible with him.

A couple of years after he was out of office, Trey III and Kerry flew to Iran to visit with Mohammed and his wife. Their plane was met at the airport by a massive crowd of Iranians there to see the former president of the United States and his beautiful wife. The international news networks covered this event, as it was unprecedented for any American to be welcomed and adored like this in Iran.

After lunch at Mohammed's palace, the four went to his young granddaughter's soccer game in the middle of the city. After the game, all of the girls on both teams lined up to hug Trey III, Kerry, Mohammed, and his wife.

Before departing, Trey III gave Mohammed a gift.

"This is magnificent," said Mohammed. "It looks ancient. Where did you get it?"

"It was a gift from my dad. He claims it is the Holy Grail. It was on my desk for the last two years of my presidency. Whatever it is, good things happened. I am passing it on to you, my friend."

"Then it shall sit on my desk as well."

29

In the spring of 2047, eighty-seven years after their initial meeting, the Lord met Satan in the field a second time. The house had been unoccupied, with the exception of some periodic squatters, since the destruction of the Pagans, for the second time, over twenty years before.

God said, "You lost, and the world has become a much better place for all humanity."

"You got lucky. Your man Trey should not have made it out of the field the first time. He was as good as dead. We were cracking open the champagne bottles when Toby had the gun pressed to his forehead. How was I to know that the son of a bitch was Trey's father?"

"Because you didn't do your homework. You're lazy, which is one or your many shortcomings."

"And the Pagans. What kind of motorcycle gang that is worth a shit can't defeat three people, one of whom is an old man who is missing a hand? I had them take Tara. That was a perfect plan. Trey was standing right out in the middle of the field before them."

"What you have never understood is that good always triumphs over evil in the end. Of course, it didn't hurt that they had Mack with them. He was a one-man wrecking machine."

"When Trey went alone to face them the second time, that was suicide. He lied to Gambotti and falsely led him to believe that the Pagans killed his brother, when in reality Trey's own father did it. Come on, how Christian is that?"

"He outsmarted you. Under those circumstances, the end result warranted the means. By the way, how does it feel to get outsmarted by a human?"

Satan bristled and said, "He didn't outsmart me—he got lucky. I should be sitting on your throne now."

"His son, Trey III, also outsmarted your Antichrist. He led Bijamadean to believe that he had a month or two to launch the missiles, and then Trey III took him out before he had the time he thought he had to launch them. And Trey III set it up in a way to make it look as though he wasn't responsible for it. You have to admit, that was brilliant."

"I will give you this. The best of man is more worthy and stronger than the worst of man. That surprised me. I honestly didn't think you had a chance."

"As per our agreement, you will never again exert your influence to corrupt man. As a result, the world will continue to flourish. Why don't you lay down your sword and join us? I will forgive you for all that you have done. It's over. You had your shot, and you lost."

"Assuming I take you up on your offer, can we play poker?"

"Oh yes, there are always poker games going on."

"Can we have a shot of whiskey from time to time?"

"Most certainly."

"But we must behave ourselves and not engage in violence or corruption of any kind, right?"

"That is right."

"Can you be specific as to what the rules are with which we will be expected to comply?"

"There is only one rule. It is called love. You will be expected to love yourself and all others. All your actions must be consistent with that rule or principle. It's not that complicated."

"Can I leave the Pagans behind? They have really pissed me off."

"No. It is all or none of you. Besides, how is that loving them? You have a lot to learn about the concept of love, but you'll get it if you give it a chance."

"And what will happen to those of us who violate your principle of love?"

"It depends on the violation. He or she will either be sent back to hell or put in a reform class to learn about love and given a second chance."

"When I see Toby, can I punch him, at least once?"

"Only if you want to go straight back to hell."

"Okay, I think I get it. So you're saying that we in hell can have another chance and join you in heaven. Those of us who comply with your concept of love may stay."

"That's exactly right."

"And we can abide by your rule of love and still have fun?"

"Oh, absolutely."

"What about sex? Can we have multiple partners?"

"There is no sex in heaven. Imagine the best sex that you have ever had. Being in heaven is ten times better than that all the time."

"You're kidding me, right?"

"No, I'm certainly not."

"Can I take a few days to think about it?"

"Take as long as you want, my old friend."

"The last time I referred to you as my old friend, you got upset with me, to say the least."

"That was when you were threatening to destroy the world and man and take over heaven. Times are different now, and forgiveness is a part of love. Also, I see a part of you that is reforming right before my eyes. I sense love beginning to emanate from you, and I can see a hint of it in your eyes."

"Really? Oh, come on; you're bullshitting me."

"No, I mean it."

"I'll consider your offer and let you know."

"Can you do me a favor and disappear in an explosion of fire and smoke like you did before? That was kind of cool."

"Now you're mocking me. That's not love."

"See, you're starting to get it already."

Satan, with a satirical look on his face, obliged and disappeared in the explosion. Two old drunks who were squatting in the Pagans' old headquarters, upon witnessing this, threw down their half-full bottles and forswore drinking.